COPSLAVES

FIRST EDITION

ALAN G. GOES

COPSLAVES

FIRST EDITION

PUBLISHED BY THE NAZCA PLAINS CORPORATION
LAS VEGAS, NEVADA
2007

ISBN: 978-1-887895-76-7

Published by

The Nazca Plains Corporation ®
4640 Paradise Rd, Suite 141
Las Vegas NV 89109-8000

PUBLISHER'S NOTE
Copslaves is a work of fiction created wholly by *Alan G. Goes's* imagination. All characters are fictional and any resemblance to any persons living or deceased is purely by accident. No portion of this book reflects any real person or events.

Cover Art, Greasetank
Art Director, Blake Stephens

DEDICATION

Copslaves is dedicated to every man who ever reads it, is stimulated by it, and wishes, even for a while, that he could become a part of it.

ACKNOWLEDGEMENTS

Fantasy fiction is highly autobiographical. Therefore, the author acknowledges the role of each of hundreds of leathermen who have provided the reality basis from which fantasy could spring.

COPSLAVES

ALAN G. GOES

Contents

CHAPTER 1

Little Mike was driving his pickup South of Market late one night heading for the Bay Bridge. He was returning home from a work-related event on Potrero Hill, not expecting anything more exciting than being in bed asleep in about 45 minutes. This was a somewhat unfamiliar part of San Francisco, but Mike figured that if he took 8th Street, he'd end up right by the Highway Patrol office where there was an on-ramp to the bridge. Little Mike had been checking out CHP motorcycle officers for years, so he knew that their office and garage were on 8th between Harrison and Bryant. But 8th Street doesn't go through from the north base of Potrero Hill, so Little Mike was forced to thread his way through a marginal area of old warehouses and dilapidated structures formerly used to serve the now-defunct Southern Pacific Railroad. Mike turned a corner and passed a dimly lit, nondescript building with a small sign that said "Hole - Men's Bar". Ordinarily Little Mike would have found this sufficiently unappealing to give no notice, but not tonight. It was 2:00 AM and Little Mike was about to say goodbye to one part of his life and begin another: Little Mike was finally going to put two and two together and come up with four for the first time as he saw dozens and dozens of men in black leather pouring out of the Hole. Mainly black leather bikers. Some bodybuilders. Some cops. A sprinkle of loggers and cowhands. Black leather everywhere, and there was no way that Little Mike, in his too-tight jeans and skimpy tee-shirt, could do anything other than stop his truck, walk over and check it out. As he did so, in a moment he realized that he had not only found his world, but also, finally, himself.

Little Mike was overcome by emotion: he wanted to be one of these leathermen and he wanted sex. It was probably a good thing that the evening was breaking up so Little Mike could calm down as he checked the men out and tried to look somewhat in control of himself. As the leathermen drifted off, alone, in pairs, or in groups, Little Mike almost cried out, "No! Don't leave! Take me with you!" He knew that he would be returning to the Hole right away. It was the same kind of no option feeling that he would come to know well later as he began to explore this new world where he had to go. He was now a slave to an overwhelming need that could only be satisfied by the men who had poured out of the bar. He'd be back right away.

******

Leather Officer knew that he looked good. That was what it was all about as far as he was concerned. Oh, yeah - there was sex. And there was a certain amount of value to being social. But looking good and being able to enforce his will on other men merely by being the ultimate leather-clad police officer was what Leather Officer was really into. Walking into a bar and knowing that whatever any of the men had been doing was now on hold, that their priorities had all been ratcheted down one slot as he assumed the number one position on all the men's radar screens - that was a major part of what motivated Leather Officer. The other part was using his power, using it to substitute his will for that of another man in the man's brain. Leather Officer could see it in a man's eyes: part fear, part resignation, part surrender, part adoration. Power over other men was Leather Officer's drug, and he was hopelessly addicted.

Leather Officer prepared himself as he always did. His 40-year-old body was lean and muscular, but not so muscular that it would upstage the leather. The leather uniform, always perfect, was his weapon, a conduit for inserting his will into his victim and taking control. The Dehners were slave-shined, gleaming in the special way of spit-shined leather. His breeches, black with a single white stripe down the sides, ballooned out from his thighs just enough. They were tight at the knees, around the ass and through the groin. If erect, it was obvious that his penis was large. The bulge was plain through the tight leather of the codpiece. He usually was erect when his slaves pulled the breeches on him, for the breeches were a major source of his power - they turned him on and empowered him.

He wore a black leather police shirt with epaulets, short-sleeved, tight around his chest and arms. His badge was chromed and gleamed from all angles in the light of the bar or the street. The badge set him apart - not just any leather cop - but Leather Officer. His leather tie, black also, was perfectly knotted and held by a chrome tie bar. Collar insignia and nametag were similarly chrome. Skintight black leather gloves and a black leather officer's-type cap completed the uniform.

Leather Officer's police gear was entirely authentic and was most effective in subordinating his subjects. Around his waist he wore a heavy black leather basket weave police belt - the kind designed to support a weapon in its holster. A gun was not possible in public, but Leather Officer was generally armed at his training facility. At the bar his belt held handcuffs in a pouch, a baton in its ring, and his keys on a key fob. All the hardware on the police belt was chrome.

His trademark was the shoulder strap which crossed his back diagonally, looped over the right shoulder, and re-crossed his chest, connecting to the police belt front and rear. The shoulder strap made it clear to all that Leather

Officer was in charge and that it would be done his way.

Some men said that Leather Officer was arrogant and narcissistic, but he took this as a compliment. Attention to detail and totality of effect required self-analysis, and the mirror was an important tool. If one of the slaves had fucked up the boots, or if something else just didn't quite work, the mirror would tell, and Leather Officer would either fix it or simply not appear. If it wasn't right, the power would not be there. The power and the wielding of it were the whole point. So it had to be right. Therefore, whenever Leather Officer strode down the street and came through the door, it was right, and the power was there, and some man would get kicked in the gut by a sadism way beyond what he had ever before experienced as Leather Officer took control.

Sometimes Leather Officer told himself that his power and what he did with it were a good thing, that he had a positive effect on men, giving them what they wanted, what they needed, and making them more than what they would otherwise have been. This was bullshit. If some guy came out of an encounter with Leather Officer a better man, fine. But that wasn't the point, and seldom was the case. More often than not Leather Officer's victims were truly bruised, badly hurt - certainly emotionally and often physically as well. Inflicting pain in this manner - conquering, enslaving, destroying - was what Leather Officer was really all about - a Sadism more severe than any found in the dungeon, a pain with no relief.

****

Dan was just at the point where he had begun to break a sweat. He had been fucking Dick for about ten minutes, easy strokes in and out, pulling his dick barely outside Dick's cherry, waiting just a bit, then opening his slave up again, slipping all the way in rather quickly, pausing briefly, then pulling out slowly, as if that would be it, but then not stopping, poking his boy again, and again. Dan felt like a god, as if he were totally in control of everything to do with this beautiful man under him. As if he owned Dick and was playing him like an instrument. Dan's dick felt great, powerful, happy, and the feeling coursed throughout Dan's body. Dick was a great fuck! Every time, every stroke. In and out, hesitate, in and out, hesitate. And Dan got increasingly excited, began to sweat profusely, pick up the tempo, pump faster, faster. Dick made a gurgling noise intelligible only to Dan, somewhere between a moan and a squeal. Dan knew that Dick would be screaming full throat in about 45 seconds. Better cum fast before the boy's screams summoned the cops. Dan pumped harder, faster, no hesitation, relentlessly in and out like it's been done for millions of years. And then came the millions-of-years-old peak, the squirt no man ever tires of. Dan's whole body shuddered, and he let out a victory shout, and shot, and hissed, and knew he'd fucked his slave good, really good, and had had a great time doing it.

Dick was melted. No man fucked like Dan! At least no man Dick had met. Dick was making incoherent noises, animal noises, fuckhole noises as his Master used his hole for play. Dick had lost consciousness, sort of, long before Dan came and was aware of nothing except the union of his hole and his man's dick. His slavery was based on this emotional state, this place he had never gone except when being poked repeatedly, incessantly, mercilessly by his Topman's stick. Dick belonged to Dan because Dan had taken away Dick's ability to say no. Dick could no longer say no. His first priority was his Master's dick, taking care of it, getting fucked by it, and having it put him on another planet. As Dan roared and came, Dick felt swallowed by his man, made one, swimming, doubly alive.

"Good fuck, boy," Dan stated, once he could again speak.

"Thank-you, Sir," Dick hissed, panted, groaned. "Thank-you, Sir," he repeated.

"On your knees, boy. You can jerk off while you clean up my dick."

"Yes, Sir; thank-you Sir!" Dick's enthusiasm was real. He began pumping his own dick with his left hand, using his right to hold his Master's now softening cock and balls steady for tongue cleaning. Dan's dick was the center of Dick's universe, and he reveled in the beauty of his Master, his Master's equipment, and the transformation that his Master had achieved in him. He was Dan's, and he had never felt a clearer purpose to his life before. Dick shot quickly - he hadn't really quite gotten the clean up finished. Dan noticed.

"Fuck, boy! Get your priorities straight! My dick first, then yours!"

Dick winced. He wanted to do right for his man, but sometimes fucked up in one way or another, not big time, but enough to feel his Master's crop. Dan slapped him, for emphasis, on the cheek.

"Yes, Sir; sorry, Sir," Dick whimpered as tears welled up.

Dan just looked at his slave. "Lick up your cum, boy. Clean it up."

Dick started lapping vigorously, hoping to make amends. His Master stood over him watching, admiring the change that had been accomplished with Dick. His mind wandered to the under-weight, under-motivated young man of just six months ago and he started to get erect again, comparing that image with the hunky little slave between his boots now. Dan had done a good job.

"I should put you in your cage for that, boy. You wait until everything else is done before you cum. That's the slave way." Dick reddened. And Dan melted. It was hard to be very rough with Dick - Dan didn't need to be. Dan had slaves in the past who wouldn't obey short of bloodshed. But Dick just wanted to please Dan, to do the right thing, to be a good boy. "Get in bed, boy. You'll sleep with me tonight."

Dick leapt on the bed with a huge grin. Dan climbed in too, held his slave against his body, his dick positioned just outside Dick's asshole, and chewed briefly on the boy's collar. The bite marks were familiar. They fell quickly asleep. They were as happy as men can be. They had fallen in love.

****

Little Mike had looked close enough at the men pouring out of the Hole to see that a pair of biker boots and a black leather belt would be a start. So a couple of nights later, he put on some borrowed engineer boots and a recycled work belt, added his usual jeans and tee shirt, and set out. He was very scared and very happy and pretty much out of control. Control was coming from elsewhere - he'd figure out from where later. Right now it was time to act.

He got to the Hole just before 8PM. Swallowing hard, he pulled on the door handle. Locked! Fuck! Now what? Mike was crestfallen. This had to happen. He had to go to the Hole and be with these leathermen. There was so much bottled up need in Little Mike's heart that he got panicky. He felt a near sob coming. But wait - get a grip - it said "Men's Bar" right on the sign! So calm down and get control. Be a man.

Just then the lock was turned from inside. Little Mike grabbed the handle and rushed inside.

"Whoa, man! Cool your jets!" A hunky guy in a leather vest and chaps grabbed Little Mike by the arm and stopped him. "You look like you need a beer!" Mike was speechless. Horrified and giddy at the same time. "Slow down and I'll see what I can do," the guy said. Mike was ready to take orders, so he went up to the bar and the leatherman went behind it and popped the cap off something, handed the bottle to Mike who immediately downed half of it, almost choked, blushed, and then finally stabilized more from exhaustion than anything else.

"First time to the Hole, boy?" the guy asked.

Mike swallowed and said, "Yes." It didn't sound like his voice, it sounded like someone else's voice, and maybe it was in a way, for Little Mike was now inside the Hole having a beer with the first leatherman he'd ever met. In less than a minute he had gotten further than in his previous twenty-seven years.

"Yes. I've never been here before. It's my first time," Mike admitted, as if he were admitting to virginity. "I'm excited to be here," he said, explaining what must have been pretty obvious to his new friend.

"I'm Alan," the guy said. "Welcome." Alan extended his hand and shook Little Mike's and Mike got hard. Alan looked Little Mike over and said that he thought Mike would like it at the Hole. "What's your name, boy?"

Little Mike wasn't exactly clear why Alan kept referring to him as "boy," so he responded thinking that Alan could then call him by name. "My name's Mike," he said.

"Mike's a hot name, boy." Alan said this with enough authority that Little Mike was very pleased. He was also very pleased to be talking to Alan who was becoming more and more exciting to him with every moment. "Gotta get some shit ready for the crowd, so I'll leave you to check the place out," Alan said. Mike was relieved. He'd take a deep breath and delay falling in love for another few minutes.

Little Mike was the only patron in the bar. He was 5'7", 145 lbs., of average build, average in many ways, at least he had thought so until discovering the Hole. Now he knew he was special, in a special place, and something special was sure to happen to him. As Alan arranged beer, glasses, bottles, fruit and other bar stuff, Little Mike had a chance to check out the Hole.

It really was pretty much of a hole. There was a fairly large front room with a bar against the left wall, a smaller back room toward the left with a pool table and lockers, and a bathroom to the right. The bathroom was unique, at least in Little Mike's experience, in having a long trough in which to piss, rather than individual urinals. There were two toilets, neither of which had seats, and neither of which appeared capable of accepting more than urine. And there were two sinks, both filthy, which seemed not to be where a man could clean up.

The whole place was painted black and was "decorated" with posters advertising bars in places like Hamburg, London, or New York, or events which had occurred years ago. There were a couple of musty plaques congratulating organizations Little Mike had never heard of for an achievement of some sort eight or twenty-three years ago.

A lot of the wall space had narrow benches built in, under which boxes of beer were stored. Mike wasn't entirely sure what the benches were for. There was a pool table, but it looked pretty worn out. All in all, Little Mike was unimpressed with the place, and was beginning to wonder whether he hadn't made a mistake, when the front door swung open, and two men came in whose appearance informed Little Mike that it was the clientele which were the draw, not the venue.

The men were virtually identical and almost nude. Each was completely shaved from head to toe. They wore nothing other than a black leather collar around the neck, black leather shorts, and black leather lace-up work boots. One had a bag; the other had nothing. They approached Alan, who was still getting the bar ready, obtained a key, and proceeded to the group of crumby old gym lockers by the pool table. They opened a locker, removed a bag, replaced it with the one they'd brought, locked the locker, returned the key to Alan, and left.

Little Mike was totally bewildered. He knew enough to know that these men were leathermen - after all, they wore nothing except leather. But the rest was a cipher. "Who were those guys?" Mike asked Alan.

"Leather Officer's slaves. They were here to exchange equipment. Leather Officer has a locker full time," Alan answered, knowing full well that this would answer no questions, only raise many more. Leather Officer? Slaves? Little Mike really had no idea what Alan meant.

"We allow a couple of customers to keep lockers here full time, although most are available just for the evening. Leather Officer has a full time locker. His slaves came to remove some stuff and bring some new stuff, I don't know what," Alan explained further, only adding to Little Mike's confusion.

Slaves? Mike's mind drifted to images of Mississippi, or Mesopotamia. Slaves? "What are slaves?" Little Mike asked Alan.

Alan hesitated...Shit this guy was green. Well, somebody had to explain it. Why not the bartender at the hottest leatherbar in town? "Some men enslave other men for fucking, cocksucking, and general service," Alan explained, feeling a bit like an anthropologist. "Since you haven't been here before, it would be a good idea for you to just observe what goes on as the place fills up. You'll pick it up fast. You'll like it," Alan assured Little Mike.

That was enough for Little Mike to think about for the moment. But who was Leather Officer? Alan had mentioned Leather Officer so matter-of-factly that

Little Mike chose not to ask any more questions, opting to just follow Alan's advice and observe. He also followed the bartender's advice by ordering a shot of high-end vodka and another Stiefelknecht imported beer, downed the shot, and wandered off with the beer to see how the place he had only seen empty would fill up. He knew that the men in the street at last call were what he wanted, so it only stood to reason that they had to have gotten here earlier, and would again. All Mike had to do was wait.

Little Mike re-read every poster, every plaque. He finished his beer, ordered another, finished that and finally came back to Alan with a question. "Are any men coming here?" he asked, already a little tipsy.

"Yeah, boy, they will. It'll start to fill up around 2200," Alan stated.

Little Mike could translate military time quickly enough to realize that there was still about a half hour to hang out. So far Mike was just wasting time, he thought, but at least he had already learned not to show up when the doors opened.

"Let me show you something," Alan stated. "Come on back here." Alan beckoned Little Mike to come back behind the bar and through the doorway labeled "Staff Only."

"Is it OK?" Mike asked.

"Yes, it's OK. I'm the manager, more or less," Alan responded.

So Mike followed Alan to find out what he was to be shown. The staff room was cluttered with what you'd expect in a dumpy bar - nothing special. Little Mike followed Alan until the latter abruptly turned around and confronted Mike face to face.

"Ever suck a man's dick?" Alan asked.

"Why - uh - I - uh - well - I - uh," Mike stammered. In fact he had sucked dick before, but not much, and certainly not in a bar!

Alan unsnapped his leather pants, pulled out his handsome cock and balls, and played briefly with them, looking Little Mike dead in the eye. "Give it a try, boy," Alan said, almost like a command.

So Little Mike got his first taste of leathersex. It wasn't the best blowjob Alan had ever gotten, that's for sure, but Alan enjoyed it as much for the fun of corrupting the young man as for the usual pleasure. Basically, Mike's mouth was used as a receptacle, Alan's strong hand behind Mike's head. A bit of in-out, a squirt, and that was it. A quickie. Alan was pleased to do this for a green recruit.

For Little Mike - well, it is hard to overstate the depth of emotion a first-time event can have. Alan knew this, so after he squirted and Little Mike swallowed, and Little Mike looked up at him with big eyes that said "I love you. You're the man for me - I want to be with you for the rest of my life," Alan wasn't very surprised. To check this rush to the altar, Alan gave Little Mike a sharp slap on the ass, told him to get himself together and get his butt out from behind the bar. Mike obeyed, a little disappointed that the engagement was off, but quickly warming to the realization that he had just had sex with a leatherman! In a leatherbar no less! Wow! Zow!

Mike was walking on air. Ecstatic. It's a good thing the bar was still empty or Little Mike would for sure have made a fool of himself by rushing up to some guy and telling him what just happened, and how fun it had been, and how hot Alan is, and... "Have another Stiefelknecht, boy - on me - to wash it down," Alan offered, grinning in a way that Little Mike felt was the most erotic facial expression ever. "No charge for the cum shot, either," Alan added, grinning even more broadly.

Mike knew for sure that Alan was his best friend. He really liked Alan. Alan was so hot, so cool, so handsome, so...sigh. Mike took a big gulp of beer and leaned against the bar in that sexy way that many men are wired to do after four beers and several shots, staring enthralled at his hero. Already it was a great night at the Hole, and it had hardly begun. Same with Little Mike's career as a leatherman - great already, but hardly begun. Mike was very, very happy.

****

Groggily, Dick awakened. At first, he wasn't sure where he was. In his bed in Twenty-nine Palms? Alone? No. Neither. Where? Oh, yeah. His Master's bed! Dan's bed! In San Francisco. Quickly Dick reviewed how he had gotten here.

Dick's Dad was a Marine, a big guy from the Midwest. Dad had met Mother in Europe - she was Basque, a dancer. It was a torrid soldier's romance that had cooled on numerous Marine bases around the world, finally at Twenty-nine Palms, where Dick endured an adolescence whose only relief from desert bleakness was the plentiful supply of young Marines who taught him how to please a man. Dick had wanted to go into the Corps like Dad, but he inherited his mother's frame, so it didn't work. Dick's parents figured him out early, before he did actually, and decided that their son needed an environment in which he could bloom. So after several aimless semesters at Iron Mountain College, Dad dropped Dick off at Palm Springs International Airport, gave him a debit card with a couple grand on account, and recommended San Francisco. Dick cried a little and kissed his father good-bye. He was not oblivious to the poignancy of the moment, but it was only years later that Dad admitted that this had been the hardest moment of his life, that he hadn't even made it out of the airport gates before having to pull over, weeping uncontrollably, and that tears had come again and again, for weeks and months, and had only ceased to flow once it became clear that the decision to send his son off to be gay had been the right one.

So Dick arrived with a few bucks, a knapsack full of stuff, the body and face of a dancer, and the heart and mind of a Marine at San Francisco International Airport. A particularly hot guy from the base had mentioned a bar called "The Hole," so Dick decided to check it out. Where to spend his first night in the City should probably have been of greater concern to him, but it was not. He was focused on men, not sleep. So the cab dropped him off, he strode into a leather bar for the first time, ordered a beer, and caught his breath. Never mind that he was several months shy of twenty - Dick was motivated.

He was nothing extraordinary size-wise, but height and weight weren't what the men in the Hole noticed. Dick was incredibly handsome in an exotic sort of way, incredibly masculine in a very matter-of-fact sort of way, and the combination set the place afire. Dick was not at all self-conscious - he thought he was just a guy - but he was alone in this view. He was utterly unaware that he had seduced the whole place, so he was excited when a young bodybuilder in leather, older and bigger than he, came over to say "Hi, my name's Dan."

Well, in retrospect it seemed like something out of a porn novel, but it took these two about five minutes to connect, and Dan had a new slave. Dick was irresistible to Dan - and Dan would fulfill whatever fantasy the younger man wanted. Dick saw in Dan all the Marines he'd admired on base, but in leather, and ready to take charge fully. A "mature" man of twenty-five.

So less than twelve hours after kissing his Dad good-bye Dick was collared, chained to the floor, and being fucked by his new Master! - Dan! - His God! - Dan, the Bodybuilder in full leather, fucking the shit out of his brand new slave from the desert! That was the way it went for months - fucking, lots of fucking - workouts at the gym - an occasional visit to the Hole - but mostly fucking, or waiting to be fucked, hanging out at Dan's tiny studio, chained to the floor, constantly erect, thinking about his Master, waiting for his Master's return, picturing his Master's prick, feeling it up his ass, feeling it pump him 'til he screamed, feeling the muscled, leathered man on top of him, then hearing the key in the door, and rushing to his Master's boots, licking furiously, begging, squealing to be fucked.

Dick telephoned Dad. He'd found a "roommate." He was getting some "training, a little like 'basic.' "Everything was fine. Love to Mother." It's unfortunate that even loving, supportive parents like Dick's cannot be expected to handle the reality of a young gay man's intimate life, but so be it. Yet, Dick knew that, somehow, Dad would already be proud of him.

Dan had a job - he drove a MUNI bus, so the boys were OK financially. All Dick had to do was tidy up the place, wait for his Master, serve his Master's cock, over and over, all night long, lick his Master's whole hunky body, kiss his face and his lips and his asshole, melt in his embrace. Occasionally Dick would mess something up and Dan would use the belt on him, make him cry, humiliate him, then fuck him. It only bound Dick closer. Each transformed the other into his fantasy and they held the whole thing together with a combination of simple love and boyish sex which cannot endure but which one remembers decades later as the best it ever was.

A Boner Book

CHAPTER 2

The decision had to be made shortly. It was Friday night and Leather Officer was unsure whether to take one of his slaves with him to the Hole or to go alone. Staying in was not an option tonight - Leather Officer had the itch to be out on the prowl - but he wasn't sure what his mood was, wasn't sure whether he could be more effective on his own, or whether a slave would be of service. Would it draw attention to Leather Officer, or would the slave itself be the focus of men's attention? This kind of question often confronted Leather Officer, but he was an expert, so he always came up with the right answer.

Actually, it was a lot of fun figuring this kind of thing out, fun in that it assured Leather Officer that fine tuning was all that was left, that in virtually every respect he had achieved his goal of becoming the ultimate leather cop - living the fantasy that had always animated him. He had found his stride - had made his fantasy real - and his slaves, and his training facility, and his status at the peak of the world of leathermen proved it. If he were to take one of the slaves along, which one would it be? 2 was the most reliable and had been designated head slave some time ago. Its discipline and smooth functioning had been perfected, so 2's performance was always the envy of other tops and a model for slave wannabes. 4, on the other hand, was by far the weakest slave in performance, but at the same time the most strongly motivated. It presented, therefore, an opportunity for drama, because its need for slavery and worship of Leather Officer were huge. Yet its clumsiness and poor actual performance elicited constant rebuke and discipline. 4, as the weakest slave, was ripe for termination, so it would be fun to bring it along cruising for its replacement just to watch its pained expressions. 3 and 1 were intermediate - but perhaps it was time to show them off, perhaps as a pair, attached at the collars.

Yet all these possibilities were rejected in the end, for no matter which slave or slaves were taken, they would require attention and therefore limit Leather Officer's flexibility and quickness should a potential victim present. It really was time to get a replacement for 4. Its pain was its only positive attribute - it was virtually useless for chores and chores were a major part of slavery. So Leather Officer let the slaves think that one or two of them would accompany him, but after they had dressed him, he caged them all and set out for the Hole. 4 listened as Leather Officer went down to the garage, hoping to hear the big bike fired up, but instead it heard the pickup start. Bad news for 4 since the likelihood of its replacement being brought back cuffed in the bed of the pickup was far greater than on the back of the bike.

4 began to whimper softly in its cage. It was hopelessly enslaved, yet so incapable of performance. It adored Leather Officer way beyond what was sustainable, even for a slave, but feared that it might never taste its Master's dick again. 4 glanced at 2 with envy. 2's slavery was secure. 2 got fucked by Leather Officer frequently and 2 had its own prestige as the best trained slave most men had ever seen. 4 thought it would surely die without its Master. Tears came to its eyes reflecting on the injustice of its being replaced when its need for its Master and subordination to its Master exceeded that of the others, regardless its shitty performance. 4 cried itself to sleep, ultimately dreaming of being strapped to the fucking horse, looking in the mirror, and seeing Leather Officer approaching with a full erection, ready to fuck it until the slave would scream and squeal and beg for cop dick up its ass forever.

Indeed, Leather Officer was specifically out recruiting a new slave, but 4's position was not necessarily as precarious as it thought, for its pathetic whining and begging not to be terminated pleased Leather Officer. 4 was valued for its pain. Having a replacement already on site would be good for all the slaves - it would keep them all on edge, competing aggressively with one another, scheming against one another, constantly in turmoil seeking to please and serve their Master and avoid termination. Leather Officer took great satisfaction in the manner in which he had set up his slavery system and his training facility. His power controlled the slaves utterly and extended out into the world as far as any leatherman who had ever encountered him. He knew that the power of a leather cop was greater than that of any other hyper-masculine icon, knew that he was the ultimate leather cop, and knew that virtually any leatherman was his slave at the snap of his fingers. His self-assurance was huge as he reflected on his empire.

A short run over to the bar, park the pickup, check his uniform and gear for possible minor imperfections, and Leather Officer grasped the door handle fully intent on plucking a new slave trainee from the crowd inside, regardless what wreckage and damage were caused to the victim or anyone else. In fact, the more damage and wreckage caused, the better - to the victim, men populating the victim's world, and the witnesses, wannabes, and casual bystanders. It was Leather Officer's job to see to it that Sadism continued to be spelled with a capital S.

****

Dan punched out a bit early at the bus yard on Friday evening - it was probably about 2230 - and hopped a 14 Mission for the quick ride to the small place where he maintained his slave South of Market. For six months, ever since they had gotten together, Dick and Dan had not gone bar hopping much - they stayed in and fucked. The boys were very young and it seemed to make sense to fuck for several hours every day. Dan even quit doing aerobics at the gym. Aerobics? Come on!

The tiny studio had been Dan's alone before Dick moved in. Dan installed an eye bolt on the floor in the center of the place and chained his slave to it. The boy had a series of minor chores to accomplish each day, but mostly he just hung out waiting for his Master, waiting for his Master's prick to penetrate him, thinking about Dan hour after hour, constantly erect.

Dick didn't know the difference between God and Dan. Dan was totally committed to his job of enslaving his fuckboy - little else mattered. These were young leathermen, sickeningly in love, constantly fucking, unknowingly fulfilling the fantasy of millions of men.

Since for a change there would be enough time to actually get leathered up and get to the Hole, Dan said, "Get your ass going, boy. I'm going to show you off and drink a beer or two." Sounded good to Dick, too, so the young top and his slave boy, who really was hardly more than a boy, walked the few blocks over to the Hole. Entering, they noted that the place was well filled. Alan the bartender remembered that Dan favored a particular brand of domestic beer, so he opened two.

"On me," Alan stated, and Dick and Dan felt immediately like the stars that they were. They waded into the crowd and bathed their egos in the appreciation beaming from every man's eyes. Every man there wished to exchange places with these two very young, very hot, very in-love leathermen who were apparently so effortlessly and beautifully fulfilling every man's dream of how it could have been for him at that age if only he had had his shit together. Dick and Dan didn't quite understand their stardom, but they were aware of it and they were very happy knowing that they were embraced by their brothers, that they were in love and that they spent several hours each day fucking.

But Dick and Dan's moment of leatherbar stardom ended abruptly as the door opened and Leather Officer entered. Suddenly the emotions of the crowd became far more complex and contradictory. Leather Officer lived for these moments, when he could stimulate irreconcilable, multiple emotions in his victims, distract them from whatever had been their previous focus and enslave and torture their imaginations. He was feared and craved, hated and deified simultaneously. He had succeeded, en masse, in creating the classic slave's dilemma for the entire patronage of the Hole - the dilemma of wishing to be with him from whom you also must flee, panicky to escape him who draws you uncontrollably. Leash & Collar vs. Whip. Leather Officer owned these men, all of them, they knew it and he knew it.

Alan's response was typical in many ways. The bartender had been taken to Leather Officer's training facility once and had been reduced to abject slavery, only then to be rejected and kicked out. That was the essence of Leather Officer's sadism - a huge and ultimately immoral sadism - to enslave and then abandon. To create in a man the complete need for a Master, to present as that Master, and then to put the destroyed man out on the street defenseless, damaged. Alan hated Leather Officer with a hatred so intense that it was dangerous to his well-being. But at the same time, if Leather Officer were to snap his fingers and point down at the heel of his gleaming, slave-shined boot, Alan would still zoom in tongue-first and start cleaning the heel, desperate to serve, trying again to be chosen by Leather Officer for permanent slavery.

Leather Officer came up to Alan's station. "Why me, always?" Alan asked himself. But if the cop had gone to any other bartender's station, it would have been worse, far worse. Alan was a good top, but he could never really be entirely comfortable as a top because of his lust for Leather Officer. At the same time, he could not be a bottom, because no top could take him effectively once he had been topped by Leather Officer. So he was stuck. And Leather Officer loved it. Lived to create such pain. To make wreckage of men's egos, sexuality, lives. But hey, he was just a great top, right?

When the hawk circles high over the noontime prairie, many rodents are in view, but the hawk must, at some point, make a choice, and vulnerability will often be a factor. Why make the dive if lunch isn't guaranteed?

Dan should have stayed late at work, crashed at home, fucked Dick, jerked off, gone for pizza, whatever. But he hadn't. He brought his slave to the Hole and himself to his destruction.

Dick saw the cop first. "Wow, Sir! Check it out!"

Dan did, and as was so often the case with Leather Officer's prey, it was over before it even began. The inevitability, the utter helplessness of the victim inflamed Leather Officer. He saw it in the eyes - a glassy resignation, capitulation even before he started his seduction. Leather Officer got his drink from the near robotic Alan and strode immediately over to and adjacent to Dick and Dan. He addressed Dan.

"Hot boy," the cop said, referring to Dick. "Is he yours, boy?"

"Yes, Sir! This is my boy, Sir!" Dan retorted.

Well, that did it. Dick was shattered. In one minor exchange, Dan had blown it totally, allowing himself to be called "boy" and then referring to the cop as "Sir." It was so quick that even Leather Officer was momentarily taken aback. Dick was breathlessly damaged, wounded to hear his top, his God, so automatically subordinate to the cop. But Leather Officer was just getting started.

"You boys should quit fucking around with one another and find yourselves real tops. You won't be satisfied with boys once you've been fucked by men." Leather Officer cupped a black leather gloved hand on each boy's crotch and began gently, but then more assertively, to massage and take charge of the boys' organs.

Dick pulled away, but Dan didn't. "Fuck you, asshole!" Dick yelled. He quickly realized that his love and his life were in grave jeopardy. Leather Officer tried to slap Dick's face, but the boy was too quick. Hot tears welled up in Dick's eyes. He ran, but Dan stayed put. Leather Officer continued to play with Dan's cock and balls and moved closer to the boy, so that the heat of his cop body would warm the boy and loosen him up. Dan looked deeply into Leather Officer's eyes and saw timeless emotions and a reflection of his own eyes and an inevitable near future. Dan moaned as Leather Officer continued to stimulate his cock, moved in closer, and placed a gloved hand behind the boy's neck.

"So you're a top," Leather Officer allowed, blandly.

"Well, yes, Sir, uh, yes, most recently, with Dick, my slave, yes, with Dick I have been, uh, I have been a top, but I can be flexible, uh, you know, with the right guy."

"FUCK YOU!" Leather Officer yelled, grabbing Dan by his shirt, lifting him off the ground, and slamming the kid into the adjoining wall. "Don't give me that shit! You're no top! You're a fraud! You're pussy through and through, and you are going to be my slave! Isn't that right?"

Dan was dazed, speechless. He wanted to run, to try to find Dick, to fix this, to get away from the cop, but he couldn't. Leather Officer was too powerful, too quick. While Dan was trying to collect his thoughts, figure out a rational response, the cop slapped him across the mouth, once, twice, again, and again. "Answer me immediately! You are going to be my slave, aren't you?"

"Yes, Sir," Dan whispered.

"Louder!"

"YES, SIR," Dan shouted. Leather Officer slapped him again, harder than before, and the boy dropped to his knees. Quickly the cop circled around behind, handcuffed him, lifted him up by the back of his shirt and again slammed him into the wall, this time face first. Dan yelped and felt tears welling up in his eyes, as the full reality of what had just happened to him, to his slave, his love, his life, and his entire future flooded in. He began to yell.

Leather Officer again slapped Dan's mouth and yelled, "Shut the fuck up, asshole," and slapped him again, and again. He forced the broken boy to his knees, against the cop boot, totally enslaved in less time than it would typically take Leather Officer to piss.

But it was now time to piss, so a collar came from the cop's locker, and by leash and hood, Dan was dragged to the trough. Leather Officer inserted his big copdick, semi-hard, into Dan's throat and off-loaded a pint of warm, sweet piss. Dan choked and spit up some of the honey. Leather Officer's boot crashed down on Dan's neck, forcing him to suck up the spilt juice.

"Don't waste a drop, fuckhole!" the cop hissed. Bladder drained, he dragged Dan out of the pisser, half crawling, half sliding across the bar floor and out the door into the street, paying no attention at all to the young man collapsed on the sidewalk, but now howling at the sight of his former Master thrown into the bed of Leather Officer's pickup and hauled away.

Alan had seen the whole thing. He saw Leather Officer deliberately choose the sweetest, most in-love pair of men in the bar, bust them up, and leave the younger guy devastated and abandoned. He saw Dick fleeing out the door before the cop dragged Dan out and figured that the boy, having nowhere to go, was probably not far away. Alan called for relief and headed out into the night. Sure enough, the young man was on the sidewalk just outside the door. Not a word was spoken as Alan picked him up, embraced him, and gently urged him to rest his head on Alan's shoulder. They stood together this way for several minutes until the boy's chest quit heaving and he was able to take normal breaths. At that point, Alan took his handkerchief, wiped the boy's eyes and face, told him to blow his nose, and led him by the hand back into the Hole and into the "staff only" support area behind the bar.

"I'm Alan, boy. What's your name?"

"Dick, Sir. I'm Dick," the boy stammered.

"OK, Dick. Get yourself cleaned up. You're among friends here. Everything's going to be all right," Alan assured Dick, and returned to his station.

Alan's motives were several and complex. He was a good man and probably would have gone to Dick's aid no matter what, but also Alan had a history with Leather Officer himself and was formulating even now a plan for some sort of statement, possibly even revenge. Additionally, of course, being a horny bastard always on the lookout for a fuck, Alan saw in Dick a particularly luscious possibility. Getting more possible by the moment.

Dick emerged shortly, largely composed and approached Alan to thank him for his help. Dick had no idea where he would even spend the night, but his most immediate concern now was to get rid of the fucking collar that Dan had locked around his neck! Dan! Oh, God, Dan! Dick almost lost it, recalling the recent sight of his Master being so easily turned and dragged out by the leather cop. Fuck! Dan! What a fraud! Dick touched Alan's forearm. "Thank you, Sir," he stated quite genuinely.

"You're welcome, boy," Alan responded. "We're short handed tonight. Can you barback?"

"I - I don't know, Sir. What do you mean?"

"Can you circulate around the bar and pick up glasses and bottles. Sort of like a bus boy. And just keep an eye on the crowd, make sure everyone's having a good time but not too good of a time," Alan said with a sly smile.

"Well, yes, Sir, thank you, Sir, I can do that, Sir!" Dick said. "But Sir, can you help me get this collar off?"

"Not now, boy. I'll take care of it later when things slow down," Alan said, returning to his customers. "Get to work."

Dick felt ill-at-ease, collared and wearing nothing more than tiny leather shorts and black, lace-up boots. But he needn't have, for he and his new job were suited to one another, and the clientele of the Hole readily accepted the new barback.

Dick was so young and inexperienced that he really didn't know how attractive he was. Dan, of course, had known, but Masters are advised not to go on and on about how pretty their slaves are. Even Dan, not much of a Master as it turned out, knew this. So the remainder of the evening Dick collected dead drinks, generally tidied up and became the hit of the party. Repeatedly, his thoughts turned to Dan and the leather cop, what had happened, and what was probably happening now. But he was able to keep it together and after awhile, he began to have a good time.

As the evening wore down and the men began to drift out, both Dick and Alan had increasingly less to do, and Alan's plan began to unfold. Dick, of course, had no plan, had only lived his Master's plan for months, and now no Master. He just naturally fell into Alan's plan pretty much unaware. Dick just knew that he liked Alan. Liked him more and more. Alan's plan was pretty straight-forward: here was definitely a potential new boy. Dick had already proven he could work. Let's see if he can play, Alan thought. Alan also began to formu-late, ever so vaguely at this point, the idea that Dick, given his probable view of Leather Officer, might participate in some so far unimagined slap back at the leather cop.

The door closed behind the last patron. Alan's thoughts quickly changed as the still-collared boy approached him, a truly handsome boy, with a big wide grin for the first time all evening, and gently stroked Alan's crotch. Ah, yes! This plan was unfolding right on target! Alan unsnapped his leather pants. "How about showing me some appreciation for getting you a new job?" he teased.

"How about getting rid of this fucking collar, like you said you would, Sir?" Dick retorted. He was quite serious, and Alan could tell it. So a pair of tree pruners, useful when bondage demonstrations went awry and long kept behind the bar for such emergencies, was produced, the flimsy lock was snipped off and Dick unbuckled the collar. It was unceremoniously tossed it in the trash.

"Sure you want to do that, boy? It's probably worth fifty bucks and you might want it as a memento," Alan said. He realized even before Dick's face turned dark with anger that he had said the wrong thing. The young man had been deeply wounded earlier and Alan could see that he was going to have to be very careful. "Sorry. Bad idea, huh?" Alan admitted.

"Yes, Sir. Real bad idea," Dick said. Tears came again. Alan held Dick tightly, saying nothing. Alan was horny as hell - he definitely was of a mind to fuck Dick - but he realized that he had other obligations to the boy that might be more important.

Alan's thoughts turned momentarily to Leather Officer. What an asshole! Here Alan was cleaning up Leather Officer's mess. Why? Alan didn't have a real clear-cut answer, but if he had, ethics would have probably played a part. He would have recognized that Leather Officer, although he was probably the hottest thing on the planet, had ethical gaps - he was irresponsible and his sadism was unethical.

Dick was thinking nearly the same thing. He was as angry as a man can be, angrier than a man should be for his own good. He was angry at himself for believing, incorrectly, that Dan was the Earth and Sky. And at Dan, for not being the ultimate topman Dick had imagined, for melting in a flash. But most of all, Dick was angry at Leather Officer. He flat out hated the motherfucker. It was a hatred that needed some release or Dick would sicken. Maybe Alan could help.

Alan thought he could, so after Dick got it together, Alan finished unsnapping his pants, pulled out his cock and balls, played with them a little, and grinned broadly at Dick. Dick grinned back, knelt, and began to clean Alan's balls with his tongue, up and down and around each one, sneaking underneath, then starting in to clean the cock, licking and cleaning every square inch of it from the pubic hair all the way out to the tip. Dick took the glans into his mouth, teased the corona lightly with his teeth, darted the tip of his tongue barely into the meatus, and looked up at Alan to see a thoroughly delighted new friend.

Alan was gentle with Dick. He knew that the boy had been a real slave and that he was capable of handling fairly rough stuff, but Alan had the sense to realize that Dick needed careful treatment and shouldn't be pushed into anything that would remind him of his former Master. Or what was now happening to his former Master. So Alan sort of did a "We're fuckbuddies - you be the boy for now" routine on Dick, figuring he'd work the boy back to full slavery gradually - and have fun doing it. Alan just let Dick blow him, didn't force anything, no tough talk, no real leathersex. Just fun for boys.

And Dick had a great time, because he really liked Alan, and he really liked sucking Alan's dick, and he needed a man to be with after having his universe imploded by Leather Officer. "Let's go to my place," Alan offered.

"Yes, Sir. Thank-you, Sir," Dick responded. Dick had nowhere to go. Still, Alan was a very hot man, and Dick would have been eager to get it on with Alan no matter what. Of course he wanted to go. Problem was, he was virtually nude and even a short ride on the back of Alan's old Harley would be hypothermia for sure.

"No problem," Alan said. A riding suit was produced, and the two emerged from the Hole, Alan clad in his jacket and leather pants, and Dick in an ill-fitting riding suit. Alan kick-started the old hog, which caught this time, and the two mounted the vintage machine for the ride over to the basement flat Alan rented off Potrero Hill. Alan pulled the bike up into the courtyard in front of the place, shut it down, chained it up, and the two entered Alan's home, Dick for the first time. It was Spartan, barracks-like almost, but to Dick, considering his captivity at Dan's, Alan's place seemed palatial. There was a living room, a small galley, a bedroom, and a shitter, with shower. Heaven.

The living room was pretty conventional - a place to hang out. But the bedroom was not conventional at all. There was a four-poster bed with cross members up top. Leather gear was strewn everywhere, including a sling, still half hanging from the bed superstructure. All sorts of bondage gear, whips, rope, chains, and more were just thrown everywhere, as if a major scene had just ended. Which was pretty much the case - Alan found time to tend bar, work out, and fuck men, but not much else - certainly housework was a low priority. Dick felt at home immediately.

"Get rid of the suit, boy," Alan said, starting to take control. Dick complied, meaning that he now was clad only in lace-up boots and skimpy leather shorts. "Lose the shorts as well," Alan demanded. Alan caught his breath at the sight of Dick's ass! Perfection. The globes floated independently in the air. The musculature of the back swept down and leapt out to form the cheeks, a deep, secret, inviting cleft between the two. The prick and balls were not in any record book for size, but they were large for a smaller man, and beautifully formed, gracile. Alan realized now fully what he had understood only less clearly before - Dick was an incredibly beautiful, masculine young man. Alan was on fire.

Alan was still clad in his leather jacket and pants. Again he unsnapped the fly, but this time Dick was on it in an instant, licking Alan's still gloved hands as they undid the snaps. Dick squealed with delight at the sight of Alan's cock. Overly eagerly, he started to slide up and down the enlarging shaft, way too excited. "Hold it, boy. We have all night," Alan cautioned.

"Yes, Sir," Dick responded, blushing.

"Just give it some nice strokes, real sweet," Alan said.

Dick nodded and set to work. It had to be admitted - Dan had taught Dick how to suck cock. He was good! Alan moaned, curled his toes in his boots and thought fleetingly how lucky he was to be a leatherman. Dick slid up and down Alan's shaft, doing it the way only leathermen know how. The men were ecstatic.

Then suddenly Dick stopped sucking - Alan didn't immediately know why. Remembrance of Dan and Dan's fall flooded back into Dick, he gasped and trembled. Alan responded quickly by pulling the boy against his leathered leg, holding him tightly, letting him know that, although abruptly cast adrift, he was now again safely ashore. The incident passed quickly, and Alan noted with satisfaction that Dick's episodes of angry remembrance were already fewer, more far-between, and of shorter duration. Alan knew that his effort now assisting Dick, guiding him, would bind the two forever - exactly what Alan sought.

"Enough cocksucking, boy. Get your ass on the bed," Alan demanded. Dick complied, sweeping aside a bunch of clothes, books, leather gear, etc., lying with his ass open and available for a hoped-for first fuck from his new friend. Alan quickly readied his prick and the boy's hole. He checked out Dick's body from the perspective of a fucker. Sweet, very sweet! Very youthful but very masculine - perfect in every way. He spread Dick's legs and positioned his eager prick against the boy's hole.

"There's only one first fuck, boy," Alan said tenderly.

"Yes, Sir! Please fuck me, Sir!" Dick responded, somewhat surprising Alan with his raw eagerness.

"You got it," Alan responded, inserting his glans just through the boy's sphincter.

"Aannggh," Dick cried, "Aaiy!"

"OK, boy?" Alan asked.

"Yes, Sir. Yes," Dick breathed, gasping, trembling. "Only one first fuck," Dick repeated. "Yes, Sir. Thank-you, Sir."

Alan gently forced his way completely into the boy. It wasn't as if Dick were a virgin, but considering what had befallen him, Alan felt, correctly, that tenderness and restraint would pay dividends. Alan pulled almost all the way out, then shoved back in and held his man tightly. Out again and then in. Alan grabbed Dick's ears, gently, to control the boy's head, and chewed the neck, again gently, like lions do. Alan fucked Dick like Alan fucks. Dick liked it. He began to coo, to hiss, like when Dan fucked...Dan! That fraud! That asshole! Dick gasped and let out a strange guttural yelp, but then recovered and remembered that it was Alan's prick pounding his hole.

Alan was oblivious to Dick's momentary remembrance. He was focused on his work, like men are in such a situation. Focused on the old in-out, the oldest excitement, but still the best. Alan loved to fuck. He wondered if fucking wasn't what he did best, whether everything else wasn't just a day job. More quickly now, and more violently, Alan continued to fuck Dick's ass. Dick began to scream. Alan shoved his fist into the boy's mouth and pounded harder. He gnawed too hard at the boy's neck, where a collar should have been, making Dick squirm with pain. But Alan was oblivious - at one with the beautiful man he was fucking - but also alone in the way a man is king alone when he squirts, alone in the exquisiteness of the sensation as the glands and tubes shudder and shoot. No poet has described it - none can - and none needs to, for every man knows. So Alan shot cum deep into Dick and made the boy his, but pumped a few more strokes, sliding his prick through his own cum, because he couldn't accept that the first fuck was over.

Dick felt owned and like he had a future again, held tightly by his new man, the prick still lodged in his ass. And Alan felt like God, a benevolent conqueror, a great hero. The men lay there, their breathing gradually softened, their hearts beat together as they fell asleep and began another chapter in the story of leathermen.

CHAPTER 3

The drive from the Hole to Leather's Officer's training facility took about fifteen minutes, during which he observed his new victim handcuffed in the bed of the pickup through the rear-view mirror. The boy was quieting down, finally, no longer struggling. Leather Officer figured that fear was now sobering him as the realization crystallized how truly dangerous a situation he was in. The pickup arrived at the training facility, which was also Leather Officer's home, and the home of his slaves. Clicking the garage door opener, Leather Officer thought about how much effort it had taken to convert this derelict Victorian house in the marginal Mission District into what was arguably San Francisco's premier training facility. If any one had a set up better than this, Leather Officer was unaware of it.

As the garage door rolled shut behind the pickup, a slave appeared in a doorway at the rear of the garage. It was shaved from head to foot, collared and shod in lace-up short boots, but otherwise completely nude. Leather Officer mounted a staircase up to the first floor as the slave went to work on Dan. It followed standard orders in such a case and required no further direction from its Master. It also knew exactly what the consequences would be if its work was not satisfactory.

The slave grabbed Dan by his feet and dragged him toward the back of the pickup's bed. Dan was still handcuffed and could not resist as the slave locked a loop of heavy chain around his neck, ordered him to follow, and roughly led him by the remainder of the chain through the doorway. Dan noticed that the slave was somewhat older, somewhat larger, and definitely more muscular than he. Cuffed, chain-collared, and chain-leashed as he was, Dan saw that resistance would be futile. Indeed, from the moment he first had seen Leather Officer, now less than an hour ago, resistance had been futile.

Dan stumbled behind the muscular slave into a dimly lit room. A hook on the end of a cable hung down from the ceiling to which the slave attached Dan's chain-leash. The sound of an electric motor alerted Dan to the fact that his leash was being drawn slowly upward, ultimately to the point where he was close to being hanged by the neck. At this point Dan's initial emotions were completely banished by pure terror. Was he going be executed? What the fuck was going on here? How had this happened? Dan began to plead loudly. "No! No! Please! Don't kill me! Please, no!" Dan could feel warm piss running down inside his leathers and into his boot. He was beside himself with fear.

"Shut the fuck up, asshole!" the slave hissed. "If you want to make it out of here in one piece, you better do exactly what the fuck you are told and do it immediately! Get this straight right now - blind obedience is your only option."

"No! Please!" Dan continued, not really having comprehended what the slave had said. So the electric motor was heard once more, only more slowly, and Dan could feel the chain-collar tightening as he was pulled up by the neck. He shut up. He had to. He couldn't breathe!

Dan couldn't remember very clearly what had happened next, but the slave knew. It let Dan hang only for a few seconds, released the tension and proceeded with its work on a now totally compliant victim. Dan came around to the wisdom of blind obedience in that breathless moment - the moment when Dan became a real part of Leather Officer's system - the moment when Dan understood for the first time that there was only one way - Leather Officer's way.

Breathing again, Dan was strangely calm and could take a moment to check out his captor. The slave was handsome, obviously in very good shape and equipped with a very presentable set of cock and balls. Dan was tempted to thank the slave for not killing him, but instead just kept quiet. The slave produced a handcuff key and freed Dan's hands. Dan thought briefly about trying to escape, but quickly realized that the chain-collar and chain-leash attached to the ceiling were enough to hold him.

"Strip!" the slave demanded. Dan obeyed and removed that portion of his leather that he could reach. The slave pulled Dan's pissed-in pants and boots off, put all the leather in a sack, and tossed it through a small cabinet type door to...where? Dan was about to protest, but thought better of it. Dan was totally nude now, and getting no empowering feedback from his leather. He wasn't cold - indeed it was quite warm in this strange bare room - and Dan began to perspire. Looking around, he noticed that the walls were pretty much bare concrete block with a couple of additional cabinet-type doors, like the one that had received his leather. The floor was concrete, sloping to a small grated drain in the center, just below where Dan was chained. The place was bare and clean. This theme was to be repeated a lot in Dan's new life.

Three more slaves suddenly appeared, shaved, collared, and booted like the first. One opened a door and brought out a hose, quickly turned it on and sprayed Dan from head to foot with cold water. He yelped. That brought a slap on the ass from another slave, using a dog-slapper obtained from behind another door. "Shut the fuck up, asshole," one slave commanded, and Dan got sprayed again. He again made some kind of unintelligible noise, got slapped on the ass twice and sprayed again. Finally Dan got the drill and had the sense to just take it.

The next half hour was the greatest humiliation of Dan's life. Each slave had apparently been assigned a portion of Dan's body to denude, starting first with scissors, then clippers and finally, razors. A full body shave requires a great deal of time and effort. Very few Masters will attempt it on their own more than once or twice, realizing soon that it's really only feasible if several slaves are available to shave one another. Dan had had a fairly hairy chest of which he was quite proud, but no more. No hair around his cock and balls, around his ass, on his legs. His head was shaved, his eyebrows were gone, and even his eyelashes were trimmed. He had less hair on his body than a newborn.

After the shave, Dan was again hosed down. No complaints this time. The slaves dried him off, and rubbed oil over him to make him glisten. Finally his chain-leash was removed from the ceiling hook, and he was dragged / led up the stairs, forced to his knees, and chained to a ring in the floor such that he could kneel but not stand.

As Dan looked around, he began to understand that his previous life was over. The room was structured much like an arena, or throne room. The walls were all black, covered with a bewildering array of equipment which Dan recognized from leather stores and Masters' spaces he had visited. But a lot more, with a bank of cages on one wall, and on another a very imposing large black leather chair, upon which Leather Officer sat. The four slaves took positions in a row, sitting like dogs in front of their cages.

"What took so fucking long, slaves?" Leather Officer demanded. "I didn't bring this piece of shit here to wait all night while you fuck around with it. Is it ready for me to start its training?"

"Yes, Sir." Dan thought it was the voice of the first, and apparently, head slave. "It's ready, Sir."

At the Hole, Dan had been completely enthralled by Leather Officer's appearance and manner. But if possible, in this new setting, now that Dan was chained to the floor with no leather, not even any hair, Leather Officer appeared far more dominating, far more threatening, far more irresistible even than before. Dan felt himself melt as the handsome leather cop strode over to him. It is arguable whether Dan, even if he weren't chained to the floor, would have been able to have fled at this point. Even facing certain death at Leather Officer's hands, it is doubtful that Dan would have walked away even if he had been free to do so. He was that far gone.

Dan noticed that the cop was somewhat changed in appearance since an hour ago. What was it? Leather Officer answered the question by slapping his gloved hand lightly against the holster on his belt which now held the largest revolver Dan had ever seen. ".44 mag. It'll blow a hole the size of a football in a man's chest at close range. It's useful for keeping all these shitheads in line," the cop said, indicating the squatting slaves in a row. The same slaves that had seemed so powerful to Dan only moments ago as they humiliated him with their razors, now were clearly shown to be completely and utterly under Leather Officer's control.

"Get this straight, fuckhole, and get it the first time: you are now a slave train- ee. I have already begun your training. Your past life is over. I own you. You will serve me until I no longer have a use for you. Do you understand?"

Dan hesitated, as the cop anticipated he would. "Well, I, uh..." A gleaming police boot shot out in a manner all the slaves knew well and kicked Dan in the chest, not with the toe, but with the sole and heel, on an angle, abrading Dan's now hairless left pec, leaving a series of reddening welted lines. "Ahyeee!" Dan screamed, and retreated as far as his chain-leash would allow, failing in his attempt to get out of reach of the cop boots.

"DO YOU UNDERSTAND?" Leather Officer shouted.

"Sir, yes Sir, I do understand, yes Sir!" Dan wasn't sure what he understood, but he was learning quickly that whatever Leather Officer said was the way it would be and it was better to agree and obey than to risk the consequences.

"Come over here. Kiss my crotch," the cop ordered. Dan obeyed. He crawled over and began lightly kissing Leather Officer's black leather codpiece, steal- ing a glance at the god-like figure towering above him. The presence was increasingly overpowering. The cold stare downward from the handsome, officers-capped face. The perfectly fitting black leather police uniform, the weapons and gear, the gleaming boots. Dan was melting, mindlessly compar- ing his own hairless, chained self with the man invading his brain and insisting that Dan be a slave.

Dan felt oblivious to everything other than his Master, for Leather Officer had already mastered Dan completely. Dan might never make a particularly good slave, the cop would find that out, but he would be easy to train - the fight was already gone. Dan began to make a low moaning sound as he continued to kiss the cop's codpiece, as the man in front of him became increasingly indistinct, mesmerizing Dan.

Suddenly, Leather Officer ripped off the codpiece and pressed the inside of it against Dan's nose and mouth, also covering the victim's eyes, so the odor of the cop's cock and balls was drawn deep into Dan's lungs, deep into his body. Dan nearly fainted from the power of the odor, nearly forgot where he was, who he was, only thinking about the man who was becoming his Master. Again, without warning, Leather Officer pulled the codpiece off his trainee's face and tossed it aside. Immediately one of the slaves leapt up, retrieved the prize and placed it on a shelf handy to Leather Officer's throne. Momentarily distracted by the slave's rush, Dan returned focus to the cop and gazed for the first time upon the center of his universe.

Leather Officer's dick and balls hung in the air in front of the trainee's face. The cock was only semi-erect, but already long, thick and veiny. The corona was more darkly colored than the shaft, the tighter skin demanding service. The balls were in many ways more impressive than the penis, filling their sac, promising sweet juices later, stating their pride as the source of Leather Officer's power. Dan saw it all in a flash, it all came together, where he had been, more clearly where he would now be taken. The cop's cock and balls finished Dan off. The place began to spin, churn. Dan fell to the floor without even a blow.

The slightest nod from the cop was all it took to dispatch slaves 1 and 3 to raise Dan back up off the floor and onto all fours. As the trainee regained consciousness, Leather Officer took a moment to survey his facility. The walls were painted black and shiny, the lighting was mostly red, but some clear. Equipment was arrayed against one wall, hung neatly and with a specific organization: hoods together, by type and size, and similarly for collars, restraints, harnesses, ass-work equipment, tit-work equipment, floggers, crops, bullwhips, and much more - each piece reminding Leather Officer of a particular time in his career, a particular slave, a particular training session.

One very unique item, which Leather Officer had had custom made years ago, was not leather at all. It was a replica of a Dungeon Master shirt he had seen in a Boy Scout magazine when he was just a boy. It was a comic strip format cartoon that showed how unpleasant it would be to live anywhere other than in America - patriotism for boys. In Europe, in the past, prisoners were tortured in dungeons for their beliefs, the cartoon explained. It showed several emaciated victims shackled to a stone wall - Albigensians perhaps - about to be abused by a huge, muscular man wearing black boots, black leather pants, and a shirt of some kind of stretchy material - a shirt unlike any the young boy had ever seen. The shirt was tight on the man's large, muscular chest and arms, black, short-sleeved, sort of like a t-shirt, but with a difference. The shirt included a hood covering most of the man's head and a mask, so that only the eyes and the face below the mask were visible - like an executioner's hood. The man was gloved, carried a bullwhip and was standing next to a three-legged charcoal brazier in which he was heating a thick poker to red hot. The Dungeon Master's expression was pure sadism.

The immediate effect on the young boy was dramatic; a huge and sustained erection for his boy-dick. A debut almost, with the usual dawning adolescent confusion about what was going on and what to do about it. The magazine was kept and the cartoon referred to repeatedly over the years, kept with other images from the mainline press of athletes, soldiers, cops, heroes of all kinds. The Dungeon Master was as much a hero to the boy as the others. Maybe more so.

The custom-made shirt was now itself twenty years old, seldom worn anymore, but still highly cherished, a symbol of Leather Officer's first overt sadism - the first clue. Scouting had certainly had a positive effect on Leather Officer.

The spontaneous survey continued. Against another wall was a row of four large dog cages, large enough for the largest of "dogs" to stretch out and sleep. In front of each was a pad upon which the slaves sat on all fours, dog style. When not involved otherwise with their service, the slaves would be found sitting at the ready, or caged. Experience had taught Leather Officer that four slaves was the right number. Enough to serve him fully, but not so many that their upkeep and management became a burden.

Against the back wall was a large jail cell with bunks - for guests, new trainees, whatever. Also against that wall was stored an array of larger equipment such as the fucking horse, torture table, suspension pyramid, etc., and all of Leather Officer's uniforms. From the past, there were conventional biker leather, military uniforms, and even sports gear. But over the years, as Leather Officer had become increasingly focused, little had been added that was not specifically motorcycle cop gear. Lately, very few authentic motorcycle cop uniform items had been added. The focus had been almost exclusively on custom-made leather motorcycle cop uniforms. A little white, a little silver, gold, dark blue, and dark crimson were seen, but these colors were only sparsely scattered on a mass of black leather. The survey only took him an instant, the instant during which Dan was hauled up on all fours to confront the cop's dick once again.

"OK, fuckhole, let's get started," Leather Officer announced. Slaves 1 and 4 scurried back to their pads. "In lesson one, you learn what your throat is really for, who controls you, and that there is no alternative to obedience."

Leather Officer glanced briefly at one of several strategically placed huge mirrors and saw the beginning of a process he had taken many victims through - copslave training. He saw himself without any noticeable flaw, uniformed in black leather, armed, balls heavy and full of promise, penis erect and threatening, standing directly in front of the new trainee, a glistening drop of precum a fraction of an inch from the trainee's lips. Leather Officer had no idea what the shithead's name was and didn't care. Hell, even the four slaves had no names Leather Officer used, just numbers. "Open up, fuckhole!" the cop demanded.

Dan obeyed as Leather Officer straddled Dan's leash-chain and plunged the entire organ entirely inside Dan's mouth and throat, zipping right past the sphincter at the junction of the two as if it weren't even there. Dan had no hair on his groin, but Leather Officer did, and Dan now felt it against his upper lip and nose. He shouldn't have been surprised by this assault, but he was. He was unable to breathe. Automatically, he retreated back off the copdick. He was panicky.

As Dan retreated on all fours, desperate to get off the cop's prick, desperate to get a breath, Leather Officer merely took a step forward and the copdick stayed put in the trainee's throat. Through the tears, Leather Officer could see real fear replacing mere panic. So he pulled his cock out for a moment, keeping Dan's mouth full but allowing him to suck in lungfuls of air through his nose.

Two deep breaths were enough, Leather Officer felt. Back down Dan's throat the copdick was shoved, eliciting the same desperate retreat on Dan's part, followed by Leather Officer's advance. Again two breaths, plunge back in, trainee retreat, cop advance. A few cycles of this and Dan became aware of a pressure on the back of his neck as his serial retreats had caused him to now be at the end of his chain-leash. No more retreat, and the copdick was advancing once more. In it plunged and Dan was stuck with nowhere to go and no means to get the prick out of his throat. He felt Leather Officer's slave-shined boots kick his legs wider apart, felt the leather of the cop's breeches against his hairless chest, felt the chain around his neck holding him fast and realized that he was in danger of being killed right here, right now.

Leather Officer stepped back slightly - just enough for Dan to get two breaths - then back in he went. He continued to fuck Dan's throat, occasionally abrading the trainee's cock and balls with the soles of his cop boots, occasionally jabbing at the insides of the thighs with the boot toes or treading on the tops of the thighs with the boot heels. Once Leather Officer felt that the trainee was ready, had accepted the inevitability of the fuck, he began pulling his copdick all the way out of Dan's mouth before the return plunge, increasing the length of his strokes and then began to hesitate slightly before plunging, keeping an eye on Dan's reaction to discover how long it would take before Dan's eyes would begin to plead for the next stroke, dread that the previous had been the last. How long would it take before Dan developed slave eyes?

Not long. As Leather Officer began to take a moment to smack Dan's face with the hard copdick, to tease the victim, he could see clearly in Dan's eyes that there was now a new slave. Less than two hours from top to slave! Dan's slave wiring was fully activated and Leather Officer was his universe. The easy conquest made Leather Officer cocky. He began to swagger as he fucked, enjoying the huge power chasm between his godlike self and the servile object on his dick. He increased the tempo of the fucking and Dan began to make gurgling, animal-like noises between strokes. Quicker and quicker the strokes came down Dan's throat as he reached out to grasp his Master's breeches for support. No chain was now needed. Dan was owned totally by the leather cop fucking his throat. Dan caught Leather Officer's rhythm perfectly and could imagine no future other than being throat-fucked forever.

Suddenly, Leather Officer let out a low groan which then raised in pitch, and the copdick strokes changed in rhythm, becoming jerky and impossible for Dan to follow. Cum went everywhere - a lot of it - down Dan's throat, in his mouth, up into his nose, into his eyes, all over his face and his hairless chest, dripping down onto his erect cock and twitching balls. 3 rushed forward with outstretched tongue and quickly cleaned up Leather Officer's copdick. The cop took a step back and surveyed his new slave.

"Your throat is for me to fuck, slave! I control you totally and completely. You will obey me without question. Immediately!" Leather Officer yelled. "Remember what I just said. It's Lesson One. 1 and 3, take this piece of shit downstairs and get it cleaned up. Then strap it to the horse and you can fight over which one of you will get to fuck its ass." Leather Officer watched 1 and 3 grab the trainee by the arms and lead it downstairs to be cleaned. 2 and 4 remained on their pads. Leather Officer addressed 2. "You know what's next, right?"

"Yes, Sir, I believe I do, Sir," the head slave responded.

"Which one of you will fuck the trainee, do you think?" the Master asked.

"Sir, I imagine, if it be your intention that this competition go in the way it has in the past, that I will fuck the trainee. But, Sir, my anticipation is only a service to you, Sir. How it goes, Sir, is entirely a function of your will," 2 responded.

Addressing 4, Leather Officer questioned similarly, "What about you, fuck-head? Who do you think will fuck the trainee?"

"I - I - I don't know, Sir. I hope you will fuck me, Sir," 4 said.

Leather Officer grabbed a leather riding crop and was on the fuck-up immediately. He stood in front of 4, his now-soft dick inches away from the sex-starved slave's lips. In spite of the pleasure Leather Officer took inflicting pain and in spite of the pleasure he derived from witnessing 4's distress, Leather Officer was genuinely angry. He struck at the collared animal savagely with his crop, smacking it repeatedly on its naked ass. As he struck, Leather Officer's penis grazed 4's face, as close to its Master's dick as the failure might get. "You fucking jerk!" Leather Officer yelled. "Answer my question! Answer it now!"

The distraught 4 just burst into tears, not so much from the blows as from shame and remorse for having fucked up the most important thing that it had ever had, its slavery to Leather Officer. Leather Officer rained blow after blow on his slave, until it collapsed, howling in pain and shame.

"Answer my question!"

The fact was that 4 couldn't answer the question because it didn't remember what the question had been, had never known, because it didn't listen closely. It allowed itself to get distracted by its own needs, allowed itself to be so filled with craving for its Master's cock that it didn't pay close enough attention to its job, which in this case, had been to answer the fucking question. So 4 just cried and added more demerits to its record, inching closer and closer to what it dreaded most - termination.

"2, tell this idiot what the question was," Leather Officer demanded.

"Yes, Sir. The question was 'who do we think will fuck the trainee?' Sir," 2 responded, getting it right as always. 4 would have been better off if it had spent more time emulating 2 than envying it.

"Ok, moron, what's your fucking answer?" Leather Officer again asked.

"Sir, I think 2 will - *sob* - fuck the trainee, Sir," 4 blubbered.

4 was so hapless that even its Master upon occasion almost felt badly for

it. "Sit up!" the Master barked. 4 did, immediately and stared up at Leather Officer through its tears with a level of adoration that few tops ever see. But slave eyes, even these 100% slave eyes were not enough reason to keep an otherwise dysfunctional slave. Leather Officer looked deeply into 4's slave eyes. "What's the cardinal rule?" he demanded.

"Sir, a slave obeys its Master!" 4 shouted.

"Good boy," Leather Officer said. 4 grinned and made a cooing sound in response to its Master's compliment. Its slave eyes shone. Leather Officer glanced at 2, about to continue the interrogation. But at that moment, cursing and commotion were heard on the stairs as the trainee was wrestled back up by 1 and 3. Leather Officer's attention was diverted from 2, but not before he noticed, ever so briefly, something that was new in the head slave. Perhaps it was just the comparison of the moment to 4, but Leather Officer, as his attention was diverted to the struggling trainee, fleetingly noted 2's slave eyes. And the question was raised, just in an instant, whether 2's slave eyes were as bright as Leather Officer had come to expect. Again, perhaps it was just the comparison with 4, but Leather Officer made a brief note to check further. Perhaps something was up.

"No! Fuck, no! I don't want to stay any longer! I want to go! I want my boy!" the trainee was yelling. "You can't keep me here!"

2's slave eyes would have to wait. The trainee was having a crisis and Leather Officer's skill was needed. He grabbed the trainee's cock and balls with a gloved hand, encircling them with his thumb and first finger like a cockring, squeezed tight, twisted, and pulled out and up.

"Shut the fuck up, asshole! You are going nowhere! You are my copslave trainee and you will submit! You will obey or I will rip your fucking nuts off and serve them to these slaves for dinner!" The trainee made a sort of sucking, hissing sound in response to the excruciating pain being administered by its Master. It shut up. It obeyed. It learned the cardinal rule. "Strap it to the horse!" Leather Officer shouted.

2 and 4 were up in a flash, running to the far end of the room where the fucking horse was stored. They dragged it front and center, whereupon 1 and 3 quickly bound the trainee to it using the many attached leather straps, binding its arms and legs and torso. The trainee's face was toward the arena, its ass toward Leather Officer's throne. Both the mouth and ass were at cock level. "I have already taken control of your throat and made it my fuckhole, isn't that right, shithead?" Leather Officer asked the bound trainee as he circled

around in front of its face, still holding the crop recently used on 4. The trainee hesitated. "Obey me! Answer me immediately and truthfully!" Leather Officer thundered, and struck repeated blows against the trainee's exposed ass, much the same treatment given 4.

"Sir, yes, sir," the trainee murmured, eliciting more strokes from the crop.

Leather Officer's penis was becoming engorged with blood, threatening to again demonstrate to the trainee the answer to the question. But rather than fuck its throat again, Leather Officer circled around to the dangling cock and balls, grabbed these again and re-asked the question. "Have I already taken control of your throat and made it my fuckhole?"

"Sir, yes Sir," the trainee stated, more loudly, more affirmatively and with greater conviction. More rough handling of its balls coupled with more crop strokes on its naked back informed the trainee that the answer was still not correct.

"4, tell this jerk what the correct answer is," Leather Officer offered to his weakest slave.

"Sir, yes Sir, thank you Sir. The correct answer, Sir, is 'Yes, Sir, you have already taken control of my throat and made it your fuckhole, Sir,'" 4 responded.

"Good boy," Leather Officer stated, blandly, making 4's slave eyes shine with pride. "Now you say it, dickhead!" Leather Officer commanded the trainee.

"Sir, you have taken control of my throat and made it your fuckhole," the trainee responded, hoping it had gotten it right.

"Fair," the cop noted, "but you'll soon do better, much better. Now listen up, fuckhead. You are my trainee. If you succeed with training, you will be my slave. If you fail, you will be terminated. In either case, it is my decision, not yours. I own you. You are my property." Addressing the slaves, he asked, "What is the cardinal rule?"

The chorus responded immediately, in perfect harmony, born of hundreds of repetitions, "Sir, a slave obeys its Master, Sir!"

"That's right, 'a slave obeys its Master.' Trainee, you will obey me completely, immediately, and with no hesitation or doubt. Do you understand?" Leather Officer asked, again circling around in front of his victim, lightly snapping the crop into his gloved hand.

"Yes Sir, I understand, Sir," was the trainee's response. Well after all, it was not more than three hours ago that it had been a top itself, so it really should be familiar with the rituals of slavery. The issue, Leather Officer knew, was whether the slave wiring could be activated to the extent that the former top would fully function as a slave. Leather Officer figured that it would be easy, but what kind of a slave would result was always hard to tell. He'd see.

"Obey me and it will be relatively easy. If you fight me, I'll rip your fucking skin off," Leather Officer whispered in the trainee's ear, patting it on the cheek. "Now, let's get down to brass tacks." Leather Officer pulled a pair of handcuffs from his belt and threw them on the floor in the middle of the arena. "Who wants to fight first?"

The slave chorus shouted, "Me, Sir, me, please, me, me first, please, me!" They all knew that the choice was entirely their Master's, but they also knew that to appear less than eager to fight could produce serious repercussions.

"OK, let's go with - 1 and 4: on your marks, get set, go!" Leather Officer said, and the two were off their pads in a blink. First to grab the cuffs would have the advantage.

Surprisingly, 4 grabbed the cuffs; perhaps a result of how well it had recently been treated by its Master. The game was no-holds-barred wrestling, the winner cuffing the loser. Sometimes it was over fast, sometimes not. It was Leather Officer's favorite spectator sport: the sadism inhered not only in the humiliation of the loss, but in the fact that as the fighters became fatigued, it became increasingly difficult for either to get the advantage, leading to greater fatigue, and so on. As the fight dragged on, it was the cop's habit to abuse the fighters and goad them to a resolution, usually employing his copboots.

No-holds-barred meant just that, but each slave knew that it would live to fight another day, and it had to live day to day with the opponent as well, so restraint of a sort was built in. Hurt the guy too bad and you'd likely get payback soon. This structure was Leather Officer's design and it served to reinforce the general relationship between the slaves: they were rivals but they had to coexist.

4 grabbed the cuffs, then circled quickly around 1 and grabbed it by the cock and balls. It squeezed and pulled back and up, just like the cop had done to quiet the trainee. 1 squealed as 4 shouted, "On your belly, right now, hands behind your back!" 1 obeyed, and 4's triumph was quick as it clicked the cuffs onto 1's wrists with its free hand. "Ahyeee!" 4 elated. "Ahyeee!" "Ahyeee!" Leather Officer smelled a rat. This unexpected victory was a little too easy,

and coupled with the cop's recollection of the unusual look in 2's slave eyes, alerted him to a possible conspiracy. Leather Officer played it cool - if something was up, he'd uncover it soon enough - he knew the slave mentality far better than any of them did. Watchful waiting.

"Good boy, 4!" the cop stated, with apparent enthusiasm. "Put it in the stocks." Leather Officer sat on his throne. 4 opened up the stocks, which were set up along the side of the arena and moved 1 onto the bench behind. 1's ankles went in and were fastened. Then, already immobilized, its head went in and was similarly fastened. The wrists would have to wait for Leather Officer to come with the cuff key, and the cop was in no hurry, starting his investigation into whether the fight had been thrown. A second set of cuffs was thrown into the arena. "At the command 'home!'"

"On your marks, get set, go." It was 2 and 3. Again, the unlikely fighter to grab the cuffs first was the one that did - 3. 2 was the head slave for many reasons, and combat was one of them. 2 was always the favorite, as both it and 4 had stated earlier. Now Leather Officer's suspicions were really up. The cop began to formulate his response to what had the appearance of a full scale revolt, and it was clear who was the Spartacus. But quickly the fight went the other way: 2 clamped a massive biceps against 3's windpipe, pulling it against the muscular chest. A few seconds of this were all it took for 3 to realize that the cuffs should be dropped, which they were, and 2 moved 3 down to the floor, effortlessly picked up the cuffs, snapped one on the loser's right wrist, ran the short chain between the legs and snapped the other cuff to the left wrist. 3 was now in a cumbersome and humiliating position. Apparently there was no slave revolt after all.

"Motherfucker," 3 muttered, feeling correctly that its humiliation was gratuitous. That won it a slap across the mouth; then the head slave hauled it over to the stocks. Quickly 2 fastened its conquest in and turned toward Leather Officer.

"Sir, permission to gag this smart-mouthed slave, Sir!" 2 requested of its Master.

"Denied, slave. I want the throat available for fucking. That will teach it to smart-off better than gagging it. But hood it - deny it the fun of watching the training," Leather Officer commanded.

"Yes, Sir! Very good, Sir!" 2 responded with real admiration for the cop's sadism. The hood had only a mouth hole, nothing more, making 3 into nothing more that a prick receptacle, not even a spectator like its bench mate 1. Leather Officer arose and unlocked the handcuffs on both slaves' wrists as 2 quickly placed those same wrists in the stocks and locked the apparatus.

"Home!" the cop commanded 2, guiding 4 over to right home. Home and right home, the most comfortable places in the universe for slaves, kneeling at their Master's boot, cheek against his breeches and arm around his boot. The slaves' lips can occasionally kiss the Master's leather breeched leg, their hands can caress his boots, they can hold tight to him, gaze up lovingly at his handsome face and receive pets from his gloved hand. Home at the left boot, and right home at the right boot: the positions that slaves who lose their Masters often say were their favorites.

"You boys have done well," Leather Officer said. 4 glowed. It had never been happier! 3 fumed. It sensed that it had been fucked-with and it was correct. 1 was pleased. It would have liked to fuck the trainee, but was willing to sit it out for a good cause. 2 was cautious. It thought that it and its lone confederate were fooling the cop, but although Leather Officer had suspended his suspicions, they were only suspended. The Master had sensed something and would be alert, for there was still the issue of 2's slave eyes.

Leather Officer laid a gloved hand on the heads of the two slaves in home position, 2 and 4, the winners of the first two fights. Normally, these two would fight for the right to fuck the trainee. Indeed, all the slaves expected that this would occur, that 2 would easily dominate 4 and go on to fuck the trainee. But Leather Officer had something else in mind - a twist. After all, who was in charge? "Well, boys, this is an unexpected result, isn't it?" he asked rhetorically.

Only 2 was quick enough to come up with the right answer: "Yes, Sir," 2 responded, but although it was the right answer in that it was the correct answer, it was the wrong answer in that it confirmed Leather Officer's suspicion that the slave under his right hand was there only through some kind of chicanery. The cop's job now was to expose the plotters and smash the revolt. Any agenda other than Leather Officer's constituted a revolt, and revolution would be dealt with mercilessly. The game continued.

"Since the unexpected has occurred, let's up the ante and dispense with the playoff. 4 is declared the winner. 4 will fuck the trainee," the cop proclaimed. "2, take the place of the loser!"

The plotters felt a bit sick. Both 1 and 2 suspected that Leather Officer had caught on. In fact the cop had not yet figured out quite what was going on. 3 was not a part of it and was hooded anyway. But most alarmed of all was 4. Fuck the trainee? 4 was not a fucker. It was 10,000% slave and lived only to have its mouth and ass fucked by its cop Master. Fuck the trainee? 4 began already to experience performance fears way beyond anything most men can imagine. Fuck the trainee?

"Stand up. Get ready to fuck its ass," Leather Officer commanded 4, as the cop himself stood and moved over in front of the trainee's mouth, readying his penis to fuck its throat again. "C'mon, fuckhole! Get it up! Fuck it!" Leather Officer commanded as 2 knelt adjacent to the head end of the trainee. The loser in the play-offs was the alternate throat-fuck, and Leather Officer liked to switch back and forth between the two throat fucks, trainee and loser, while the winner exulted its slave cock up the trainee's ass. "Fuck him! Fuck him!" the cop yelled at 4.

Poor 4 looked down at its tiny, shriveling dick. It was completely inadequate to this task which was totally new. 4 had never fucked any man before, it wasn't possible for it, it only got erect for its Master, sucking its Master, getting fucked by its Master, awaiting its Master, dreaming about its Master. 4's penis was not meant for what was now demanded. Leather Officer came back over to 4, grabbed it by the neck, and forced its tiny cock against the trainee's ass. "Fuck it! Fuck it now! Fuck it or you're gone tomorrow!"

4's worst nightmare. It was totally incapable of fucking the trainee, especially with its Master yelling and threatening it. 4 collapsed in horror, in a despondence deeper than any man can know. It wailed and shrieked, its body shook, it grabbed its head and curled up in a ball and sobbed.

"Fuck," Leather Officer spat with disgust. He kicked 4 once, then again, hard. "Get the fuck out of here! Wait downstairs. I'll deal with you later." The broken, humiliated slave dragged itself down to the cleaning room and collapsed. The others were white. This brutality was beyond what they had experienced before. "OK, I'll fuck it myself," Leather Officer announced. The scene with 4 had left the cop hugely erect and ready for release. Leather Officer had been tremendously aroused by the humiliation of 4 and that arousal would now be directed to the penetration of the trainee's ass. "2. Stand up and fuck its throat."

2 stood, but it was soft. 2 was shaken by how badly its plot had gone. The slave which was to be helped ended up hurt worse than anything 2 had ever seen in its several years of slavery. 2 slapped the trainee across the mouth, hard. It yelped. "Get me hard and make me cum! Do it or I'll cut your fucking nuts off! I'm serious! Do it or you'll leave your fucking balls here!" 2 hissed at the trainee, not loud enough so that Leather Officer could quite get it. 2 was serious. Things had gone badly off track, and 2 was desperate to fix it. A suc-

cessful face fuck was all it could think of.

The trainee was frightened and obeyed. It did its damnedest to get 2 hard and was successful. 2 began the throat fuck slowly, more or less emulating the technique of its Master. This was tough on the trainee, for it needed a lot of oxygen. That was the point of the alternate throat fuck, to give the trainee enough breathing time to endure a throat fuck simultaneously to having its ass slave-fucked. No alternate for this trainee and no slave fuck either. The ass would be conquered by an enraged Leather Officer instead. Not a randy but empathetic slave up the ass, no. The trainee was about to take the full wrath of Leather Officer, who had confirmed that some shit was up with the slaves, but clearly the best solution would be brutality.

The trainee was not a virgin, of course, but had been a top exclusively for quite some time. Leather Officer's copdick was purple with rage, larger and more vicious than ever before. The cop strode up to his victim's asshole, spat in it, and briefly poked the head of his cock barely into it to spread the spit around. "Pay attention, slaves. You're about to find out why I wear the boots and you wear your collars."

2 was now hard, and pumping away at the trainee's throat, trying to focus on the fuck and forget about 4. 2 glanced at its Master, whose cock was pressed against the trainee's sphincter, only a moment away from penetration. Leather Officer's eyes met 2's. The cop saw it in an instant. The slave eyes were gone.

2 was unaware. It continued to perform, banishing all thoughts from its mind except its cock down the trainee's throat. It would time its strokes to its Master's, and cum on demand. It would grin and act cocky afterward. But everything had changed. Leather Officer had seen that 2 had, at least for the moment, lost its slave eyes. The plot to save 4 had backfired badly and the punishment would be severe. Seeing 2's dull eyes only enraged the cop more. *What the fuck is going on here?* he asked himself. Whatever it was, the trainee would very likely be critical to maintain full staffing. Leather Officer could smell two terminations, so better break it fast and hard. The little bit of spit was the only care Leather Officer gave to his victim. This evening was turning out to be far more brutal than any of them had imagined.

"Keep your prick down its throat while I give it the first several rape strokes!" Leather Officer barked at 2. "Do it now." 2 complied, burying its penis deep in the trainee's throat. Simultaneously, Leather Officer thrust through the sphincter with the head of his angry cock, held momentarily, withdrew completely, poked against it as if he were about to enter again, hesitated, but then shoved the entire member all the way home, so that the cop's pubic hair tickled the trainee's ass. He pulled completely out, again teased the anus with the point and slammed back in the whole way. 2 felt the convulsions in the victim's throat, the screams stifled by its cock.

"Pull out!" Leather Officer yelled. 2 obeyed, and the poor trainee sucked in gallons of air, then bleated it back out along with a noise that sounded more like a machine than an animal, certainly not like a human. "OK, fuck him normal," the cop commanded, and 2 did, in and out deeply, hesitatingly, teasingly, allowing breathing enough to survive the double fuck but not more, to emphasize the full level of control over the trainee's life held by Leather Officer.

The cop fucked this ass as well as he had ever fucked. He was angry and determined to regain control of his empire. The rebellion was already long over, but Leather Officer wasn't entirely sure of it and wanted to make it clear that nothing of the kind would ever be attempted again. This ass fucking was the best ever, if brutal is best. In, out, in, out, relentlessly, no break, no recovery, constant strokes, full strokes, all the way in, all the way out, snap the hole shut, pop it back open, thrust all the way in, pull all the way out, on and on.

The trainee was delirious, screaming between throat strokes, sucking in air and screaming it back out. 2 came simultaneously with its Master, grunting unintelligibly as the cop hissed in and out rapidly, finally spasming in his heaving chest as his tubes contracted and his juice squirted up the trainee's ass. 2 grinned at its Master, but received no grin back, only a cold stare. 2's slave eyes had returned, but it was too late - where had they gone? What slave has moments where its slavery is in abeyance? Neither Master nor slave had a plan, but both knew that a crisis was at hand. Each kept quiet, better to control the outcome.

"Clean it up! I'll deal with the rest of you in the morning!" Leather Officer commanded. "3! Come upstairs." 2 released 1 and 3 from the stocks and removed 3's hood. 3 climbed the stairs to serve the Master, 1 went to its cage, 2 threw a blanket down to 4 and itself went to its cage to spend a restless night pondering a way out.

3 was the only slave that wasn't in trouble, so it was the one that would prepare Leather Officer for sleep. The cop unholstered his weapon and laid it aside to be locked up. 3 removed the entire leather cop uniform and got erect in the presence of its Master's naked body. The uniform was hung up for care in the morning. Leather Officer removed 3's collar as the slave removed its boots. The two showered together, the slave washing and drying the Master's body. They dressed for bed: the Master was booted and gloved with softer

than usual leather and wore a plain Sam Browne, also designed for comfort during sleep. The slave was recollared, but not reshod, fettered and fastened ass up to the bed.

Leather Officer inserted his copdick into the slave's ass and pumped it leisurely, more as a reward for the boy than anything else. Leather Officer had an active night already. The cop fucked for a while, came a little, but then left the slave plugged to give it sweet dreams. 3 fell asleep easily, the only one in the facility to do so.

The trainee was still strapped to the fucking horse, exhausted. It reviewed the day briefly, thought about Dick, hoped that he was OK, but then simply fell unconscious to await whatever would come in the morning. Next to sleep was 1, who knew that its Master suspected that it had thrown the fight and knew that it would be interrogated at length about the suspicion. It fell asleep regretting that it had allowed 2 to corral it into the scheme. 4 was downstairs alone on the concrete with just a flimsy blanket, desperate about its fate, tearful as usual, and wishing it were strapped to Leather Officer's bed with the copdick up its ass. 4 resented the fact that it, the best wired of all the slaves, was probably going to be terminated. A sigh of resignation preceded its fall to sleep.

Leather Officer realized that something was up. 2's slave eyes had clearly dimmed, although they had brightened up later. Still, something was up with the head slave. It did appear that 1 had thrown the fight, suggesting some kind of conspiracy. 4 might be a part of it as well - this was unclear. The new trainee was an as-yet-untested quantity. Only 3, under him now and being fucked as the cop did his planning, was not currently a problem. Leather Officer considered stretching each of the four in turn on the St. Andrew's, whipping them to tears and eliciting the information he needed. Each whipping would be in private so the conspiracy would crumble. The cop would have no trouble getting the whole truth out of each of them, the whipping would be good for them, and once the story was clear he'd take whatever action was appropriate. Including multiple terminations if necessary. Leather Officer had not invented slavery or slave wiring, he merely administered it. If any of these assholes had fucked up, Leather Officer would simply fix it. He fell asleep confident that resolution would flow quickly.

Last to sleep was 2. It reviewed its disaster. It had plotted with 1 to throw the fights. They had agreed that if either fought 4 they'd allow it to win, boost its standing and to help it stave off termination. 1 cooperated because 2 had a certain control over it in slave debts. 3 could not be brought into the plot. 3 had no current debts. 4 was actually unaware; it didn't know that 2 was out to help it. 1 was persuaded that it was actually valuable to have 4 around, a cushion so to speak. As long as 4 was fucking up, the scrutiny was off the others. There could only be one weakest slave at a time, and 4 was it. Without 4, 1 might be the goat. 2 had persuaded 1 with this argument.

2's real motive was fatal. 2 had come to have affection for 4. It had spent a lot of effort trying to bring the fuckup to a higher standard, but had been largely unsuccessful. 4 just couldn't do very well at any of the slave activities: it messed boot polish up, burned food, was untidy with the leather and gear, made very slow progress at the gym, never got the answers right, etc. 2 had thought at times that 4 should be terminated, that the slave was just not cost effective. But 2 was affected by 4's slave wiring. Although its performance was bad, its devotion to its Master, its complete subordination to Leather Officer, its total lack of any thought ever for itself other than to be with its Master, to serve, to have its ego melt - its level of slavery was really beautiful, regardless the chores. 2 thought that in many ways, 4 was really the best slave and plotted to protect the fuckup.

But the fatality of 2's motive was that it had substituted its view for that of its Master. In essence, it disagreed with Leather Officer's priorities, felt that the cop was incorrect in his judgment and his action and sought to thwart him. This kind of thinking is fatal in any slave. It is incompatible with slavery and was the cause of the dimming of 2's slave eyes - which Leather Officer had seen immediately.

An observer might argue that 2's view had great merit and that Leather Officer would be a better slavemaster in the long run if he considered it and implemented it. But such was not to be the case, and cannot be the case - it is not the way of slave and Master. 2 had broken its connection to its Master. Even though its slave eyes regained their brilliance, damage was done, and the inevitable would have to occur. It knew what it must do. Like a character in a Greek drama or a Wagnerian opera, 2's course of action was now fully determined. There would be no way out.

CHAPTER 4

Alan was the first to awaken. Since Dick was far from the first man to share Alan's bed, it took the top a moment to remember who it was that he held in his arms, whose body was causing Alan to get hard even before his eyes had opened. Oh yeah, it was Dick, Alan's hot new slave-to-be, the boy he had rescued from Leather Officer's attack. Yeah, handsome Dick.

Alan was ready to fuck again, but Dick appeared sound asleep and Alan recollected that he had decided to go slow with this wounded little stud, giving him a chance to heal. Alan gently slid out of bed and proceeded to the pisser, off loaded and then to the galley to start coffee. Dick made an unintelligible noise, and Alan returned to see if the boy was ready to fuck.

Not yet, apparently. But Alan then noticed nasty bite marks on Dick's neck, marks that Alan had inflicted in his passion during their first fuck. Alan loved to bite - he'd gotten into the habit years ago - and most of the collars Alan used on his boys were all bitten up. It was a part of fucking with Alan. Thinking to avoid further damage to his new man, Alan selected a thick dog collar from the pet store, very chewable, and gently started to buckle it around the still-sleeping boy's neck. Dick was up in a flash. "No! No! Get away from me, motherfucker! No! Fuck! No!" Dick was still half asleep, but in full panic. He didn't know where he was, or whom he was with, but he would kill whoever tried to collar him!

"Fuck!" Alan muttered, realizing his error. How to fix this? "Whoa, man. Whoa," Alan said softly. "It's me - Alan. It's OK."

Dick was now awake, backed into a corner of the room, his fists clenched to defend himself against - whom? Leather Officer? Dan? He realized quickly that he had over-reacted, also realized why and was again overwhelmed by the horror of his loss of Dan to Leather Officer the previous night. The huge anger welled up in Dick. He let out a truly frightening cry, like a mortally wounded animal, and slumped to the floor.

"Oh wow, man! I'm sorry, man!" Alan exclaimed. He was nearly as emotional himself, taking the blame for the hurt the boy was suffering. Alan tossed the collar aside, angry at his stupidity. He picked the young man up and held him tightly, smoothed his hair, kissed his face, and told him that everything would be all right.

Dick and Alan had now gone through several of these meltdowns together, so they both pretty well understood what was going on. Alan quickly forgave himself for hurting Dick again, because it was Leather Officer who had done the hurting, not Alan. Alan had merely been clumsy, and he vowed not to do it again.

Dick was ashamed of himself for his inability to control his emotions, but he, too, realized that it was Leather Officer and Dan who were the malefactors. Nonetheless, Dick would attempt to get control of himself and move beyond the incident. Dick was now OK and the men were embracing tenderly, just about ready to get hot, when the unmistakable lub-dub of a large Harley could be heard outside the building. Then, the crackle of a police radio. Alan and Dick peeked through the window and their eyes widened. There in the courtyard, checking out Alan's old bike, was a California Highway Patrolman - a CHP motor officer!

The cop was huge, about 6'4" Alan thought, with a very handsome face, dark sunglasses, and of course, full CHP motorcycle cop uniform with gear. Blue and gold helmet, black leather jacket with gold badge, tight tan wool breeches with blue and gold stripes, tall black leather cop boots, black leather utility belt with baton and pistol and all the rest! He was apparently writing down the plate number of Alan's bike.

Alan rushed to put on his pants, in order to find out what the scoop was. Emerging into the courtyard, he found that the cop had remounted his bike and was just roaring off. All Alan saw was the broad, leather-covered cop back as the officer sped away. He returned to Dick, perplexed, not knowing what to make of the visit, and filled with some disquieting emotions. Dick was taken aback as well. Both men held rather complex attitudes concerning motorcycle cops, including both real ones and iconic ones like Leather Officer. But man! This CHP was gorgeous! If only he had come to the door! If only...

Dick and Alan settled in and finally made coffee. Dick had absolutely nothing other than a pair of leather shorts and a pair of boots - no other clothes or stuff whatsoever. Getting the basics for him was obviously the first priority of the day. Alan suggested that they hit a second hand place that dealt with the kind of things Dick needed. Getting Dick's stuff out of Dan's place was also a priority. They fired up the old Harley, which obliged this time, and headed over to Dan's to scope it out. Locked tight for now, and they really had no way of contacting Dan, so Dick was pretty much stuck dependent on Alan.

They went to find duds for the new barback. He chose a couple pair of ultra-tight Levis, some skimpy t-shirts, a fat black leather belt and some engineer boots. A change from the slave boots he came with. Alan was about to charge the stuff when Dick let out a shout. He'd found a complete leather California Highway Patrol motorcycle officer uniform! The swishy clerk said that the cop outfit had been around forever - nobody could fit into it. It had been marked down repeatedly. The price was still a bit much for Alan's bartender budget. But when the boy emerged from the changing room with the CHP leathers covering his hot, young body, Alan said, "Fuck! - It was made for you, boy!" They'd work out the finances later.

It fit Dick almost perfectly - the leather tailor could quickly take the shirt in a bit - and it seemed that the boy was fulfilling some sort of destiny, that the leather uniform had lain dormant waiting for him to animate it. The upshot of it was that Alan had found a new slave, or at least a sort-of a slave. Well, a former slave that was still anxious to suck dick and get fucked. Dick had found a benefactor and fuck-buddy - a good man who was willing to help the boy out, help him get back on his feet, was hot to fuck him and show him some stuff that Dan hadn't known about.

Was it a long term relationship? Between a bartender in a worn out leatherbar and a barback on the rebound? Of course not, but it worked for the moment. Both men were realistic, not in love, but crazy for sex and fun, and they gave each other that.

Later in the day, Alan and Dick checked back at Dan's place and found a note stuck on the door saying that Dick's stuff would be delivered to the Hole. The author of the note had no way of knowing that Dick was now employed, sort-of, at the very same bar to which his stuff would be delivered. Two slaves delivered a package early in the evening. Thus Dick, the very same day, was able to pay Alan back and contribute his share to their maintenance, work his new job in his new leathers and zoom ahead to the front of the pack in the world which was his destiny. To say that Dick was naive or green would of course be laughable - too much Marine cock sucked to say that - but he was undeniably young, so the phenomenon of a (practically) teenaged leather CHP bike cop barbacking at the Hole was really something. Dick became a celebrity.

Despite the fact that Alan was a great bartender, that Dick was the barback to die for, that the rest of the staff were also hot and fun and that the clientele were all one could ask for - in spite of all this, the rumor was that that the bar would close. The entire building, including the already closed laundry next door, would be sold, and the Hole would be no more. All the more reason to get it on now, before everyone is forced into exile at the Falcon, forced to commingle with other men who were just not dedicated to leather in that same way as the men of the Hole had been for decades. Closure would be hard and sad, but bearable. And for now, everyone figured, let's honor the history of the place and continue to do it right.

Alan and Dick gave it their utmost, and gave to each other. Dick played the role of bottom and Alan was the top, but both knew that it was just an interim thing - therefore not of less value - but each was aware that their tenure with one another was about as solid as the continuation of the bar. So enjoy it for today! Not a bad approach to life, if you think about it.

One morning, Alan awoke with Dick in his arms. Alan was now 33, Dick was almost 21. Alan had fucked hundreds of guys, Dick had been fucked by two. Alan reflected on how fortunate he was to have this beautiful, ultra-masculine young man in his bed, how extraordinary it was that his rescue of the boy from Leather Officer's assault had produced this gift. What a funny world. He looked over the boy's body, only partially cloaked by the bedding and became inflamed not only with desire to fuck the boy, but also desire to possess him forever. Alan was falling in love; a dangerous situation, very dangerous, since Dick was evolving rapidly away from slavery and was clearly ripe to grow. And after all, a man of 21 can hardly be expected to be faithful! Dick was becoming increasingly hard-edged. Alan was fucking a 21 year old boy who was beginning to evolve into a top.

Bar receipts were up - markedly. Why? Guys were coming in to check out the hot young CHP barback, acting rowdy just to have him hard-ass them. Desperate to interact on any level, they'd misbehave just to get Dick to get into bouncer mode, also his job, and fuck with them. Dick was a one-man psychodrama. Only Dick and Alan didn't get it but all the rest of the City's leathermen did. They put away their videos to come out to be involved at whatever level with the hot, young motor officer transforming before their eyes.

Alan's thoughts returned to the present. He was ready to fuck. He pulled Dick to him, pulled the boy's ass toward his anxious dick and slipped it into Dick's asshole. The boy groaned at first, but as Alan plunged in and out, Dick began more to sing than to groan, to give voice to Alan's lust, to speak for Alan's cock which had no voice of its own. His singing continued as Alan continued to pump - pump, pump, pump, like it's always been. Nothing new here, just the same old fuck, the fuck that's never new, but also always new. The fuck that is as exciting this time as the first time.

Alan was breaking into a major sweat, pounding Dick's ass, informing Dick that Alan was the boss and that Alan was in charge. Dick didn't doubt it for a minute. When a man has his dick up your asshole, you know who's the boss. Dick was fucked harder and harder, quicker and quicker, more and more viciously, as Alan began to scream. To shout - unintelligibly - garbled - frothy - finally mute. He shot. The boy felt it, and felt that there would never be another man in his ass like this, that this would be the ultimate.

After the fuck, the men got dressed and headed out for a late lunch before opening the bar. They were on Folsom at 13th, just under the elevated free-way, when Alan saw the red light in his rear view mirror. Shit! Now what?

He pulled over and shut down the bike. Both Alan and Dick dismounted. The CHP motor officer stopped and parked his bike behind the boys, leaving it running, idling, lub-dub, lub-dub, lub-dub. As the cop approached them, Alan felt sure it was the same guy who had checked out his bike recently in the courtyard that time early in the morning just after they had gotten up, and who had ridden off before they could meet him. The CHP was big – 6'4" probably, well over 220, a very handsome man in his 40s. Full CHP gear, of course, but particularly well done and particularly attentive to detail.

"May I see your license and registration?" the cop asked, with professional courtesy. The pistol and baton which he carried on his belt indicated that courtesy was merely the first overture. Failure to respond adequately and quickly, it was clear, would result in a dropping of the courtesies and falling back on force.

Alan pulled out his wallet and removed his driver's license. He handed it to the cop and began fumbling around inside the small leather pouch attached to the bike which contained the registration. Alan handed the registration to the offi-cer as well, confidant that everything was in order. Alan had no idea why they had been pulled over. He had mixed emotions about motorcycle cops. On the one hand, like many leathermen, Alan found bike cops tremendously attrac-tive, mesmerizing almost. The boots and breeches were a part of it certainly, but also the sexy machine, the motorcycle jacket and above all, the cocky attitude that motorcycle cops often seemed to have. Like they knew they were the hottest, that's why they were doing it, and enjoyed the envy of mere mortal men. This was why Alan had been drawn so strongly to Leather Officer. At the same time, much as Leather Officer had hurt Alan and had stimulated Alan's hatred, Alan knew that the CHP Officer now confronting him also had the power to hurt. Should the cop choose to mess with Alan, he could surely find some reason to issue a citation, impound the bike, even arrest the two leathermen. Alan was uncomfortable in a situation where another man held so much power over him - like right now. Very confusing emotions, on top of which Alan was aware that he had developed a very noticeable erection!

The Officer's name was T. Stockton according to a chrome name plate on the right side of his chest. He took a long time to review Alan's documents it seemed, but then the cop handed them back to Alan and said, "Seems entirely in order, sir. Thank-you." But then, addressing Dick, T. Stockton asked, "How about you, young man? May I see your license?"

It was only at this point that Alan first noticed Dick's demeanor - Alan had been so busy dealing with his own emotions and the cop that he'd momentarily ignored Dick. The boy had that dark look on his face that Alan had seen before. Oh, shit!, Alan thought. He's going to lose it, going to melt-down! Dick was by no means over Leather Officer, Dan, the abandonment, being torn unwillingly out of slavery, any of it - still a very fresh hurt for Dick. Would this big, hot motorcycle cop be too much for Dick to handle? Would he snap?

Dick hesitated, trying to pull himself together, trying to make the distinction between Leather Officer and the policeman now demanding identification. T. Stockton was a professional and could tell that there was something out of the ordinary here. The cop put his muscular, leather-jacketed arm around Dick's shoulders and said, "It's OK, pardner. You're the passenger. You don't have to have a driver's license, but you should have identification."

The officer's voice was like honey as he spoke to Dick. The cop's arm around him was reassuring. Dick was going to be OK. "Oh, yes Sir. I do have an ID. It's right here," Dick stated, happy to work with the cop. Dick whipped out his wallet and showed T. Stockton his Marine Corps dependent ID from Twenty-nine Palms. It showed a picture of Dick, a bit younger, and a picture of Dad as well, giving information about both.

T. Stockton checked this out thoroughly, continuing to rest his arm on Dick's shoulders. "Well, pardner, this looks fine," the cop said at length. "Your father looks to be about my age."

It was true. Perhaps this was why Dick's initial negative emotions had been so readily swept away by the handsome motorcycle cop who seemed to consider Dick to be his "pardner." T. Stockton advised Dick that he should get a new ID from the DMV since he was no longer a dependent. Dick agreed wholeheartedly. He figured that any advice T. Stockton gave would be good advice and he promised to take care of it right away.

T. Stockton addressed Alan: "You should teach Richard here how to ride the bike so he can get a driver's license with a motorcycle endorsement. It's something a young man should have."

This astounded Alan. He thought the cop's counsel was wise, but still very unusual, not the kind of advice one normally expects at a traffic stop. Alan noticed that Dick had developed an erection - no surprise there - but he also noticed that Dick's eyes had developed a sort of strange, comfortable quality Alan had not seen before.

T. Stockton's boots gleamed. Dick always checked out motorcycle cops and always checked out their boots. Yet he had never seen boots like these, like black mirrors, reflecting 100 percent of the sun's rays that touched them, nearly blinding Dick. The cop's tan breeches were tighter than Dick had seen before, about as tight as Dick's leather CHP breeches hanging at the bar. The gold in the stripes down the sides glinted, and the blue was especially deep. Officer Stockton wore a heavy black leather motorcycle jacket, very shiny and well maintained, to which his badge and name plate were attached. The jacket squeaked slightly as the officer moved. As Stockton removed his arm from Dick's shoulder the officer bumped the side handle of his baton, which accidentally thumped Dick gently in the groin.

"Sorry, pardner," T. Stockton said. The cop turned to address Alan, at which point Dick got a good look at the big pistol which was holstered but ready for action floating on the officer's heavy duty belt. Additionally, Dick noticed that the cop's crotch seemed to bulge - as if he were wearing a jock and the jock were full. T. Stockton's pistol was large and looked as if it could defend the officer if need be. Probably it could defend Dick as well.

"I'm giving you a verbal warning," the cop said to Alan. "You need to see to it that your young friend gets licensed. He needs to be able to ride the bike in an emergency. Take care of it right away and contact me when you have." T. Stockton handed Alan a business card with Highway Patrol insignia. Alan was speechless. The cop then turned to Dick: "Since you come from a military background, you should consider a career in law enforcement. Do you have any college credit?"

"Yes, Sir. Some, Sir," Dick responded.

"Well, consider taking some Administration of Justice at City College. Contact me if you need any help with it. And be sure to get licensed - it's important, pardner," the cop said and handed Dick a card as well. "I'll check back." With that, the Highway Patrolman straddled his motorcycle, kicked it into gear and sped off toward the freeway onramp. Dick and Alan could hear the machine roar onto the elevated highway as Officer Stockton accelerated up to full speed.

"Wow!" Dick said. "Wow!"

Alan looked at the card. "Officer Tracy Stockton, State Traffic Officer, California Highway Patrol, Golden Gate Division," it read. Below was a phone number and an e-mail address. Dick read his card, too.

To Dick, it seemed that Officer Tracy Stockton was an excellent public servant, had provided the men with good advice, and Dick was keen to report back about getting licensed and enrolling at City College. Alan was less enthusiastic. He thought the entire encounter was quite strange, that there was something going on with the cop which was obscure and he was not at all comfortable with Dick being anybody else's "pardner." Particularly not T. Stockton's. Alan wasn't sure, but he wondered whether the whole traffic stop wasn't just bullshit - just a way for T. Stockton to make a move on Dick. "Well, wasn't that something?" Alan said to Dick, probing. "Going to sign up for classes right away?"

"It sounds like a good idea," Dick responded, confirming Alan's fear that Dick had already come under Officer Tracy Stockton's spell. "Do you think I could be a cop?"

"Well, I don't know," Alan responded. "I doubt they'll let you wear your leather uniform," he teased.

Dick smiled. "No, probably not."

It was clear to Alan that Officer Tracy Stockton had had a big effect on Dick, probably had nudged him in a direction in which he was already interested in going. Well, Alan thought, why not? If that's what the boy wants. Maybe we'll both do it. Why not? Few routine traffic stops have had this much long-term effect. T. Stockton certainly was, as Dick had decided, an excellent public servant.

CHAPTER 5

2 spent a restless night. It awakened before the others and began preparing for what would be an eventful day. It brewed the half gallon or so of coffee which was consumed each morning and then set to work on the trainee. "Wake up, asshole," 2 demanded, slapping the still horse-bound trainee's face.

"Ungh, no," the trainee responded unintelligibly, only half conscious.

A slap to the face. "Wake up, now!" 2 had no affection for this trainee, feeling that trouble had come with it. 2 wasn't being fair: slaves do not choose to be slaves, they simply are slaves. They're wired for it. The trainee had not chosen to be enslaved by Leather Officer - it was as inevitable as gravity. Still, 2 was rougher than it otherwise would have been as it locked the chain-collar back around the trainee's neck and unstrapped it from the fucking horse. 2 dragged the still half-asleep trainee downstairs for cleaning.

The routine was familiar: the chain-leash was attached to the hook, the hook was raised and the trainee was forced to stand tall over the drain as 2 scrubbed it with a stiff brush and strong soap. Then a cold spray rinse. The trainee was allowed to drip dry as 2 itself showered, leisurely, using warm water from the wall-mounted shower head and mild soap. 2 lathered up its muscular body and played briefly with its handsome cock and balls. It bent over slightly to lather its ass, giving the trainee a full view, suggesting some possible fun slave-to-slave action to come once the trainee graduated to full slavery. 2 rinsed, toweled off, and then finished drying the trainee. It then applied a coat of light oil to the trainee's body, only hours ago shaved completely clean of all hair save the eyelashes. The trainee glistened, warm and pink from the scrubbing, tight from the cold rinse and now slick from the oil. 2 got erect applying the oil and thought briefly about copping a quick fuck. It was clear looking at the trainee's dick that it would not have objected. 2's hands, all over its body applying the oil had aroused it as well. No. Better not, 2 thought. Already in enough hot water. 2 brought the trainee back upstairs. It was now fully awake and seemed almost to trot eagerly after the hunky head slave. It was fastened to a ring in the floor at the side of the main arena.

"You will wait here for your Master. You will obey him immediately, completely, and eagerly. All the functions of a slave derive from obedience. Obedience produces joyful slavery. Disobedience produces punishment. The choice should be obvious. How's your asshole?"

"Raw, Sir, but good," the trainee responded.

2 immediately stepped on the chain-leash as close to the collar lock as possible, forcing the trainee's head to the ground and then placed its other boot sole on the back of the trainee's neck. "Do NOT refer to me as 'Sir!' I am a slave! You will reserve the title 'Sir' for your Master," 2 bellowed, having half anticipated this standard error.

"Yes, ..." the trainee murmured, lips pressed against the floor.

2 really was an excellent head slave. It was able to function almost like a top with the trainees and other slaves, yet had been totally enslaved to Leather Officer. 2 never failed to spring an erection immediately upon the cop's appearance and was utterly dedicated to his service. Of the current slaves, only 4 had stronger slave wiring. Additionally, 2 pretty much ran the nuts and bolts aspects of the facility. Reflecting on this, 2 was momentarily concerned about what would happen to the Master and the slaves without it, but it set this aside and got back to work.

"Now sit. I have some questions for you." 2 didn't bother to ask whether the trainee wished to continue with training. That was Leather Officer's decision and 2 knew what the cop's intentions were. Additionally, last night when Leather Officer was fucking the trainee's ass and 2 was fucking its throat, it was very clear to 2 that the trainee's slave wiring was quickly becoming fully activated. Formal designation as a "slave" was not yet at hand, of course, but 2 knew that this would be a successful training. The trainee's throat had told 2's penis so.

2 pulled up a short stool and began the entry interview. It would be necessary to close down the trainee's previous life. 2 needed information about where it had lived, worked, banked, etc. Also whom to contact, lest individuals such as the trainee's former slave, family, etc. cause problems. Slaves in jerk-off novels are simply enslaved, but in real life a great deal of effort is required to maintain even one slave, much less four. Real slaves have to be fed more than cum and piss and they have health care issues that can't be dealt with by a sadistic personal trainer at the SM gym. Leather Officer had delegated all this non-erotic stuff to 2 in order to devote himself fully to issues such as electrifying slave wiring, making slave eyes sparkle and deepening the power chasm between Master and slave. The issues where Leather Officer had demonstrated over and over that he was more skilled than any other man.

As 2 was interviewing, Leather Officer awoke. He had rolled off 3 during the night and lay on his back next to the still-bound slave. Leather Officer wondered why any man, given the choice, would not choose to sleep wearing slave-shined cop boots, a Sam Browne belt and skin tight gloves. Any man could, he reflected, but most men, even leathermen, probably slept nude or wearing some sort of dopey pajamas. Was it arrogance to realize that he, and probably he alone, had the mind and heart required to bring slave mastery up to this level? No, not arrogance, just a recognition of what it takes in order to own slaves in the real world. Leather Officer was not a character in a porn story, he was a real Leather Master, a Leather Cop, running a string of slaves out of a slave training facility on a full time basis. Who in hell else had anything like this going? It wasn't a fantasy, it was real and only a mind like Leather Officer's was clear enough and strong enough to pull it off. Arrogance? Not at all.

His copdick was beginning to swell. He glanced over at 3's ass. Yes! But first he needed to modify his plan. It was imperative to think and plan ahead of the slaves, especially 2, in order to maintain control. This would be the plan: after the morning workout and feeding, the slaves would set up the suspension pyramid. Then, while the others were off wrapping up the trainee's affairs, he would torture 1 and break the conspiracy. Leather Officer had the skill to get the truth from any man, slave or not. He could, if he chose, simply torture 2, who he suspected was the author of the conspiracy, but it would be more fun to keep 2 guessing. He'd fuck with 1 while 2 and the others were off serving him otherwise. Also, 1 would quickly betray any additional conspirators, whereas 2 might require considerable blood-letting before totally fessing up. So that would be the plan.

He smeared a bit of spit on the tip of his copdick, now fully engorged, wet a finger as well and quickly stroked 3's asshole. 3 murmured something, but had not awakened. Good. Leather Officer leapt on top of 3, digging the heels of his boots into the backs of 3's calves, grabbing the slave's forearms with gloved hands and positioning the cockhead just outside but touching the victim's hole.

"Up and at 'em, copslave!" Leather Officer accompanied the deep male scream emanating from below him as he shoved the entire thing in and pounded into the slave's ass cheeks with his hairy groin. It was in situations like this that Leather Officer was reminded of the value of a fully and freshly shaved slave. The smooth slave skin felt great against the cop's hairy chest and legs. The difference heightened the difference between the two - Master and slave, fucker and fuckhole.

This was not intended to be a major fuck, just a good morning ploughing to make 3's slave eyes glow, stir up a little jealousy among the others and prepare the cop for the real work later. So he just pumped awhile, carefully avoiding cumming, for the effect on the slave rather than his own release. After a few minutes, just as the slave was beginning to slip into delirium, Leather Officer abruptly pulled out, jumped off the slave and slapped it on the ass, hard. It yelped and got slapped again. It shut up.

Master and slave stripped and showered. The slave then brought the cop black leather gym shorts for the morning workout and things proceeded at the facility in a fairly routine manner, except for the presence of the new trainee and the anticipation among the slaves of being sent out to attend to severing the trainee from its past, a process they had all been through. Leather Officer had a plan in mind beyond what the slaves expected. So did 2, which was to make this an unusual day. But for now it was time to workout and then prepare the ultra-high protein after-workout meal that was standard. Both plans would unfold later.

After the post-workout feeding, Leather Officer said, "4, come upstairs and serve me. The rest of you, be about your chores." The slave followed its Master up to the cop's quarters. "Get the leather torturer's shirt out, and the breeches without stripes, and a smooth Sam Browne. Do it now," he commanded. 4 scurried to comply, pulled out the demanded leather, and dressed its Master. That completed, 4 sat dog-style in front of the cop, penis erect. "What's the cardinal rule?" Leather Officer demanded.

"Sir, a slave obeys its Master, Sir," 4 responded.

"Good boy."

4 looked up at its Master, at his gleaming slave-shined boots, at his perfect, shiny leather breeches, at his fitted shirt with attached executioner's hood, at his shiny Sam Browne with bullwhip and keys attached on the left. 4 was mesmerized, enthralled.

"Do you know why it is that you continually fuck up, asshole?" Leather Officer asked.

"No, Sir," 4 stated, although by now it should have known.

"You forget the cardinal rule. You allow your emotions to guide you rather than your obedience. You focus on your needs, your desires, and forget that your first priority is to obey: to do what the fuck you are told. I'm not interested in a highly motivated slave that cannot perform. I want performance. I want obedience. I want results." Leather Officer wasn't sure whether this speech was getting through to the fuckup or not. He recognized 4's strong slave wiring, and realized that there was big potential. But if it could not be realized, so what?

4 stared at its Master. Its eyes were glazed. It so wanted to do the right thing. It vowed, to itself, that it would control itself and would improve its performance. Therefore, it said nothing, merely staring at its Master. All slaves would do well to follow 4's example in this situation: a slave cannot say or do the wrong thing if it says or does nothing. 4 got it right. It just stared at its Master's crotch - stared and stared - and shortly the copdick was hauled out and inserted down its throat. 4 learned something. It learned obedience. It learned who was in charge. It learned self-control.

It was a fuck of a lot better to obey and get throat fucked than to disobey and get the shit whipped out of it. Well, maybe 4 had a brighter future than had seemed the case previously. Maybe obeying the Master was the best avenue to the Master's cock. Sounds simple, once you get it, and it appeared that perhaps 4 had finally gotten it. Finally gotten that if a fucking slave just fucking does what the fuck it is fucking told, it'll get fucked! Pay attention, slaves! Obedience! A slave that consistently and fully obeys its Master will almost always enjoy a long, joyful, sex-filled slavery. Is this not what every slave craves? "Copslaves!" Leather Officer shouted, "Take your places!" The cop descended the stairs, followed by 4.

The other three ran to the fronts of their cages and sat, dog style, facing their Master. 2 knew something was up, for Leather Officer had changed into torture gear. 2 understood the meaning of this gear. Leather Officer had a black leather rendition of the Dungeon Master's shirt from the Boy Scout magazine cartoon made. Not fabric, but leather! A zipper closed the executioner style hood in the back - the hood being one piece with the tight fitting short-sleeved shirt, also zippered down the sides. It was fearsome. He also wore plain black breeches, no stripes, and slave-shined cop boots. As always, a Sam Browne completed it. In this case, smooth, shiny black leather, holding his keys and bullwhip. It fully captured Leather Officer's youthful sadism. 2 knew that at least one slave would have a rough time.

Thus confronted, all the slaves and the trainee developed big hard-ons. Moments like this were especially rewarding for Leather Officer. There was no room for doubt that these slaves were real slaves when their dicks were competing with each other to see which could be most excited about their Master. Slave wiring was fully activated, slave eyes were glistening with adoration for their Master. Great! "1 - replace your boots with the suspension boots. 2,

3, and 4 - set up the pyramid. Do it now!" Leather Officer commanded. The slaves jumped to obey, each figuring out pretty quickly what was about to come down, at least partially. Although none knew, including Leather Officer, what would be left at the end of the day.

The pyramid required three slaves for set-up. It consisted of three 12 foot long steel pipes with small, strong rings at each end. The slaves spread the pipes out on the floor, one end of each pipe together in the center in a star pattern, 120 degrees between each pipe. Then the center rings were fastened together and a block and tackle was attached. The slaves each grabbed one pipe and raised the center of the star toward the ceiling, which it almost touched. The ends still against the floor were then chained together using 12 ft. long chains and the pyramid was complete.

In lieu of the charcoal brazier and poker in the cartoon, Leather Officer plugged in a soldering iron. He grinned. He alone grinned. All the slaves looked worried, except 1, which looked positively ill. The trainee hadn't seen this before, so it remained clueless. "OK, 2, 3, 4, get your fucking shorts on and get your asses out of here. You know your job. 3, you're driving. Damage the pickup and this is up your ass!" the cop threatened, brandishing the soldering iron. He threw it the keys and a wallet containing all the slaves' driver's licenses, a credit card and some cash. Everything they might need. They each pulled on their "errand shorts," shorts they wore when out of the facility on their own without supervision. The shorts were tight, reinforced with latigo on each leg, which came a bit above mid-thigh. There was no fly. The shorts zipped up in back, the zipper attached to a chain loop pierced by a stout latigo belt riveted to the waistband of the shorts. The belt buckled in back, held closed by a good sized padlock. These shorts, designed by Leather Officer, assured that the slaves would not be engaged in any illicit sex. But they also precluded shitting or even pissing, forcing the slaves to return to the facility promptly. Suspenders could be attached as well. Leather Officer felt that they looked boyish and therefore humiliating. It was not cost effective to send slaves out in public without humiliating them. Still, the slaves were safe, for never fewer than two went out, they all worked out regularly, were in very good shape (except for 4) and were very, very proud. Off they went, down the stairs, into the garage, piled into the pickup and out into the City to facilitate the enslavement of the new trainee, now chained around its neck and attached to a ring in the floor at the side of the arena.

Leather Officer turned to 1, which had by now removed its own boots and replaced them with the suspension boots. "Put on some wrist restraints as well, fuckhead." The slave was white with fear. The trainee was getting worried, too, although its role was largely to be an observer. Yet, in spite of fear and worry, both the slave and the trainee were entirely erect and Leather Officer also was finding that his own cock was uncomfortably restrained within the now too small codpiece. He strode over to 1's cage, in front of which the slave had changed boots. He kicked the slave boots aside and stood directly in front of his slave, towering above it. 1's breath could be seen on the surface of the cop's gleaming boots. "You can either make this easy or difficult. One way or another I will extract the truth. Your torture will continue until I am convinced that you have been truthful. Once I am convinced, then the punishment will begin. Do you understand?"

"Yes, Sir," was the barely audible response.

With that, the cop grabbed his slave by one boot and dragged it to the center of the pyramid. He quickly attached both boots to the end of the block and tackle and hoisted 1 up until it was suspended upside down, scalp about four feet from the floor. The arms hung down, unable to touch the floor. Leather Officer squatted down to address his slave. "This is a legitimate judicial proceeding. You will tell the truth, the whole truth, and nothing but the truth. It is a slave's duty to be truthful with its Master. I have instructed you repeatedly for months concerning truthfulness. I suspect that you were involved in a conspiracy to thwart my will. You should have informed me immediately when approached to conspire. That you did not constitutes untruthfulness for which you will be punished. Do not compound your crime. As far as I am concerned, perjury is a capital offense. If I must sacrifice your life as an example for this trainee, I will do it. I will not be lied to. Do not fuck with me. Your life is on the line."

Leather Officer stood and walked away. 1 was shaking with fear. It had had no idea that its transgression would be thought so serious. A capital offense! 1 saw its body being served for dinner to the other slaves, soup made from the bones, entrails down the toilet. It was no longer hard. It felt its own urine running out its dick, downward across its hairless chest splitting into several rivulets at its face, in its nose and eyes while mixing with its tears.

The cop returned with a galvanized bucket, perhaps two feet deep, three feet in diameter, and a hose. He placed the bucket directly beneath his slave and filled it with water. The trainee now began to shake as well. 1 began to scream, incoherently, babbling, beside itself with fear. "You have said nothing yet to indicate to me that you are ready to be truthful," Leather Officer said coldly, and released tension on the block and tackle such that 1's head would have gone into the water had it not supported itself with its arms and hands. "Are you ready to be truthful? Are you ready to salvage your slavery?"

"Sir, yes Sir! I'll be truthful, Sir! PLEASE, SIR, PLEASE!"

Leather Officer hoisted it back up, but now attached the d-rings on the slave's wrist restraints to a short chain running between its legs, the same humiliation inflicted on 3 after it lost its fight against 2 the previous night. The slave was now powerless to keep its head out of the water. "Did you allow 4 to win the fight? Did you throw the fight?" Leather Officer asked.

"Yes, Sir, I did. I allowed 4 to win although I probably could have beaten it. Yes, Sir, I did," 1 responded.

"Why did you do this?" it was asked.

"Sir, 2 asked me to. It said I owed it and that it would be smart to protect 4 so it wouldn't be terminated and I might end up as the weakest slave, Sir," 1 responded, quite truthfully.

Leather Officer's sadism began to show: "What was 2's motive?" he asked.

1 really didn't know, so it was truthful, and said so. Leather Officer released tension on the block and tackle and immersed 1's head and shoulders in the bucket of water. He kept its head under water for a ten count, then pulled it up. The poor slave was sputtering and coughing and gasping for breath, writhing on its suspension, and it screamed, "I don't know! Please Sir! I don't know!"

"Well, think about it, and figure out why. You're a fucking slave. You know how slaves think. What was its fucking motive?" the cop demanded, and lowered the boy again under the water, this time for fifteen seconds.

At this point, the trainee lost it. "Stop! Stop!" it pleaded. "Don't drown him! Please, Sir, don't!"

Leather Officer hauled 1 back up, gasping, vomiting breakfast, convulsing, truly afraid for its life. He turned his attention to the trainee, who paled. The bullwhip was removed from its keeper on Leather Officer's belt. He cracked it several times in the air for effect. Good, he thought. The trainee was making this easy. The whip sang through the air, but before the song could be heard, struck the trainee across its chest with a thin thudding sound, leaving a linear raised welt on both pecs. 1 could see, even upside down, small drops of bright blood seep from the line. The trainee screamed. Seeing its chest bleeding, screamed again.

Leather Officer used the same technique on it used earlier by 2: He placed the junction of boot sole and heel on the trainee's chain-leash as close to the neck as possible and stomped the boy to the floor, then placed his other sole and heel on the back of its neck, grinding it further down. "Shut the fuck up! If you want to make it to sunset with your fucking balls still in their sac, just shut the fuck up!" the cop bellowed. He ground his boot again more viciously into the trainee's neck, but it appeared to have gotten religion and it uttered not an additional peep.

Leather Officer returned his attention to 1. "Again, asshole, what was 2's motive? Even if you aren't sure, you must have a guess. Tell your Master. You have no slave friends. Your Master is your only friend. You have no loyalty to any other than I - I forbid it. Obey or die."

1's voice now had an eerie, gravelly quality to it, quite calm: "Sir, I am your slave and nothing more. I owe allegiance to none other than you. You are my sole friend. Thank you for teaching me this, Sir. I believe that 2 sought to protect 4 from termination because of affection. I believe that 2 cares for 4."

"Excellent! Finally I have a slave that understands truthfulness! Finally I have a slave worthy of me! Excellent!" Leather Officer exulted. "Note it well, trainee. You are here for your Master exclusively. There is no brotherhood among slaves. Learn this lesson the easy way, by 1's example, or learn it the hard way by repeating its trial." Leather Officer pulled the bucket out of the way and dropped 1 to the floor. It was unhooked from the block and tackle.

"Move over under the trainee," Leather Officer ordered, addressing 1. "Lie down on the floor, on your belly, head to head. Trainee, lie on top of 1. Put your cock and balls in the small of its back and spread your legs. 1, spread your legs as well." They were now positioned such that the trainee's body held 1's down, lying about six inches ahead so that both victims' asses were exposed. The trainee was still chained to the floor and 1 still had a short chain from one wrist restraint to the other running between its legs. Leather Officer stepped momentarily away, then returned and stood astride the trainee's chain-leash, between both sets of legs. He spread the legs further apart kicking with his boot toes and kneaded the muscles of the backs of the thighs. He kicked the trainee's ass, moving it slightly forward, then held 1's legs apart with his boots as he took a wider stance. Both 1 and the trainee wondered which one of them would be fucked first.

But again, Leather Officer demonstrated that his sadism was not merely psychological. Of the three, only the cop had not forgotten the soldering iron, only he had the lifelong image of the Dungeon Master requiring fulfillment. What had the Dungeon Master done, after all, with that red hot poker? "OK, assholes. Don't move an inch, either of you. Trainee, keep 1 down. If you let it move, I'll hurt you bad. 1, you have now achieved a higher level of slavery where you have stated, and stated truthfully, that you have allegiance to none other than I. Therefore, I mark you."

The trainee heard a searing, sizzling sound, then a gut wrenching scream from the slave under him, which convulsed, triggering the trainee to hold it down as ordered. It was over fast, then the trainee felt all of 1's breath expelled, its body shake and then re-expand. 1 seemed to explode and threw the trainee off it, as it rushed to Leather Officer's left leg and seemed almost to try to climb inside the leg, to get inside its Master's body and exclaim, "Oh, Sir, thank-you, Sir. Oh, thank-you, thank-you, Sir."

The trainee saw black, burned flesh on 1's right ass cheek. The letters L. O.

CHAPTER 6

Leather Officer's pickup pulled up in front of what had been the trainee's studio, where it had maintained Dick as a slave for months and fucked him a thousand times, centuries ago. 2, 3, and 4 popped out and entered the tiny place. Their emotions were complex, for each had had its previous world invaded similarly by Leather Officer's slaves. They treated this trainee's space and its former life with respect.

What the slaves were sent to do, essentially, was to literally "wrap up" the trainee's former life, at least the physical parts of it. They boxed up all its shit for storage, just as all their shit had been, should the day ever come when Leather Officer no longer had use for them and they were terminated. The trainee had told 2 what stuff was Dick's. These were kept separate to be delivered to the Hole, since the trainee had no idea where else Dick might be found.

The place was small and its former inhabitants were young, so clearing it out was not as complex as one might think. A lot of the "wrap up" of a trainee was handled by telephone: employer, bank, family - not requiring on-site slave activity. It was surprising, really, how easy it was to close down a trainee's life. The slaves were always amazed at how quickly it went - even Leather Officer was sometimes startled how a trainee's entire past could be wrapped up in less than an afternoon. Very different from the cop's elaborate empire.

"Let's get out of here," 4 said. "I need to take a leak."

"Well, brain-dead, didn't you go before you put the fucking shorts on?" 3 queried.

"No. I was too fucking hard. I couldn't," 4 responded. Understandable, 2 and 3 thought, although they had thought ahead and weren't in the same fix. It was easy to see why 4, which in its simplicity was probably truest to the slave way, would have forgotten to piss. It was just so focused on its Master that it fucked everything else up. There was a tragic irony here: Leather Officer was probably, unless someone else was very secretive, the best top in the City. Hundreds of slave wannabes would have given their left nut just to be his trainee, much less his slave. And 4 was arguably the clearest manifestation of the slave way on earth - it would have died in an instant if Leather Officer had ordered it, died gladly, proudly, erect. But probably with its boots untied, or boot polish under its nails. Yet termination was always on the agenda, and not just for the stimulative effect, but real termination. It just didn't make any sense.

At least to 2 it had made no sense. But to Leather Officer it made perfect sense. And who was in charge? This was the nub of what happened next. Everything was in the pickup; 4 was squirming noticeably. It knew what the cop would do to it if it pissed its shorts.

Then 2 said, "I better take one last look-see - to be sure we haven't missed something." So it returned to the place and shut the door.

3 turned on the radio: it was Beethoven, the Choral Fantasy. Probably Silvesterkonzert with Abbado and Kissin. Just starting. 3 could listen to it 20 times a day forever and not tire of it. 4 loved it as well. In fact it was almost an anthem for the slaves since it was among their Master's favorites and there-fore theirs. They relaxed as the solo piano performed what seemed initially like a sonata, but then added an orchestra behind it, transforming into a concerto, and then 14 or 15 minutes later adding solo voices, soprano and baritone, and then full choir, reiterating the melody initially introduced by the solo piano but now in full voice, and the whole thing seeming like a dress rehearsal for the 4th movement of the 9th Symphony, but with words not Schiller's:

> Schmeichelnd hold und lieblich klingen,
> Unser's Lebens Harmonien,
> Und dem Schönheitsinn entschwingen,
> Blumen sich die ewig blühn.

Beethoven - so mächtig! 3 and 4 were pretty gone when Kissin finally closed on piano and the crowd at the Philharmonie erupted in applause. But where the fuck was 2! It was just going to take a quick once through! What the fuck!

Both slaves leapt out of the pickup at once and rushed the place. They banged on the door. No answer. More banging. Still no answer. 4 checked around the side, found the bathroom window open, crawled in, found no one, and unlocked the door from the inside to confront 3. As their eyes met, they knew: 2 was a runaway! Not only a runaway, but a runaway from them with 20 minute head start!

Fuck. They closed and locked the window and the door, returned to the pick-up, and 3 called in. "Sir, 2 has run away.... It went out the bathroom window....

I accept full responsibility, Sir.... Yes, Sir, 11th and Harrison in 15 minutes if we can't find it, Sir.... Yes, Sir." Frantically they began combing the area in Leather Officer's pickup. They had the sense to focus the search in the direction of the Hole, thinking logically that a collared slave wearing only boots and bondage shorts would have to head toward a leather venue for safety - where else? Fifteen fruitless minutes later they met Leather Officer as ordered. The cop was on his bike, still wearing the Torturer shirt, but with the hood pulled down in front, and a helmet. His search had been equally fruitless.

Leather Officer was not in charge. He knew it and once the slaves saw him, they knew it as well. His eyes had a hollow quality to them neither slave had ever seen, nor would they ever see again. This was not the first runaway - there had been two before, but only two - and they were quickly caught and "rehabilitated." Now the head slave was on the run and it looked as if it were going to escape. "Wait for me in front of your cages," Leather Officer said, in a voice so laden with emotion that it seemed devoid of emotion. Wordlessly, they obeyed, returning to their cages, knowing that their world was in crisis and determined to hold it together if they could.

2 had slipped immediately out the bathroom window and hit the pavement running. Predictably, it did head for the Hole. It took smaller streets, alleys, constantly looking for cover with adrenaline pumping. It was about halfway to the Hole when it heard the unmistakable sound of a large displacement motor-cycle behind it. It ducked into an entryway. The bike came closer. How could the Master have gotten here so quickly? How did he know where to look? But the sound was not right. It was not the sound of Leather Officer's bike. Leather Officer's bike didn't make the sound 2 was hearing, Leather Officer's bike was much smoother, less lub-dub. The motorcycle and its rider came into view and stopped, right in front of where 2 was hiding. Busted! "Is there a problem, Officer?" 2 asked, trying to bluff its way out of this.

"You tell me," the cop responded, dismounting and approaching 2. "Considering your outfit and the fact that you are apparently fleeing something for no clear reason, you tell me if there is a problem."

The motor officer was a California Highway Patrolman. Why he was cruising these South-of-Market alleys would await explanation, but the Bay Bridge and 101 were not that far off, so 2 didn't ask questions. The cop was about 6'4", maybe 230, 45 or so, and drop-dead Hollywood handsome stunning. Blonde mustache, mirrored sunglasses, blue and gold helmet, black leather jacket, gold badge, blue tie on a tan shirt, tight tan breeches with blue and gold stripes down the sides and - could it be? - slave-shined boots? His basketweave gun belt carried two sets of cuffs, a radio, baton, keys, and a huge revolver.

The cop put an arm around 2's shoulder and said, "Are you in some kind of trouble, pardner?"

Pardner? What the hell did that mean? 2 was without a plan. What to say? "Well, yes, Sir, I guess I am."

2 was wearing a collar locked to its neck, bondage shorts of a peculiar custom design, also locked on, combat boots and nothing else. It had been found running for no apparent reason in seedy alleys in a marginal part of town. Identification? Money? Destination? Motive? Well, none of these. 2 decided to just lay it on the line.

The officer's name was T. Stockton, according to a tag on his chest. T. Stockton said, "Well, that's quite a story. Looks like you do need help. I'll put you into protective custody until we can figure out how to get you back up and running. Put your hands behind your back."

2 was used to taking orders from cops, so it didn't occur to it that this demand was a bit unusual until after T. Stockton had clicked the cuffs on and double locked them. The officer then called on a cell phone - odd, since he could have used his radio - and said, "Send the van to Natoma just beyond 11th. Do it now. Just do it."

The cop addressed 2: "My name's Tracy Stockton. You can call me Officer Stockton. I know what your situation is and I also know what you need. You shouldn't worry. You won't be taken back, and you won't be taken anywhere you don't want to go. I guarantee that within one hour you can be a free man, rid of the gear you are wearing, and totally independent if you want to be. But I also know that you will choose something far more exciting and geared to your tastes. Trust me. You and I are going to be good friends."

2 was drawn to the Highway Patrolman and did trust him and did want to be his friend and was interested in something "exciting and geared to its tastes." But this was a very odd encounter indeed - even by the standards of a runaway slave. Odder still it became as a black van drove up and Officer Stockton escorted 2 to the back doors, which opened revealing two leather clad, armed police officers who jumped out, put a hood over 2's head, threw it into the van and climbed back in themselves. 2 heard the doors shut and the van sped off.

CHAPTER 7

No slave had ever before successfully run away from Leather Officer. 2, the former head slave, was the first. So a period of adjustment for the cop, the three remaining slaves, and the new trainee was required. It was not easy, but it occurred, gradually. It looked as if 1 might become the new head slave and as if the trainee would be fully functional shortly. Time would tell. But it was certain that staffing was again too low, so the cop determined that it was time for a recruiting venture.

Leather Officer summoned 3 and 4 to his quarters and ordered them to pre-pare his black leather cop uniform and gear for a night of recruiting at the Hole. The cop had many uniforms and many were full leather, but the newest one, the black leather one with a white stripe down the outside of the breeches was his current favorite, and his choice this evening. It was modeled after the uniforms worn by the paramilitary cops who got busted up in Capital City. The story had been in all the papers. A big scandal. Leather cops with slaves had taken over the Capital City Police Department somehow. But one of the slaves squealed and the whole thing crashed down. Leather Officer had seen photos of the cops in the paper, had been impressed, and had had a near replica of their uniforms made. His slaves dressed him in this newest leather uniform and he set off to look for a new trainee.

Leather Officer was slightly apprehensive as he pulled the bar door handle toward him. Hell, he was always apprehensive when entering the Hole, even after a thousand times. This was his world, where he was Top. But it was a continual struggle to stay on top, and he was constantly apprehensive of slip-ping into second place, that another man might do it better, might walk off with the prize that was rightfully Leather Officer's. Apprehension melted, however, as Leather Officer inspected his Serengeti like a lion. No apparent predator competition; plenty of game. This was just what Leather Officer thrived on: not only would he collar his choice, but plenty of also-rans would be stuck stand-ing as he removed his prey. In many ways, the look on the face of a man not chosen was as exciting to Leather Officer as anything he would get from the one he cuffed.

Alan, the bartender, spotted Leather Officer right away. He was glad that Dick was not working tonight. Dick was not ready to deal with Leather Officer yet, if ever.

"Hi, Alan," Leather Officer said.

"Good evening, Sir. Your usual?"

"Nah. Give me a draft. Ammunition."

"Coming up," Alan responded, understanding immediately what the cop meant by "ammunition," and remembering with mixed emotion the time he had been pissed all over by Leather Officer. That was a while ago. Alan wondered if Leather Officer even remembered.

"You're about due for another hosing down yourself, eh?" Leather Officer sparred. Well, that answered Alan's question. But Leather Officer's question was harder for Alan to answer: was he "due?" Would Alan ever get involved with this guy again? The cop was so fucking hot, but... There was still a bad taste in Alan's mouth, even though Leather Officer's piss had been as sweet as honey.

"Just about due," Alan responded, slightly off balance. Leather Officer was clearly winning this encounter, and they both knew it. "On me," Alan said, placing Leather Officer's beer on the bar. As if this would somehow fix it for Alan.

"It'll be yours, if you're ready," Leather Officer said, ending the conversation and fucking up at least the first half of Alan's shift, until things got so busy he couldn't obsess about the cop any further.

"What an asshole! But God, he's so fucking hot," Alan thought, 'round and 'round, until he became dizzy. Leather Officer was getting off to a very good start.

The bar was only about a third full and it was relatively early. Leather Officer timed his hunt to the minute for maximum effect. If he could cuff the guy and drag him out when the joint was just peaking, that was perfect. Leather Officer immediately downed a quarter of his draft, set it on the side bar and checked himself out in the mirror. Tie straight, ditto the tie bar. Tucking the shirt in, slightly pulled out from the ride over. OK. Perfect. Nobody else had ever seen any flaws in Leather Officer's appearance, but that was because of constant monitoring. Is there really an argument against excellence? Leather Officer didn't think so.

The bar door opened and a guy walked in wearing racing bike leathers. He was smaller and younger than Leather Officer, attractive in a fresh, naive sort of way. He gave Alan his helmet and ordered a shot of some clear liquor,

Leather Officer couldn't tell what. Then a bottled beer. He chatted with Alan as if they knew one another, briefly. He then headed back to the pool table area, although the table was closed. The biker seemed a bit nervous, Leather Officer thought, his interest kindled. By now Leather Officer had finished half his draft and had sufficient excuse to check out the pisser. He cruised by the young biker, beginning to unsnap his codpiece before he got to the door of the restroom. Leather Officer looked the biker dead in the eye. The guy's face reddened. Leather Officer figured that if he took his time at the trough, he'd have company.

Leather Officer finished unsnapping the codpiece, freeing his dick and balls. He played around with them watching his dick grow. It looked good, caressed by his black leather gloved hand. No hurry. He really didn't actually have to piss that bad anyway. He'd take his time, waiting for the biker to show. A virtual certainty.

Chapter 8

Little Mike had fast-tracked himself. It was now only six months since he had first blurted into the Hole, but he was a regular. He'd played around here and there, as much for experimentation as to satisfy real lust. And he got a bike - used - from a guy he met through Alan. The guy was trading up and going for a big road machine. So the helmet and racing leathers came with the bike. A quick course in riding, a trip to the leather tailor for minor alterations, and Little Mike was a biker. In fact, some guys started calling him Biker Mike. Mike was joyous.

Before Dick came along, Alan had taken Little Mike to his place a couple of times and had shown him the ropes. Alan liked Mike a lot and had been very careful to bring the boy along at just the right speed. Alan protected Mike, too, warning him about who might be "too rough" or "insincere." Mike was very excited and happy to be a new leatherman. And he was doing a good job!

Mike decided that Friday night would be a good time to leather up, hop on the bike and drop in at the Hole. He pulled up outside, shut the engine down, got his shit together and swung easily through the same door that had been such a challenge only recently. He was still very excited each time he entered, but now could at least appear largely under control. Mike approached the bar and Alan poured him a shot of high-end vodka and brought him a Stiefelknecht imported beer. Mike found this combo got rid of butterflies. Alan had recommended it. Mike had taken a lot of advice from Alan, and it had largely been good. Generally, Mike followed Alan's advice, but not always. Alan had warned Mike about a handsome leather cop who, Alan said, Mike should avoid until he was more experienced. Well maybe, Little Mike had thought.

Little Mike turned around with his beer to check out the place. About a third full - it was still early. But across the front room Mike saw a man that stopped his heartbeat. It all happened in an instant, and an observer probably would not have noticed anything at all as Little Mike checked the man out and then moved to the pool table area, to escape as much as anything. The panic of six months ago flooded back.

Mike saw it all in an instant: the guy was six feet tall, athletic, maybe late thirties, and very handsome. But what was unusual, particularly for a rookie like Mike, was that the man wore a black, full leather police uniform. Black cap, black short sleeved shirt, black tie, black breeches, black boots, black gloves, and all leather. The cap was trimmed with chrome that glinted, as did the tie bar, insignia, and badge. The man wore a gun belt with a lot of equipment and a strap over his right shoulder. This too was heavy black leather with chrome metal hardware. The breeches had a white stripe down the outside. The boots gleamed. The codpiece bulged.

Little Mike's flight had encountered major turbulence. Unlike some costumed leathermen that Mike had seen, this leather cop appeared to be entirely one with his leather and with his gear. Mike knew that, of course, this was not a sworn officer on duty. They were, after all, in a bar called "The Hole." But there was no getting past it; this man was a leather cop. Little Mike's dick went rock hard instantly. Mike leaned against the unused pool table and tried to calm down. Good thing he had had the shot! A new set of emotions flooded over Little Mike. He thought about sneaking out of the bar and just getting away. But he also thought about the fact that he was so powerfully drawn to the leather cop that he really could not go. He was stuck. He was well on his way toward copslavery in just an instant.

Mike's dick hurt. What to do? No time to think. Then Little Mike realized: the leather cop was coming toward him! And unsnapping his codpiece! Oh, shit! Mike realized quickly that the cop was on his way to the piss trough, and as he passed he looked Little Mike deep in the eyes. Mike was mesmerized, enslaved really, and he flushed deeply. The leather cop was now past, but Mike could imagine copdick being prepared to off-load into the trough. Little Mike followed the leather cop into the pisser. It was really all over already.

Mike washed hands that weren't dirty and stole a glance at the cop's prick. It was large and semi-hard, held in the cop's black-leather-gloved hand, ready to gush. Street lamp light came in a high window and lit the cop's uniform in a way to be forever burned into Little Mike's brain. The shiny leather almost seemed alive, getting power from the cop's body, giving power back, drawing Mike in, getting its power from Mike. Mike felt suddenly that he was almost a part of the leather cop, some kind of electric connection, or magnetic. The leather cop was all Mike saw, the copdick, the leather uniform, the man. Little Mike's universe had shrunk down to this powerful man and nothing more.

"What are you staring at, asshole?"

Little Mike paled and broke out in a sweat. He murmured something unintelligible.

Leather Officer repeated his question, louder, "What the fuck are you staring at?"

Little Mike really had no answer. What could he say? Nothing. He could hardly admit to staring at the leather cop's dick. How'd he say that? So he hesitated and fell into Leather Officer's trap.

"Look here, asshole. I asked you what the fuck you were staring at. Are you staring at my dick?" Leather Officer said, attacking as he had often before, but in a way that Little Mike had never experienced. Mike still had no answer. "Answer me, motherfucker!" Leather Officer yelled, and slapped Mike on the cheek with his gloved hand. Mike yelped. He stepped back, but Leather Officer was on him fast, grabbed him, slapped him again and again. Forcing him to his knees, he confronted Mike with a now swollen copdick, waving it in the air in front of Mike's face. Even if Little Mike had had any resistance to summon, it would have been too late. This game had been over several minutes ago, when he had first seen Leather Officer. The cop was just mopping up - claiming a prize already won. Little Mike was delirious. Leather Officer was delirious, too, in a different way. Ecstatic. Joyfully out-of-control, yet completely in control. Leather Officer performed as any top would at this point, as he had many times before. He drew the soon-to-be copslave to him and shoved his copdick down Mike's throat, all the way down. Why fuck around? Might as well make the point clearly, right now.

Little Mike gagged and spat up his shot. For that he got two slaps, back to back. Leather Officer then shoved his copdick back down Mike's throat and held it there until Mike's gag reflex subsided, then pulled it out, gave Mike a chance to take a breath and focus his eyes briefly on an ever-swelling copdick, then shoved it back down the new trainee's throat, held it there while Little Mike struggled, then pulled it out, and slapped the boy again. "Now, again, what were you staring at, boy?" Leather Officer asked.

"Your dick," murmured the new copslave trainee.

Mikey got slapped again. "Wrong answer, fuckhead. You say, 'Your dick, SIR.' Now say it."

"Your dick, SIR! Your dick, SIR!" Mike shouted.

"Good boy," Leather Officer conceded, now for the first time merely stroking and not striking the boy's face. "Suck."

Little Mike had no choice. He leaned forward and took Leather Officer's big copdick in his mouth and caressed it with his tongue, sealed around the meat with his lips, and slid to and fro, up and down the length of the shaft. Leather Officer made a low noise which Little Mike understood to be a sign of pleasure, and he knew he was doing good. He had never felt better before, ever. In less than 90 seconds he had practically fallen in love and was well on his way toward becoming another man's slave - a copslave, and he realized that he was now where he had always been destined to go. Little Mike could have sucked forever, but Leather Officer pulled out, replacing the copdick in Mike's mouth by several leather encased fingers. These were used for inspection, to state ownership.

"Whose slave?" Leather Officer asked.

Mike got it quick. "Your slave, Sir!" he answered with enthusiasm.

"Good boy," Leather Officer responded. "Put your hands behind your back."

Leather Officer produced handcuffs and quickly clamped them around Little Mike's wrists. Mike hadn't expected this, but even if he had, he wouldn't have resisted. It was way too late. The cop hauled Mike to his feet and shoved him out of the toilet. He grabbed the front of Little Mike's jacket and pulled him over to a locker by the unused pool table. Inside the locker was the equipment Leather Officer kept at the Hole for these types of situations. A collar, thick black leather, went around Mike's neck. A leash was attached. A hood with no eyeholes went over Mike's head and was zipped tight. Sight was impossible, hearing was impaired. The mouth and nose were open for breathing and sucking copdick. Mike was led out to the main bar. Leather Officer hadn't really needed to piss anyway, so baptism could wait.

"Kneel," Leather Officer growled. Mike complied. He slid down guided by his new Master's leg. He caressed the boot and smelled the breeches' leather. Little Mike overheard Leather Officer order another beer from Alan. As the bar filled up, it was increasingly difficult for Mike to hear what was going on. But he didn't much care what was going on as long as he was kneeling beside his Master. His knees began to ache.

Eventually, Leather Officer became aware that it was time to get rid of the beer. He dragged the collared, cuffed and hooded trainee into the pisser, up to the trough. Leather Officer let Little Mike have it full force all over Mike's racing leathers. Drenching everything. Hosing the boy down for what was to come. Leather Officer's dick spewed out sweet, drinkable piss, but Mike swallowed little of it as his new Master soaked him with cop urine.

Mike struggled to accept the flow, but he intercepted only a portion of what had been draft beer only moments ago. Mike thought it might matter to the cop if some piss hit the floor, but it didn't. Leather Officer only wanted to hose the boy down so he'd be wet for display. Bladder emptied, the cop stowed his cock and balls and led his leashed trainee out to the main bar.

"You're moving quick, Sir," Alan said, as Leather Officer again dragged his slave up to the bar. "I guess mine's already gone."

"Sorry, Alan. This boy got yours." Leather Officer stated. "I couldn't say 'No.'"

Alan's emotions could hardly have been more complex. He would have given anything to be Leather Officer's copslave, yet he hated the guy - hated him for how he had been treated and how Dick had been treated. He was worried about Little Mike, but also jealous of him. It was a mess.

"Forget the beer. Don't need any more ammo. Make it my regular," Leather Officer said.

Alan quickly mixed the gin/tonic Leather Officer favored. Alan tried to regain his composure, but was only barely able to function. He would have preferred not to be able to recollect the time he had been collared by Leather Officer and taken away for training. Leather Officer had whipped the shit out of Alan, drawn blood, and forced the boy to cry out in tears. But ultimately Alan was deemed unsuitable and was denied slavery.

So when Little Mike got dragged over to Alan's station, it was a difficult moment. It was hard for Alan to look when Mike was forced again to his knees at Leather Officer's boot, hard to look as Leather Officer essentially ignored Little Mike for the next hour as the hooded, collared, piss soaked boy became increasingly uncomfortable. Alan should have called in sick.

Ultimately, Leather Officer determined that the new conquest was sufficiently humiliated, Alan and the bar patrons were sufficiently aware of its humiliation, were sufficiently impressed with Leather Officer's power to humiliate, and that it was time to go. In other words, the show was over, and now it was time to get down to the task of enslaving this new piece of meat. Little Mike was dragged out into the night, thrown into the bed of the pickup, and transported to Leather Officer's training facility like so many before him.

Leather Officer pulled into the garage and 1, the probable new head slave, appeared immediately to take charge of the trainee. Leather Officer mounted the stairs assured that he would shortly be presented with a totally shaved victim ready for training. He noted with satisfaction that his facility had weathered the loss of the former 2 without apparent injury - the new 2, and 3, and 4 were sitting dog style in front of their cages waiting for the training to begin. There had, of course, been a few missteps as 1 began to take over the job of head slave, but not enough to cause alarm and Leather Officer congratulated himself for having erected a structure that could withstand personnel change without major disruption.

He ignored the yelling from downstairs - apparently the new trainee objected to something. He surveyed his facility, his slaves, his equipment, his uniforms, all of it. It was good. Each of the slaves' wiring was fully activated and each had shining slave eyes. Leather Officer was right where he wanted to be, and the crisis of the runaway was over. He strode over to the rack of uniforms. "4! Get this ready for me," he commanded, pointing to a leather Military Police uniform. "2! 3! Get downstairs and shave the trainee."

4 scooted into action, slave eyes shining. It adored its Master way beyond what the others did, but could it perform? Could it do the job of getting the cop ready to train the new meat? It pulled the leather off the hanger and brought it to Leather Officer, laying it on a stool. It carefully undressed its Master, pulling off the cop boots and breeches, removing the shirt and tie, the Sam Browne, all of it, until the Master's body confronted it totally nude.

4's slavery was so huge, so deep, so broad. If it could have climbed inside its Master's body then and there, it would have. Just melded. Why not? It had no ego. Why not just unite with its God right now? Why not? Because it had a job to do and it would be punished if it fucked up the job. The job was to dress the Master in the leather MP uniform. It pulled on the khaki trousers and tucked these into the gleaming paratrooper boots. It slipped the khaki leather shirt on its Master, buttoned it, tucked it into the trousers, tied the black tie, and slipped it into the second space between buttons on the shirt, in the MP way. It fitted its Master with the pistol and nightstick belt, with shoulder strap, including handcuffs and ammo pouch and slipped both the .45 and the stick into their holsters. It placed the white Officer's cap on its Master's head, and then affixed the MP brassard to his left arm, completing the leather MP uniform and outfitting its Master for training.

"Good work," the MP stated. "But give the boots some attention. Lick the edges of the soles. I see some dust." 4 licked greedily, leaving saliva on the edges of the soles and heels which still shone as the new trainee was brought before Leather Officer.

Military Police are doubly powerful, Leather Officer thought, and he felt unusually empowered by the leather MP uniform. It should be easy to break the new trainee and move it quickly toward full slavery, threatening the four current slaves with replacement and termination. This was the essence of Leather Officer's technique, to keep the slaves on edge, constantly fearing termination. The world at large was dealt with similarly. Every man that saw Leather Officer yearned to be his slave, and feared that he could not be. Most had that fear realized. Most were not selected and were left standing in the bar as the lucky one was dragged out. But even the lucky ones would also most likely be rejected, incapable of moving from trainee to slave. And even the slaves were never at ease, fearing the termination which inevitably came. A large part of Leather Officer's sadism inhered in the brutality of kindling in men a desire that would, sooner or later, be unfulfilled. In the end, they were all left standing, rejected by their God as the God moved on to his next victim.

There was a minor commotion as the trainee was brought upstairs and chained to the floor in front of Leather Officer. It was utterly hairless, even lacking eyebrows, pink, oiled, shiny, and totally vulnerable. What had been Little Mike was now but a lump of clay awaiting the MP's slave training, awaiting its transformation into whatever the cop desired. Leather Officer looked down into the eyes looking up at him. He saw fear. Adoration and slave eyes would come, perhaps, but for now there was just fear, naked fear.

"Who's in charge here, boy?" the MP shouted.

The trainee crouched mute. It was too scared to respond. Leather Officer placed a gleaming MP boot on the trainee's right shoulder and stomped it to the floor.

"I said, who's in charge here?'"

Still, the trainee apparently did not understand what was expected of it, just didn't get the drill, and was mute. The MP stepped with both boots onto its back, grinding the soles and heels into its flesh. It squealed unintelligibly. "WHO? WHO? WHO'S IN CHARGE? ANSWER THE FUCKING QUESTION, YOU PIECE OF SHIT!" the MP yelled.

The trainee just had no idea what was going on. It had been so attracted to the leather cop at the bar that it had melted into subordination, but now it just didn't know what to do, it froze. It became incapable of response. The MP kicked savagely at the trainee's ribs, again and again, out of control, screaming for it to respond. There was no fall-back position in such a case - the only option available to the MP was to press ahead, to increase the brutality until the fucker responded.

"Answer me!" Leather Officer shouted, grabbing a crop and slashing at the back, butt, and thighs of the trainee. "Answer me!"

The trainee began to sob. It had no idea what the question even was. It was just confused, hadn't understood what the exciting leather cop in the pisser was really all about, had just known that it got hard and wanted to try. Now it was here, being brutalized for no apparent reason, unclear what it was to do, confused, panicky. The trainee began to howl. It curled into a ball, to protect itself from the crop, and wailed and screamed.

4 was frantic. It knew the answer to the question and was close to blurting it out. It also understood how the trainee had become so emotional that it could not hear, could not think, could not respond. Fortunately for 4, it kept quiet, but it was excruciating to watch the trainee get beat up for the same mistakes that 4 had only recently learned not to make. 4 winced as the crop repeatedly landed, blow upon blow.

Finally, the MP stopped. "Get this piece of shit out of here," he ordered. Turning away, he pointed at 3, signaled that it should accompany him, and mounted the stairs. He took his slave up, shackled it to the bed, pulled his angry dick out of the MP uniform trousers and fucked the slave until he came. He fell asleep full of anger, pressed against a slave shaken by what had happened, shaken by an angry rape, concerned for its Master, unclear what it should say or do.

Little Mike, badly damaged, was taken downstairs, redressed in his leather, and driven back to the Hole. The slaves ascertained that he was capable of riding his bike. They bid him farewell, and watched him ride off. They returned to their facility, but it would never be the same. Never before had there been such a quick and total failure of training. It was clear that something was going wrong, that Leather Officer's approach had, at least in this case, failed.

CHAPTER 9

Little Mike was bewildered. He did not understand what had happened to him, how the handsome leather cop could possibly have beaten him so savagely. The man had been irresistible to Little Mike, but Mike had become frightened at the point when his body shave was completed, frightened about the consequences of long-term, real slavery. He had been unable to resist the cop at the bar - no surprise there - but he really wasn't ready for slavery. He couldn't run, so he froze and now bore wounds that would take a long time to heal.

Little Mike shivered as he crossed the Bay Bridge wearing piss-damp leathers. It would take a lot of thought before he would be comfortable with leathermen again. He just wanted to get home, take a hot shower, and get some sleep. He was exhausted. As Little Mike was cruising through the tunnel, he heard a quick *whooop* and checked his mirror. Shit! CHP. What was the problem? He wasn't speeding - too cold. What? So the poor boy would have to deal with another cop? Pretty cruel.

Little Mike pulled over just past the eastern end of the tunnel and shut his bike down. The cop stopped his motorcycle just behind Mike's, but left it running. The sound of the machine reverberated back into the tunnel, the lights of which outlined the figure of the policeman as he dismounted. It was not yet dawn, so Mike could hardly see the cop's features, but the cop could see Little Mike's clearly. The two were essentially alone, given the hour.

Little Mike saw a huge man approaching him, much taller and larger than Mike - boots and breeches, leather jacket, helmet, pistol and baton, badge and gloves - full CHP motor officer gear. Ordinarily Mike would have been a little apprehensive, but also turned on and excited. He jerked off thinking about these cops all the time. But right now, Little Mike was just not ready for any more cop action. He'd had enough.

"I'd like to see your driver's license and registration," the cop stated in a neutral, business-like tone.

Little Mike froze. He heard the officer's words, knew what he needed to do, but was no more capable of obeying this cop than the last. He began to tremble, to perspire. He removed his helmet, to be able to cool down. He set the helmet down on the pavement, partially composed himself, and began to fumble for the demanded documents.

"What seems to be the problem, pardner? Aren't you feeling well?" the cop asked, putting his arm around Little Mike's shoulder.

Little Mike lost it. He put his arms around the Highway Patrolman, buried his face in the officer's leathered chest, and breathed deeply in and out, again and again. Little Mike was oblivious to the absurdity of this encounter. Fortunately, light pre-dawn traffic and poor lighting shielded the two men from the eyes of passing motorists. No 911 calls.

"Whoa, pardner," the cop said. "Pull yourself together. It's going to be all right."

The officer's words comforted Mike tremendously. It WAS going to be all right. Unlike the last cop, this one was not going to hurt Mike. This one would help him.

"What the fuck happened to you, pardner? You look all beat up."

The cop could tell that Little Mike was not intoxicated - that was easy to see. This was beginning to have a familiar look to it, especially the fact that Little Mike was very upset and was apparently recently shaved clean, eyebrows included. The cop didn't have to investigate much more to figure out what had happened. Little Mike was calming down, returning to his search for license and registration.

"Well, Sir, I met a man in a bar, and he...he took me home and...and..." Mike's speech trailed off as he looked up into the CHP's eyes, at his handsome face and Little Mike knew that whatever had happened was over and that his new friend, T. Stockton the officer's name plate said, would not let him down, would help a young man in need.

"OK, pardner, I pretty much get the picture," T. Stockton said. "Now how about the license?"

"Yes, Sir! It's right here, Sir!" Little Mike said with far more enthusiasm than would usually be the case during a routine traffic stop. "And here's the registration as well, Sir!" Little Mike was very happy to be able to participate. T. Stockton's agenda was Mike's agenda, for sure. T. Stockton checked out the documents, returned to his motorcycle with them, and radioed in for a warrant check. Mike followed in order to stay close to his friend. His composure was returning. He took out his handkerchief to wipe his eyes and spruce up a bit.

He felt his newly hairless head and winced, reminded that his whole body was that way. Lucky thing T. Stockton didn't know, Mike thought.

"Full body shave, pardner?" the cop asked.

What? How did the cop know? "Uh...yes, Sir...yes," Mike answered. A part of Little Mike almost hoped that the warrant check would result in arrest, that T. Stockton would cuff Mike, put him on the police Harley, and take him away, to...wherever. They could be together somehow forever, maybe some private prison that T. Stockton had. Suddenly Little Mike realized that this was precisely the kind of action that he had been unable accept from Leather Officer. Why fantasize about it again already with a real cop? Mike was very confused, but also very happy, happy to be standing out here on the bridge with this big, handsome Highway Patrol motorcycle officer who Little Mike knew, just knew, would make sure that everything turned out all right.

"OK, pardner, you're clean. You can go," the cop stated. Not at all what Little Mike wanted to hear.

"But Sir, why did you stop me?" Mike asked.

"Because you weren't speeding. All these assholes speed all the time, like they know better than I do. Since you weren't speeding, it was an indicator of a possible DUI. It's nuts, I know, but it's the way it works, pardner," T. Stockton said. Mike was delighted to get this insider information. He picked up the thread.

"But if I had been speeding you would have pulled me over for that. I'm kind of stuck," Mike said.

"That's right, pardner, you are stuck. I can pull you over no matter what you do, figure out a reason to ticket you if I feel like it, hardass you, and probably get you to over-react, forcing me to arrest you, possibly requiring 'excessive' force, maybe even requiring some stick time," the cop said, running his gloved hand along the length of his baton, pulling it forward so that it swung up in its ring, pointing directly at Little Mike. "Then there's this firearm," T. Stockton said, letting the baton swing down against his leg, and patting his holstered revolver with his other hand. Little Mike flushed deep crimson and his eyes glazed somewhat as the cop spoke so matter-of-factly to him about police power.

"Sir! Yes, Sir!" Mike shouted, forgetting where he was, and with whom he was.

"OK, pardner, take it easy," the cop chuckled. "It's good to see that you support aggressive law enforcement. I appreciate that. Here's my card. Give me a call anytime you need my help. And try to remember which cops will help you and which will not."

With that, T. Stockton remounted his cop bike, clunked it into gear, and sped off at full speed, quickly out of sight. Little Mike was completely dazed, floored, in love. He put his helmet back on and pocketed the license and registration. He checked out the Highway Patrolman's card. "T." stood for "Tracy," Mike learned. Officer Tracy Stockton - Mike spoke the name without voicing it. A warm glow came over Little Mike. He put his friend's card away, kicked his bike to life and sped off after Tracy Stockton.

Mike wasn't sure how fast to go…he had been stopped for scrupulous obedience. Cops could do pretty much whatever they wanted to you anyway. Officer Tracy Stockton had said so. So Mike did speed, did try to catch up to his new friend, but quickly realized that the cop had probably hit ninety and could not be caught. Only the officer's card was left, that and Little Mike's memories of the event and his now huge need to be close to Officer Stockton forever. Mike rode home thinking how he could make this happen.

CHAPTER 10

It took Little Mike a few weeks to recover from his encounter with Leather Officer. At times, Mike wasn't sure he wanted to have anything to do with any man ever again, particularly a leatherman, and more particularly with any kind of leather cop. At other times, a lot really, he thought about Officer Tracy Stockton. He had dialed the cop's number repeatedly, but had always hung up before the call could be answered, not knowing what to say. But after a while, once the bruises had faded a little, he began to feel in his gut again the need to get out among his leathermen, and inevitably rode past the Hole, just to check it out. He also wondered whether he might see Officer Stockton out on patrol. Mike pulled up in front of the Hole. To his horror, the bar was closed! Fuck! He shut the bike down and read the announcement nailed to the door: *Closed for renovation. Will reopen shortly.*

Mike now recalled chatting with Alan weeks ago about impending changes. Something about the entire building containing the bar and the adjoining already-closed laundry having been sold. It was unclear what would happen. Being relatively new to the scene, Little Mike hadn't been sure what to make of the information at the time, but now it appeared that change was occurring. The idea that the site of his epiphany might evaporate was a real scare to Little Mike. But he tooled over to the Falcon, hung out there for the evening, and found out that the Hole would reopen next weekend as The Trough under new management. Well, OK, maybe the new place would be better. It would have to be cleaner! There were several familiar faces here at the Falcon, but the environment just wasn't right, so Mike went home alone, jerked off thinking about Officer Stockton, and waited for the opening of Trough.

Friday came, and at about 2200 Little Mike fired up his bike and rode over to check out the new bar. There was an unusually large number of big motor-cycles parked in front of the place when Mike arrived, many of a specific type and paint job - a lot like cop bikes. Little Mike thought this was a good sign. It was clear from the first that the change was substantial. Instead of the old haphazard Hole - A Men's Bar sign, there was a high-tech logo outside in dia-mond plate steel announcing: TROUGH. The reference was to the piss trough where Mike had been baptized by Leather Officer, now a rarity in local bars, and conserved intact and highlighted after the metamorphosis. Mike strode in confidently.

His confidence was immediately shattered. The Hole really had been a hole. It was funky and did not upstage its clientele at all. This new space was a challenge. Gone were the posters advertising bars long closed from all over the US and northern Europe, the benches over beer cartons, the gimpy pool table. Instead, Mike was confronted by acres of diamond plate steel, floors and ceilings covered with black leather and dark red paint, spot lighting, hard edges, clean angles, and an environment that challenged the patron to rise to a new standard.

This was obviously no longer a local leathermen's hangout. Trough was big-time and had a game plan that had little to do with small business and selling beer. Something entirely new was going on here. Mike entered the new era. Among the crowd there were a few men he recognized interacting stiltedly, not yet comfortable in the new environment. Mike wasn't sure how to act either. He headed for the bar. Reassuringly, Alan was there to get him his usual shot of high-end vodka and a Stiefelknecht beer.

"Hi, boy," Alan greeted. Mike still felt funny about being called "boy," but considering where he had been and what he had done and had had done to him, a far more humiliating greeting would have been justified.

"Hi," Mike rejoined. Nothing else to say sprang to mind. Mike was pretty overwhelmed by the new, challenging space.

"Hot place, eh?" Alan queried, rhetorically.

"Very," Mike responded, parroting every other old patron confronting the new bar for the first time. Well, yes, it was hot, clearly, but also something else, something disquieting. It was demanding - it seemed to demand a new, higher level of performance from every man there. No longer was the tone set by the men, but rather by some as-yet-unknown power which had been the author of the space. Mike sensed this already, but it would be a while before he would understand.

Regardless the uncertainty, each man knew that this was the place to be, that to be elsewhere would be to be nowhere. Little Mike and the other patrons from the old Hole were waiting for something to happen, something to clarify the reason for being here. The clarification was not yet at hand. These men were being fucked with; they knew it, but they stayed. Trough was where they needed to be.

Shot downed and beer in hand, Little Mike took a few moments to look around. A small fortune had been spent covering walls, ceilings, and floor with a mix of steel diamond plate, black leather and dark red shiny paint. Not normally into "decor," Mike had to acknowledge that whoever had done this had known how to get a leatherman's juices flowing. It was like a wet dream! Finally, Mike noticed one of several structural changes: a previously blank wall now had a metal, roll-up garage-type door in its center. Well, that was interesting, but with no further information, Little Mike passed on quickly and began checking out the men.

There were familiar faces and friends from the Hole, but also new meat, heavy-duty meat, formidable leathermen from, Mike guessed, far away. New York maybe, or Europe. Guys who were definitely not local, but who seemed more at home in the new bar than Mike, or even Alan, for that matter. These men might explain the large number of matching motorcycles parked outside.

Little Mike spied a well-put-together little hunk decked out in a leather Highway Patrol uniform. It was Dick, the barback. Mike approached Dick aggressively, as if Mike weren't a bottom himself, because Dick was just so fucking hot that any man would zoom right in and try to take charge. "Hi," Mike said, as if this type of first encounter between two men had never occurred before. "I'm Mike."

"Hi, Mike. I'm Dick." Well, OK, now what? Mike asked himself. Regrettably, Mike made some sort of clumsy observation about how it was fitting that such a hot number would be named "Dick," realizing too late how stupid a comment this was. Just as Dick was about to try to fix this already-fucked up beginning, both men were torn from each other's gaze as the new garage-type door in the wall rolled up with a loud clatter. A clumsy first encounter inaugurated by an inexperienced young stud was saved from failure by an outside event. As the door rolled up, a tunnel was revealed, perhaps 20 meters long, as wide and high as a garage entrance. Half-way along it was an iron bar gate, like jail bars. Beyond that, the tunnel turned, so that it was impossible to see further. All patrons had their attention diverted, Dick and Mike included. Everyone expected something to happen, but nothing did.

The boys' attention returned to one another. Little Mike was very attracted to this miniature, leathered Highway Patrolman. Sort of like Officer Stockton, but sort of not. Dick had grown into his new role - he'd gotten cocky, too cocky. He forgot about Alan, he forgot about the fact that he was working and he forgot that he was in the middle of a bar. He just went for it uncontrolled, like young men do, and would figure it out later. Little Mike had thought he'd take charge of the smaller, younger man. Wrong. Dick began squeezing Mike's cock and balls, through his pants, making Mike moan with pleasure. Dick was moving fast, taking control of Little Mike and, given another thirty seconds, probably would have had Mike down on his knees sucking cock right in the middle of the bar. Fortunately for Dick's relationship with Alan, and for his job as barback, this fast paced seduction was distracted by a loud clanging as the iron bar gate in the tunnel swung open.

Three men appeared, young men, slaves, as it turned out. They were identically fixtured. Each wore eight-inch high lace-up black boots, wrist and ankle restraints, knee pads, and a full torso harness connecting from the crotch to a collar around the neck. Each had a shaved head and no facial hair. The three slaves emerged into the bar, ordered drinks from Alan, did not pay, and spoke only among themselves, as if the other patrons were invisible.

Little Mike said to Dick, "Wow! Who are those guys?"

Pointedly, Dick responded, "Dunno. Why don't you find out?"

Little Mike was unsure whether he should obey the cop or not. When he had initially approached, Mike had imagined taking control himself, but now it seemed to be going the other way. What was it about motorcycle police, anyway? Mike was confused, but he strode over to the three slaves. "Hi! I'm Mike!" he said. He was, after all, only a recently emerged leatherman, and he did lack a certain sophistication, but still, even Mike immediately could see that this opening was a disaster. Two of the three turned their backs to Mike, and the third handed him a card. It said: "Max's personal slaves are forbidden to speak to bar patrons."

Little Mike flushed deep crimson and turned tail toward Dick. Dick was taken aback as well, once he read the card. But the diversion was fortunate for Dick - he already had Little Mike obeying him and he got a chance to think about whether it was really a good idea to get his dick sucked right here, right now. Realizing that it wasn't, he motioned to Little Mike to follow him. Again, Mike obeyed.

Dick led Little Mike into the pisser. The wall between the piss trough and the main bar had been partially replaced by glass in the area just above the trough, so that bar patrons could see men using the trough only below the belt, their identities remaining hidden. Dick pulled Little Mike away from the trough, next to the shitters, so that Alan, the ABC, patrons, or the new management, whoever that was, couldn't observe what he was about to do. Both men had quickly forgotten the three slaves and their attitude and had begun again to focus on each other. Dick wasn't sure quite how to proceed with this over-eager biker, but saw that Mike was an opportunity not to be missed.

Mike's crotch was bulging with excitement, and Dick's hand again began to caress the leather, teasing out the outlines of Mike's cock and balls. The question of who would be top was still not entirely answered. Mike and Mike's equipment reminded Dick of the Marines at 29 Palms. Also, Mike was a little bigger and a little older. Dick knelt and began to lick and slobber the outline of his new friend's bulging organ. Little Mike moaned and staggered a bit, so excited was he by the attention of this little cop hunk. Dick unbuttoned Mike's fly and sucked the equipment out with his lips. Prideful was the only word for Mike's erect penis. Dick could almost hear the organ demanding a hole to fuck; it seemed to say, "Try and stop me!"

Dick licked Mike's balls all over and made them slick with saliva. Then he focused on the shaft and took it down his throat, swallowing it whole. It tasted great, but Dick's thoughts wandered for a moment to Dan, and Dan's dick, and then to Leather Officer, and Leather Officer's dick, probably fucking Dan's throat and his ass! But wait - what the fuck! - that shit was over! Here Dick was with a new man but the old hurt was again flooding back! Dick got angry, stood up, and said, with a voice never heard before, "Now suck me, asshole!"

Mike was taken aback, but obeyed immediately. He knelt, pulled out Dick's cock and balls, and began giving them the treatment that Alan had taught him. His tongue was all over, warming and teasing, and then he began to slide up and down the shaft, rhythmically, as if Dick's prick were the center of the universe. Until he got the leather cop uniform, Dick had been 100% bottom, but he was now finding that there was a brutal side to him as well as he began to force his cock down his Little Mike's throat, slapping his cheeks, and calling him "cocksucker."

"Yes, Sir," Mike squealed, as Dick plunged again and again down his throat. Dick felt like a king, conquering this eager biker boy, maybe making him his slave. Mike was getting jelly-like, getting to where Dick was his god.

Dick pulled the belt out of Little Mike's pants and wrapped it around Mike's neck as a rough-and-ready collar and leash. He dragged the boy over next to the piss trough and recklessly displayed him through the glass, again shoving his prick down the boy's gullet, letting loose hot gushes of sweet piss. "Don't spill a drop, asshole, or I'll whip the crap out of you!" Dick yelled, surprising himself with his ferocity. This was brand new to Dick, but he had the wiring for it, and the boys were on the way to someplace new. Until suddenly, there was a clang of the steel door in the tunnel and Dick was no longer a top. No man in the room was a top. All would be slaves to the man who was emerging from the tunnel. The slaves who had been so rude to Mike fell to their knees. No man spoke a word and the background music went silent. For the first time,

MAX entered Trough.

MAX emerged from the tunnel. Every man at Trough was instantly enslaved. The man was 6' 4", 240 lbs., and solid muscle. MAX had worked out three or four days a week for forty years and carried virtually no body fat at all, just powerful muscle, bulging muscle, veined muscle, his whole body resembling the surface of an erect penis. MAX wore gleaming motorcycle boots, perfectly polished and maintained by his boot slave. Tucked into the boots were skin-tight leather breeches, with two rows of square/pyramidal studs forming glinting stripes down the sides. His belt and shoulder strap were similarly studded, five rows on the belt, three on the strap, the strap crossing diagonally across the massive, muscled chest. Huge pecs, washboard abs, all of it. Arms like pile drivers, gloved hands. A black officer's cap crowning his shaved head. A handsome, commanding face that expressed its 55 years of experience as a leader.

MAX approached the three slaves, uncurled a large bullwhip attached to his belt, and cracked it repeatedly to still the remnant of bar-room hubbub. Total silence. One of the slaves uttered a whimper, knowing apparently that it had fucked up and that punishment was at hand. One quick devastating lash from the whip and it was over. The slave howled and fell to the floor as a line of blood appeared on its back. No one in the bar other than the slaves and their Master knew what the failure had been, but everyone knew that a new era had begun, the era of MAX.

MAX recoiled his whip and re-attached it to his belt. He approached Alan and was served without having to order. Alan had already been instructed what MAX wanted - and Alan understood that any displeasure on MAX's part would mean a lash from the whip for him as well. Every man at Trough understood immediately that MAX's orders would be obeyed or the bullwhip would punish immediately. Trough was MAX's bar and if a man's behavior displeased MAX he could expect to be humiliated by a public whipping prior to being ejected. MAX was God. Therefore, in spite of the danger of being whipped if he should be displeased, men gravitated to him uncontrolled, mesmerized, to offer themselves to him, to be near him, to bathe in his eminent power.

It didn't take Dick long to figure out that he was in a very compromised position. Having dragged the eagerly cocksucking Mike back in full view of all the patrons through the window over the piss trough had been bold beyond recklessness. But as MAX emerged, Dick just went soft and quickly snapped back to reality, or at least reality as defined by MAX. "Get up, fuckhead!" Dick hissed. "Get up now!"

Less aware of MAX's entrance than anyone else at Trough, Little Mike still knew that he and the cop fucking his face were in big jeopardy, so he jumped up and went over to the sinks as Dick hastily put away his equipment and exited, hoping to blend seamlessly back into his job as barback. Mike cleaned up and rejoined the crowd as well. The mood was decidedly different at Trough now. Much more focused, but also much more calm, in a strange way, since the former patrons of the old Hole now knew why they were here, intuitively knew why the new men were here and partially knew who they were.

This was MAX's first night in his new leatherbar. All the men here, even those who had just now realized it, the old Hole patrons, and Alan, and Dick, and even Little Mike, were now on the same wavelength as the men who had come on the matching motorcycles outside. This was a celebration of MAX, what he had achieved and the major effect that, it was immediately clear, Trough would have worldwide. Even Little Mike, generally the most obtuse leatherman in the crowd, got it right between the eyes: MAX was TOP. Every man's TOP.

Dick glanced at Alan. Alan was pissed. Well, shit, Dick realized he'd fucked up. But hey...what was to be expected of an oversexed, underage leather CHP motorcycle officer? Dick moved quickly to clean up the empty beer bottles and dead drinks that had collected while he'd been using Little Mike and it was soon done. Alan could go fuck himself! Shit! Dick was tired of sucking dick. He deserved getting his rocks off, too.

Alan wasn't really that pissed - just concerned that Dick's recklessness might get Dick, or both of them, whipped and then fired. Alan already knew where Dick was evolving. He wished he could hang on to the little stud forever, but he knew better. Best bet was to just keep things going, keep up with the AJ classes at City, let the boy cop a blow job here and there, hang on to as much as he could for as long as he could, and hope there was something left when it was over. Alan had no idea that there were only minutes left.

The men who had clearly stood out earlier as not having been Hole patrons, who had apparently come on the matched motorcycles parked outside, had assembled around MAX in a congratulatory way, speaking in turn with him in a manner appropriate to colleagues. Each was dressed in biker leather, each in his own style, yet they all seemed to have a common bond. Perhaps a shared past experience. They were here to celebrate a big event for their esteemed friend, for themselves and for leathermen everywhere. The slaves who had emerged prior to MAX, including the one with the lash mark weeping crimson, were busily at work cleaning the men's boots with their slave tongues, occasionally stealing a crotch nuzzle or a prick-nip. It was a festive occasion, so the slaves' indiscretions were received as the play they were, the response being merely gentle remonstration to get back on the boots. These were slaves picked specially for play, for fun, to entertain at the celebration. No serious training here. Just fun - party favors provided by MAX.

"Gentlemen!" MAX announced, not loudly, but since it was he who had spoken, Trough fell silent. "Welcome to Trough. Honor the space. Obey the rules. Trough is dedicated to your future."

Alan then announced, as he had been instructed earlier, "Drinks are on Trough for the remainder of the evening, gentlemen. Please order top shelf. Make it memorable." The crowd pressed strongly toward to the bar to celebrate Trough and MAX. It was a big moment for every man there, but it did not mean that there was no work to be done. There was always work to be done. Especially fun work.

As the men pressed forward for their single malts, tequilas, and cognacs, MAX stepped back from the crowd. He continued to accept the congratulatory back slaps and handshakes, but his thoughts were elsewhere. The party was already a success and would take care of itself. MAX was, as always, focused ahead, on the future, his future, and the futures of the men in orbit around him. MAX moved to the back of the bar, where the gimpy pool table had been, but where a chest-high small round table, covered in chromed diamond plate steel, now stood. Dick the barback was just finishing up his backlog, about to remove a couple of dead beers and hit the table with his rag. He felt a beefy arm around his shoulder.

"Have you got a moment, pardner?" MAX demanded, phrasing it as if it were a question, although it wasn't. "We need to talk."

Dick froze. He turned white. Then he turned crimson. He was hot and cold simultaneously. He wanted to fight - he wanted to run - both - neither. He ended up accepting MAX's invitation to accompany him into the tunnel. Dick followed MAX as if there were no option. An observer might have noted that, well, Dick could always have simply bolted out the front door of the place and been gone, gone to whatever. But for a 21-year-old barback / leather CHP motorcycle officer, MAX's invitation could not be refused. Indeed, virtually no one had the capacity to say "no" to MAX. That was just the way it was. Through the tunnel Dick was led, not leashed, but as if he were leashed, past the iron-bar gates, past the 90 degree turn, and into what seemed a vast unlit space, unlit save one small spotlight which shone on a small wooden stool.

"Sit," MAX said. Dick sat. Sure, he had been clearly metamorphosing into a hot, young, leather Top - look how he had taken charge of Little Mike in the shitter. But this was different. Very different. There was nothing within Dick that he could call upon to resist MAX in the slightest. Different ball game.

MAX stood next to Dick, placing his hand on Dick's neck, squeezing it gently, affectionately really, but making it clear that he could snap it if he chose. Dick felt MAX's leather breeches against his shoulder and his thigh. He glanced laterally and saw MAX's codpiece full to bursting. He looked up, past the washboard abs and the pecs jutting out, to the handsome face, which smiled down at him. MAX began: "So, you're Richard Stark, 937-40-4706, born Camp Pendleton 25 May 1982, raised all over the place, graduated from high school in 29 Palms, have had a fair amount of college work, are currently taking AJ at City, and want to be a cop - CHP, apparently, given your outfit. You're also queer as a three dollar bill, working in a bar, shacked up with a weakly motivated bartender and were getting your fucking dick sucked in the shitter in my bar on my time."

Dick was numb. What could he say?

"Nothing to say, asshole?" MAX asked. "How about 'Yes, Sir. That is correct, Sir.'?"

"Yes, Sir. That is correct, Sir," Dick responded. It was a good response, a smart response.

"Good answer, pardner," MAX said. Dick was trying to remember: the arm around his shoulder, being called "pardner," the cocky, holding-all-the-high-cards attitude - it all had a familiar quality to it. Dick couldn't quite make the connection.

"OK, pardner, this is the way it's going to be. You're working for me now, but not as a barback. You are not to set foot in any bar. You are not to violate any law - any law - ever. You will continue with your college work toward your career and you will succeed. You will succeed because I will be your trainer, I and my men. You will be trained to succeed at my facility - I guarantee success. I know what you want, and I will train you to achieve that. The training is strictly voluntary. You can terminate at any time if you are not man enough. But I doubt you will. Do you accept training, Richard? Answer now." MAX looked deeply into Dick's eyes to find the answer to his question.

Dick hesitated, but only for a moment. "Yes, Sir, I accept. Yes, Sir. I do," he said.

What the fuck was going on here? When Dick had first landed in the City, when he met Dan his first night in town, and had become Dan's slave immediately, there had been no saying "no." It was entirely emotional, and it was the right decision, at least for the moment. When Dan had been snatched by Leather Officer, Dick remembered that Dan also lacked the capacity to say "no." Again, an emotional decision, a bad one, Dick thought. But now, confronted with MAX's offer, again the idea of saying "no" was not even there, yet it was not just an emotional decision - Dick felt that it was entirely rational - that what MAX offered was the right thing to do not just because MAX was the hottest thing on the fucking planet, but because there was absolutely no doubt that MAX was right. That whatever MAX said was the case, was the way it was. So as Dick was led away by two slaves to begin his training there was not even the shadow of a doubt that any other course of action was thinkable. MAX's way was not only the right way - it was the only way.

CHAPTER 11

Little Mike thought that Trough was a much better bar than the Hole had been. His concern for the loss of the place of his leather epiphany melted away after a short time at the new venue, probably when he was forced to suck Dick's penis by the piss trough. As the hot little leather cop poked at his throat, Little Mike could look out, over the porcelain, through the new window, and see the whole bar. It was a great place, Mike thought. But this fun had been cut short as the large man who was apparently the new owner arrived, and Dick had had to go back to work. Shortly thereafter, Dick's employer had called him aside, Mike saw, but Mike hoped that Dick would return soon and take him back into the toilet and again fuck his throat.

Little Mike downed several Stiefelknechts waiting for the hunky little leather cop to return. But nothing. Mike approached the bar to see if Alan knew what the story was. "Where'd the barback go?" Mike asked, as if Alan were some neutral observer. In fact, Alan was quite agitated on several accounts. He was very aware of what Dick and Little Mike had been doing earlier. The window over the piss trough had revealed it all. Alan was hardly keen on helping Little Mike start up again with the man Alan still considered to be his boy. Alan was the last to accept that Dick was moving on. "That big guy took him into the tunnel. What's up?" Little Mike continued.

Alan was about to lose it. He was a nice guy. He tried to be ethical toward everyone, ethical and courteous. It was his job and his nature. But this was just too much. Alan was beside himself: he, too, had seen Dick taken through the tunnel. To where? It had been a while ago, and Dick had not come back. What to do? And now this idiot Mike was asking the same question that was destroying Alan: "What's up?" Alan turned red in the face and was just about to leap across the bar and attack Little Mike when two slaves appeared.

"MAX wants to see you," one slave said to Alan. "Come with me." Alan obeyed. The slave led him away, through the tunnel, while the other took his station serving the patrons. Mike was left standing, his question unanswered. Little Mike was beginning to have misgivings about Trough. It definitely had plusses, but it was beginning to seem as if there was a lot of stuff going on that Mike was not a part of, and he felt left out. The men he knew best had been taken away and he really didn't know any of the guys from Europe or wherever. He felt a bit uncomfortable. Mike gravitated toward the door, thinking that it might be best to just call it a night, thinking that to wait for either Dick or Alan to return might be foolish. Finally, Little Mike decided to call it quits, and headed out the door, feeling like an outsider, with no friends.

As Little Mike emerged into the night in front of Trough, the many Stiefelknechts he'd consumed caught up with him. He was a little unsure where his bike was. Where had he parked it? Little Mike was busy answering this question when he heard the low lub-dub of a high displacement motorcycle approaching. The bike pulled up adjacent to the group of matching bikes belonging to the new men in the bar. Mike saw that it appeared to be a Highway Patrol motorcycle, and the big man dismounting was attired as if he were a Highway Patrol motorcycle cop. Well, Mike was impressed - the man looked great, really hot - but Mike was not entirely surprised, because leather bars were often frequented by men wearing police uniforms. After all, that was what Leather Officer was all about, and Dick had worn leather CHP duds while Little Mike was blowing him less than an hour ago. It was not entirely unexpected that a man dressed like a cycle cop would be shutting down his bike in front of Trough at this time.

But Little Mike checked the man out further. Fuck! It can't be! Mike blinked, then blinked again, unbelieving.

"Hey, pardner, how's it going?" the cop asked. Mike was speechless, unsure that he was still conscious. Pardner? It couldn't be. But it had to be. It was.

"I'm good, Sir, good. How are you?" Mike answered. He was thrilled.

"Great now that I'm off shift. Thought I'd knock back a few brews. You leaving?" T. Stockton coaxed.

"Oh, uh, no, Sir, I'm not leaving, Sir. I just stepped out for a breath of fresh air, Sir," Little Mike responded.

"Well that's a healthy attitude, Mike. It is Mike, isn't it?" Stockton asked, knowing full well that it was.

"Yes, Officer Stockton! I'm Mike, Sir!" Little Mike responded.

"Well how about joining me for a nightcap, Mike?" the cop offered.

"Well, yes, Sir, I guess one more beer won't hurt, Sir," Little Mike said, ignoring the absurdity of the fact that he was already too drunk to drive and was being encouraged by an armed Highway Patrolman to get even more hammered.

"Great, pardner." Tracy Stockton put his arm around Mike's shoulder and escorted him back into Trough. "You're looking better that the last time I saw you," the cop suggested.

Mike flushed. Well, he certainly was better, much better, which made him feel good, because Little Mike wanted to be at his best for Officer Stockton. He felt that he somehow owed it to the cop, to be "better" since the officer had helped him when he needed help. "Yes, Sir, better, much better. I have eyebrows, hair on my chest, and hair around my cock and balls!" Mike stated, realizing only after he had said it how incredibly idiotic an announcement this was, especially as he and Officer Stockton approached the bar where the slave which had replaced Alan did not have hair on its chest or around its cock and balls. "May I buy you a drink, Sir?"

"Yes, Mike. You may," Stockton stated. The slave overheard this, asked Mike what he wanted, and brought drinks for them both. Mike was served another Stiefelknecht and the cop was brought single malt Scotch, with a splash.

Mike was surprised. "How did the bartender know what you wanted, Sir?"

"Oh, just clairvoyant, I guess," Officer Tracy Stockton responded, grinning. Mike grinned too, as if he were in on the joke, even though he wasn't.

Mike frowned. "Sir, is it OK for you to be armed and drinking in a bar? Isn't that illegal?"

Officer Tracy Stockton put his arm around Little Mike's shoulder and said, "Well, pardner, sometimes it's necessary to bend the law. I can trust you to be discreet, can't I?"

"Oh, yes Sir, yes, you can trust me to be discreet, yes," Mike enthused, thrilled to be a part of it.

"Good. I knew I could trust you, Mike." Stockton unholstered the big revolver and swung the six chambers open for Mike's inspection. "Not loaded, since I'm now off duty. Ever handled one of these?"

"Why no, no Sir, I haven't," Mike responded.

The cop handed the big gun to Little Mike so he could check it out. Mike nearly fainted. He had jerked off at least a hundred times thinking about this Highway Patrolman, and now here he was in a leatherbar buying the cop a drink and handling his weapon. Phew!

"Wow, it's heavy, Sir. Have you ever shot anyone, Sir?" Mike asked, wondering half way through the question how he could retract it.

"Yes, Mike, I have, unfortunately. Occasionally I come upon individuals who simply cannot or will not accept that there are limits in a civilized society and it becomes necessary for me to defend your welfare. In self defense, I have discharged this weapon. Additionally, without it, knowing how the low-lifes among us think, it would be impossible for me to do my job. It's too bad, but there it is," the cop said.

"I wonder if I could do that, Sir," Little Mike reflected.

"You seem like a fairly level headed guy, Mike. I suspect that you could defend yourself or innocent people around you if you had to," his friend stated.

Mike was silent. This conversation had gone off in a strange direction, not at all where Mike had intended. He wasn't quite sure what was going on. Suddenly a slave appeared, addressing Little Mike.

"Sir, would you accompany me? MAX would like to speak with you," the slave said.

Mike was unclear what to say. He looked at Tracy Stockton. The officer nodded slightly in the affirmative. Little Mike followed the slave into the tunnel.

CHAPTER 12

Slaves would be well advised not to gossip among themselves, but they do it anyway. No matter how often they are reminded that the only source of valid information is their Master, still, they compare notes. So, days later, after Dick, Alan, and Little Mike were processed into MAX's system and had an opportunity to speak with one another, they realized that each had undergone essentially the same initial interview, had been made aware that MAX already knew far more about them than they would have guessed possible, and presented them with an offer which could only be accepted. But right now, each new trainee was largely uninformed about the whereabouts of the others or, indeed, much of anything else about MAX's program. Each only knew that, within minutes of first encountering MAX, he had become completely controlled by an overwhelming need to serve, and an overwhelming certainty that he was embarking on a whole new chapter in his life which, albeit challenging, was inevitable and entirely positive.

Some Tops have to go to great effort in order to convert a man into a slave. For MAX, it was easy. Certainly, molding the slave into what it would ultimately become was a process that required extensive training, but initially convincing a man that he should become MAX's property generally required less than a minute. MAX had taken his innate power and honed it to perfection over several decades, so he was as skilled as they come recognizing potential slaves, checking them out, and buckling his collar on them in short order. It was this skill, among others, which had made his empire possible.

After Little Mike, with no more than ten seconds reflection, had agreed with MAX that it would be a great idea to simply abandon Mike's entire past life, become MAX's slave and be trained for a new career under MAX's oversight, he was led away by two slaves to a dimly lit cavernous space. Little Mike was ordered to strip and then stand over a large grate in the floor. The slaves then produced a bucket of warm, soapy water and two sponges. Mike was ordered to stand still, spread his legs, and raise his arms. The slaves quickly cleaned Little Mike's body, rinsed him with warm water and toweled him dry. They then fastened one end of a pair of handcuffs around Little Mike's cock and balls - tight enough that the cuff could not be removed - but not so tight that there was discomfort. He became erect. Mike was increasingly excited and a little apprehensive, but not afraid, in spite of his recent bad experience with Leather Officer. Part of the power of MAX was that he dispelled fear - men immediately trusted him - and Little Mike was typical. Not a hint of fear, only erotic excitement, as he was led by the slaves away from the site of his cleaning to another area. The light seemed to follow Mike and the slaves as they went, finally illuminating a wooden bench with a series of 4" diameter holes spaced along it and rings attached to a brace running its length, a ring under each hole. Both Dick and Alan were seated on the bench, their cocks and balls cuffed through holes and attached to rings below. Both were gagged. Mike was directed to sit over a hole and the loose cuff was clicked around a ring below. After carefully checking the fit, one slave double locked the cuffs, and Mike was effectively restrained. He was then gagged like the others, the slaves departed and the light went out. All three were then unable to speak, unable to stand, there was nothing to see and nothing to hear. They were left this way, to think about it, for quite some time.

After a while the sound of an electric motor could be heard through the darkness. Suddenly, a large television screen was illuminated right in front of the trainees, very bright, precluding them seeing their surroundings. A video, not very high quality, began to run, a series of scenes obviously shot by hidden camera. First, there was a sequence which showed Little Mike wandering sort of aimlessly around the old Hole. Then Mike gets invited into the "staff only" area behind the bar by Alan. Alan turns, unbuttons his leather pants, pulls out his cock and balls, and gestures for Little Mike to get on it. Mike looks apprehensive at first, but quickly gets excited and involved, sucking Alan's cock. The sequence lasts a few minutes, Alan shoots, and it's over as Mike is still kneeling and Alan returns to the bar. The screen goes blank momentarily, then the word BUSTED! appeared in big block letters.

The film clearly raised a number of issues in the trainees' minds. Alan and Little Mike were perplexed and embarrassed. And Dick, of course, had not been aware that Alan and Little Mike had any history at all! But there was no time to digest this before the next sequence started.

Leather Officer is shown in the pisser, again at the Hole, playing with his dick. Little Mike comes in and stares at it. There is conversation, not audible on the video. Leather Officer roughs Little Mike up, and forces his swollen copdick down the kid's throat several times. Mike gets cuffed and hauled out.

This was different altogether. It is difficult to say which of the trainees was most upset by seeing Little Mike and Leather Officer. It reminded each, separately, of perhaps the most negative experience of his career as a leatherman. For each, it raised emotions of shame, anger, and disgust. Again the word BUSTED! and then another sequence. Dick is shown in the pisser, earlier this evening, only an hour ago, with Little Mike on his knees, sucking Dick's cock. Dick starts to get rough, both become excited, but then something seems to disturb them, and Dick hurriedly shoves his equipment back into his leather uniform as Mike stands, getting himself together more slowly, sort-of bewildered. Dick is then shown hastily collecting bottles and glasses. The sequence ends, and again, the word BUSTED! is shown. The screen then clicked off, leaving the trainees in darkness with their thoughts.

Of the three new trainees, probably Little Mike was most upset by these videos. In every one he was shown as an easily seduced cocksucker, apparently eager to administer a blow job to every man he encountered. Mike was having huge misgivings. His encounter with Leather Officer had gone so badly. Had he again made another major error by allowing himself to be cuffed by his balls to this damn bench by MAX? Little Mike was red-faced and sweating.

Dick, being so young and hot-headed, thought the videos were all about him: he had had to watch Alan, who had been topping him for weeks up until half-an-hour ago, get it on with this clueless guy Mike, then endure the sight of Leather Officer, dredging up all sorts of negative emotions concerning his loss of Dan, and then finally watch himself get "caught" getting a blow job and having to quickly put his cock and balls away - as if there were something wrong with what he was doing. Dick thought it was all designed to put him down. He developed that dark look which Alan had seen repeatedly. Dick got angry. He definitely was of a mind to get the hell out of here, but, uh-oh, that was hardly possible, was it? Was he ready to go and leave his cock and balls behind? Dick was not in control. Not at all.

Alan came closest to understanding the real message of the videos. He wasn't upset seeing Little Mike suck him off, or even suck Dick off, or even get messed with by Leather Officer. Sure, he wanted Dick all to himself forever, but that could not happen, certainly not now. He would have preferred that Leather Officer had never even existed, but this, too, was not the case. Alan saw the main point before the others did: that they all had been under surveillance and that the surveillance had been going on for quite some time. It was clear to Alan that MAX's plan was not something concocted spontaneously. Apparently weeks of planning had brought Alan to his current status - fastened by his cock and balls to the bench, gagged, and otherwise naked. He felt extremely vulnerable and helpless. Not afraid, necessarily, because MAX had done nothing to stimulate fear, but entirely without recourse. Alan understood that whatever was going on here, whatever MAX had planned, was far larger and elaborate and probably far more irresistible than Alan had imagined when he signed on. Alan hadn't bottomed in years and had sort of forgotten that funny, giddy / queasy feeling he used to get when a Top was in the process of taking control. He felt it now. Oddly, it was Alan, who had been a Top himself, who was most quickly and easily being enslaved. MAX's power was already deep into Alan's guts.

The trainees' thoughts, all so different, were cut off by the start of another video. It appeared to be some sort of interview of public officials, something from the evening news or some other TV program. With sound. A reporter was shown outside the State Capitol building.

REPORTER: "This is Bob Kawasaki in Capital City. There has been a remark-able turn-around in law enforcement here. It was only three years ago that KROK investigative reporters Dave Manhattan and Trisha Trinidad uncovered an extensive network of burglary and extortion perpetrated by officers of the Capital City Police Department."

The camera panned to the side of Bob Kawasaki to reveal a tall, thin man in coat and tie, Governor George Abachian.

REPORTER: "Governor, what has happened up here to change things so rapidly and completely?"

GOVERNOR: "Well, Bob, as you know, our great State was badly misman-aged in many ways by my predecessor's permissive administration. My back-ground as a prosecutor helped me identify a long list of problems State-wide, only one of which was the deplorable performance of the Capital City Police. My landslide victory provided the momentum to tackle these problems, and I think, although there still remains much to accomplish, that good progress has been made. The local clean-up has largely been led by Mayor John Cardinale. I think John has done an outstanding job."

The camera now pans to Mayor Cardinale, who had been standing next to the Governor, but off-camera, all along. The Mayor is a slight, handsome, well-dressed younger man, clearly excited to be seen on TV.

REPORTER: "Well, Mr. Mayor, how did you do it?"

MAYOR: "Thanks for the vote of confidence, Governor, but I think it's a bit misdirected. I certainly do feel that my administration has brought a breath of fresh air and inclusiveness to this city, but, although I strongly support aggres-sive and just law enforcement, I'm no expert in the field. If I have contributed anything, it probably boils down to simply giving Major Max McCarthy a free hand to make the changes locally which have produced such good results."

This was not network TV. It was clumsily scripted. The muffled roar of a squadron of large displacement motorcycles was heard approaching the interview site, as if by coincidence. The camera's eye broadened to include the scene of the reporter, the Governor, and the Mayor as a dozen black and white police bikes pulled up. Their riders dismounted and formed a rank, at attention, behind the civilians, with one exception. A large, powerfully built cop, obviously in charge of the others, shook hands with the reporter, the governor, and then the mayor. The mayor was noticeably excited.

MAYOR: "Major McCarthy, you probably can explain what has been accomplished better than I."

As Major McCarthy turned to face the camera, all three trainees gasped in spite of their gags. It was MAX! It was clear now that the video had been shot several years ago, but it was definitely MAX, and even more astounding, one of the officers standing at attention behind the interview was Tracy Stockton! What the fuck was going on here?

All the cops were identically uniformed. Gleaming black cop boots; black leather breeches with two white stripes; black leather shirt with white leather tie tucked into the slot between the second and third buttons, military-style; utility belt with a huge gun, a baton, and all the other cop gear including a shoulder strap; gauntlet gloves; chrome badge, name tag, and insignia. No head gear at the moment - their helmets had been left on their bikes. In fact, these cops' leather uniforms were very, very similar to what the trainees remembered of Leather Officer's uniform. Very similar. Only minor differences in detail.

Although the cuffs around the trainee's cocks and balls had been relatively comfortable previously, not so now. All three had developed major erections the moment they had seen MAX on TV, even before they recognized who it was. They only got harder as the cop began to speak.

MAJOR MAX McCARTHY: "Thank you, Mr. Mayor. With your help, and the Governor's as well, the Capital City Police Department today is among the finest in the State. I'm sure we here in Capital City don't have all the answers for every department in trouble, but we may provide some ideas."

Although the reporter and the Governor seemed substantially unaffected, Mayor Cardinale looked as if he were about to simply burst open with excitement standing next to Major McCarthy. Clearly, the Mayor was ready to provide law enforcement with whatever was needed to get the job done. Whatever. Just ask. Anything. Anything at all.

REPORTER: "Well, you are very modest, Major, but what exactly did you do to clean up the department?"

MAJOR MAX McCARTHY: "It was simple, Bob. All that my men and I did was set an example. When things fell apart at the Department, my outfit was a relatively small motorcycle detachment largely focusing on the Capitol Building and other state government activities. We had to take over, rather quickly, general policing functions at the leadership level because only we had retained the confidence of the public. It was a difficult period during which the public and the political leadership had nowhere to turn for effective law enforcement locally except the Capital City Motorcycle Detachment. Only we were unstained by corruption, so we staffed up and set standards for the Department."

REPORTER: "What kind of standards, Major?"

MAJOR MAX McCARTHY: "Bob, as the Mayor and the Governor know, my men and I are 100% cops 100% of the time. Isn't that right, men?"

OFFICERS: (in unison, shouting) "SIR! YES, SIR!"

MAJOR MAX McCARTHY: "We have dedicated ourselves to our work fully. It is not just a job. It is our life. We live together at our barracks, train together, recreate together, and work together, much like a military unit. Paramilitary police. Very different from most civilian police. Each of my men is trained to lead, to know the law and regulations, to direct the public, and to control any situation. It's all about control and authority. We do it the way it should be done. My men took over key field leadership positions and we have run street policing ever since."

REPORTER: "It sounds a little like martial law."

MAJOR MAX McCARTHY: "Yes. That's correct."

GOVERNOR: "Well, Major, certainly Mayor Cardinale, the citizens of this city, and I are grateful to you and your men for your service. You are exemplary. But can you explain why you and your officers would sacrifice so much, would choose such a Spartan life, would give up family and friends, the standard pleasures of life, to dedicate yourselves so wholly to your work?"

Mayor Cardinale and Major Max McCarthy both, quite briefly, and in quite different ways, glanced toward the Governor as if they were about to say "You fucking idiot! Why would any man, given the opportunity, not jump at the chance to do this?" But neither said it.

MAJOR MAX McCARTHY: "Well, Governor, I really don't know how to answer that question other than to say that I set extremely high standards for myself and my men. We have chosen excellence and really know no other way. Is that correct, men?"

OFFICERS: (in unison, shouting) "SIR! YES, SIR!"

REPORTER: "Governor, Mayor, Major, Officers, thank you for your time and insight. I hope our viewers can now understand better what to demand from their elected officials and their police."

Little Mike, Alan, and Dick, even if they hadn't been gagged, would have been speechless as the TV screen went dark. They sat on the bench with their hard-ons, completely freed from the negative emotions stimulated by the first series of videos, ready to go forward, understanding clearly, although not fully, that they were in some manner being trained to be one of the men they had just seen. To be ready, on signal, to shout "SIR! YES, SIR!"

CHAPTER 13

Dick, Alan, and Little Mike were again alone with their thoughts, completely in the dark, hearing nothing other than each other squirming, unable to speak. Some time passed, many minutes, enough time for them to regain their composure and to lose their erections. They were beginning to get fidgety when, again, the TV screen clicked on. It was a little difficult at first to see what was being shown. The picture had a greenish cast and was a bit indistinct. They strained to make it out, and then were shocked at what they saw. It was three men cuffed by their cocks and balls to a bench, gagged. They were looking at a live picture of themselves!

It took a moment for the implications of this to sink in. It was apparently an infra-red camera or something high tech like. But clearly, if they were watching themselves on TV, anyone else might be watching as well. Alan remembered the big TV screen that had just been installed in the bar. Christ! Were they being shown to the crowd? Was MAX watching them? Who? Where?

The image changed. What looked like a cell block was shown. Each cell held two slaves, collared but not shod, otherwise nude. The slaves were all sleeping. Another scene change: It looked like some sort of outdoor holding pen - chain-link fence, barbed wire strands angling out in both directions on the top, concertina wire resting on top of that, flood lit, a cage in the middle, a hooded slave inside.

Another image change: the pisser in the bar. Patrons were arriving, pissing, and departing, unaware they were being videoed. Yet another change: a man wearing precisely the same uniform the trainees had just seen MAX and the other officers of the Capital City Motorcycle Detachment wearing was standing behind a slave fastened to a St. Andrew's cross. The slave was apparently being punished. There was no sound, but the trainees understood. The slave was being flogged. Then the flogging was over. The cop had an erect penis. He smeared something on it, approached the slave's ass, and...the screen went blank. It came back on with four separate shots: the trainees, the cellblock, the pen, the pisser. Then eight shots. The trainees weren't given enough time to even figure out what the new scenes were before the screen went to16, and then 32, all apparently live. Then the screen went blank, leaving them to think.

How large was MAX's empire? How many cameras? How many separate facilities? How many Officers? How many slaves? What did the slaves do? How would Dick, Alan, and Little Mike fit in? What was ahead? But most of all, where was MAX? When would MAX come back?

After another period in the dark, the light came back on and six slaves appeared. The trainees were uncuffed and assisted to their feet, one slave grasping each arm firmly, as much to restrain as to assist. The gags were removed. The slaves led Alan, Dick, and Little Mike away from the bench, back toward where they had earlier been cleaned. The steel grate in the floor, six feet by ten feet, covered a drain pit. The grate was opened by two more slaves. The trainees were directed to descend a steel ladder built into the wall of the pit, the floor of which was ten feet below the level of the grate. The grate was replaced and locked. It was difficult to see, but it appeared that another, smaller drain, also grated, was in the center of the sloping pit floor.

This unusual plumbing made some sense if one recalled that the building had previously been a laundry. A lot of waste water had been generated, and the pit had held mesh to catch material that would have clogged the sewer. Waste water, such as that used to clean the trainees, could flow in from the floor above. In addition, pipes from elsewhere debouched into the pit just below the level of the grate. Although the slaves left, the light stayed on, dimly illuminating the drain pit and its captives. It was very quiet. In the distance, Alan thought he heard a toilet flush. Several seconds later a mixture of mostly water, but piss as well, burst out of one of the pipes and completely drenched Dick, splattering the others as well. Little Mike, Alan, and Dick had been inserted into MAX's hierarchy at the very bottom.

Dick was furious. Alan was worried, about Dick as much as himself, and also about Little Mike. Mike was bewildered. Although they could now speak, they didn't. What could they say? Hot-headed Dick jumped to the conclusion that MAX was an asshole just like Leather Officer. Hell, they even had the same uniform! Dick felt betrayed. He had trusted MAX, he thought he was going to be trained to be a cop and wear a hot uniform. Little Mike hoped that MAX would come back and get him, save him from this pit. It took a while for Mike to realize that it was MAX who had put them there. That confused Little Mike even more. Maturity and years of topping helped Alan realize that they were being challenged, tested, and that the best approach would simply be to accept it and obey. The only way out was up.

It was already very late when the trainees were put into the pit. The bar had closed. Their training had been handled so far by the eight slaves and some TV tape. Seven of those slaves were now asleep with one remaining on duty to monitor the pit, on camera of course, and the rest of MAX's empire.

Again Alan heard a toilet flush. He made sure he was not standing where Dick had been when it happened before. But that wasn't how it worked in the pit. This time the discharge came from a different pipe and Alan got it full force. There were several pipes and no way of knowing which one would spurt even if you did hear a toilet flush, which was not always the case anyway. Exhausted, they each slumped down and tried to sleep propped against the walls of the pit, periodically awakened by a wastewater discharge. They were miserable.

They lost track of time. How long had they been in the pit? They weren't sure, and they weren't sure what time it had been when they went in. They had no idea what time it was, and later, what day it was. At one point, it seemed that the waste water was coming more frequently, and they decided that maybe the bar was again open. But urine from the piss trough would trickle in, probably, so that idea was discarded. Unless there were some sort of holding tank for it, discharging only when it filled to a certain level. Would it be pure piss or would it be diluted? These kinds of questions were all they had to think about. Would it just be piss and water? Alternatives were scary. But ultimately the alternatives came. Alan got hit with what seemed like dishwater. Then Little Mike got hit with shit. Soon they were all shit on. They didn't accept it exactly, but they came to expect it. Hours ago, or was it days, these three had been fully functioning adult males. Now what were they? It was hard to say.

Periodically a slave would come with a hose and allow them to drink from the flow. They were also hosed off. Bags of what appeared to be dog food were occasionally thrown down. Time and all dignity were gone. They had no past and no future, only a present, an interminable wait for release from the pit. Finally they heard the sound of boots approaching which were not slave boots. MAX's cop boots sparkled as he stepped onto the center of the grate and looked down at them. He chuckled.

MAX was ready for slave training. He wore the same gear he had worn at the opening of the bar: slave-shined cop boots; black leather breeches with square-based pyramidal studs for stripes, two rows; bare chest; Sam Browne with five rows of studs around the waist, three across the shoulder; officer's cap with studs encircling the base. Attached to his belt were keys, on the left, and his bullwhip on the right. He chuckled again. "You don't get out of the drain until you have learned to perform a trick," he stated, as if this were common knowledge. "Stand up." They did. "Open your mouths as wide as you can and tip your heads back," Max ordered. They did.

MAX removed his codpiece and tossed it aside. His cock and balls hung free. Little Mike gasped. Considering MAX's stature, it would have been no surprise if his equipment were larger than average as well. And it was. Actually somewhat larger even than might have been expected. Not freaky huge like super-icons in porn stories, but larger than average even for a large man. Beautiful as well. Not all penises are exactly pretty - some are distorted and scary. MAX's penis was classically proportioned, neither thicker nor longer than it should have been. Just what you would choose if it were your choice. Choose to have between your own legs or choose to take care of, if MAX would permit it. And the balls: well, again, a bit larger than might be expected even on a very large man, but completely in proportion to the penis. All-in-all, a very hot package.

MAX already knew the trainees better than they knew themselves. He knew that Alan and Little Mike would obey, but he was unsure about Dick. Dick was hot-headed for sure, but MAX knew that Dick could excel ultimately. Harder to enslave, but worth the effort. "Hold still and we'll see how good my aim is," MAX said. Alan saw that Dick was on the verge of balking and started to coach him, but MAX cut it off. "No talking, asshole! Your mouth has a higher priority right now. The more piss you take, the faster you'll get out of the pit and start formal training!"

They shut their eyes, opened their mouths as wide as they could and held still. MAX took a wide stance, steadied his cock with a gloved hand, aimed through the bars of the grate and filled each open mouth in turn. First Dick, then Alan, then Little Mike. Very little was lost. The trainees swallowed as MAX went around again. On the third time around, MAX ran nearly dry before Little Mike's mouth was quite full. Mike was scared because MAX had said the ticket out of the pit was hooked to the amount of piss drunk. The last few squirts were impossible for MAX to aim, so he just sprayed them generally.

"Rub it in. It's good for slaves," he said. "M7, a few drops got on the boots. Take care of it"

A slave clambered out onto the grate and carefully tongued up the few drops, taking care not to lick indiscriminately. M7 knew that bootlicking was not generally allowed - bad for the boots - but that in a case like this, urine was worse, even MAX's urine, so it was a real slave treat. M7 got rock hard. The trainees in the pit also became erect at the sight, from below, of the slave carefully removing the piss drop by drop from the gleaming leather copboots. And MAX got hard, assuring that the trainees in the pit would have pleasant dreams next time they slept.

"Clean the piss off the tip of my dick," MAX commanded. M7 leapt to the task and carefully removed just the urine from the tip, making sure not to do anything more. It pulled back when finished. "Good boy," MAX stated, patting the slave's cheek affectionately. "Maybe we can find you a treat later." M7 just beamed and grinned. Its dick got even harder. MAX walked off, M7 following, leaving the trainees to wonder whether they had done a good enough job and what would happen next.

CHAPTER 14

Little Mike, Alan, and Dick continued to exist, barely, in the drain pit for sometime more. Hours? Days? It was impossible to tell. MAX deliberately scheduled dog food deliveries at odd hours, randomly, so that they would be more disoriented. Everything that happened to them, which was not much, seemed to have no periodicity to it, no night, no day, no time. Boredom, disorientation, humiliation - but especially boredom. With no end in sight.

There was one and only one exception to this torture. MAX came regularly to piss. His visit, every few hours or so, became the singular structural event in the trainee's lives. They realized, after a while, that the longer MAX was gone, the greater would be the volume of piss he provided them. If MAX was gone for a long while, presumably while he slept, then there would be much urine for them - morning piss, they figured. If he visited more frequently, it was, they assumed, during his waking hours and each such visit provided them less volume. Also the taste changed during the cycle.

So MAX's life pattern, communicated to them by the periodicity of his urination and the taste of his urine, became their marker of time, like the movements of the sun are for primitive people. They came to crave the structure he gave them, the gift of his urine and the opportunity to perform well for him. MAX, his movements, his regular appearance, his periodic gift to them, his penis, the source of the gift he brought them - it all blended into something approaching a simple religion. MAX, MAX's cock, MAX's urine. This was all they had.

Every time MAX appeared he bantered with them and teased them in a friendly way and gained their confidence. It came to be that they would become erect prior to hearing his boots because they knew it was time. Their entire focus became MAX. They forgot about the promises he had made. A new career, military-style brotherhood, all the rest. All they wanted was to get out of the pit and be closer to MAX, serve him in the manner of one of the slaves which he invariably brought along to clean up the few droplets of urine on his boots. Always a different slave...there must be dozens! Often MAX wore a different uniform. Sometimes like in the TV interview, sometimes like the first night at Trough, sometimes almost nude - just boots and his officer's cap. There was absolutely nothing going on in these trainees' world except MAX. From this base he would rebuild them into instruments of his will.

Then, at a point where they began to become fidgety, had begun to become erect anticipating MAX's impending visit, the pattern broke. Twelve slaves appeared, unlocked the grate covering the pit, and ordered the trainees to climb out. They responded quickly, scrambled up the ladder, and were ordered to stand apart for cleaning. They were hosed down, sprayed with disinfectant soap, scrubbed, rinsed, lathered up and shaved from head to toe with only the eyebrows and eyelashes remaining. Alan and Little Mike remembered what the loss of eyebrows meant, and were thankful that these were left merely trimmed. MAX knew that eyebrows protect slaves' eyes.

One slave addressed the trainees. "This is the most important day of your lives. Pay close attention to everything you are told. Obey every order immediately and unquestioningly. Be wholly truthful, always. Do this and you will experience the joy of slavery. Fail to do it, and you will be returned to the pit, or worse, dismissed."

The trainees were, of course, stark naked. Each was circled by four slaves, close to naked as well, except for slave boots and slave collars. The trainees were led by the slaves away from the drain into an area which, like everything they had experienced since coming through the tunnel, seemed large and empty but was lit by a light that seemed to follow them. Then something entirely unexpected happened. The entire interior of the building was suddenly illuminated as if at midday. The trainees, accompanied by four slaves each, had been brought before an assembly of hundreds of men! The men were in a military formation, all facing and focusing on the three trainees. Little Mike gulped.

In front was MAX, wearing the Motorcycle Detachment uniform the trainees had first seen on TV, and had also seen several times when he had visited them in the pit to give them his piss. Dick could feel his penis swelling. Behind MAX was a line of officers identically clad - fifteen armed, black leather cops, in a rank much as the trainees had seen before on the TV. Behind these were what appeared to be about twenty platoons of slaves, not necessarily the same number of slaves in each platoon, each headed by a man in a uniform the trainees had not seen before.

The men apparently in charge of each slave platoon were outfitted in tan leather police uniforms - tan leather breeches with two black stripes down the sides, a tan shirt with black piping and a black tie tucked in military style. The remainder of these men's gear was black leather - cop boots, utility belt, shoulder strap, gloves, officer's cap. No firearm. Each carried a whip of one kind or another attached to his belt and a baton.

MAX spoke. "Men, do you welcome three new slaves?"

Hundreds of male voices responded, shouting, in unison, "SIR! YES, SIR!"

"Will you train them to serve?" MAX asked.

"SIR! YES, SIR!" the men thundered.

"Will you lead them to excellence?"

"SIR! YES, SIR!"

Alan could feel the sound of this huge chorus beat against his chest. He knew he wanted to be given an opportunity to shout the same words.

MAX addressed the trainees. "Will you be truthful?" he asked.

All three, even Little Mike, knew from example what to say. "SIR! YES, SIR!" they shouted, as loud as they could.

"And will you obey?"

"SIR! YES, SIR!"

"Good. Join us," MAX said. With that, each trainee was guided to stand directly in front of and facing the sergeant in charge of the platoon to which the trainee was being assigned.

"Kneel, trainees, and receive your collars," MAX said. Each then had a brand new black leather collar buckled around its neck and locked in place. "Your new names are stamped on your collars. Your brother slaves will read the new names and tell you. Your old names are gone. Take your places at the back of your platoons."

The trainees were still being guided by four slaves each. They were shown their places at the back of their respective platoons, and given brand new slave boots to put on, which they did. Their slave guides then took their own places with their platoons. A brother slave, a platoon brother, read the new name stamped on the new collar and informed each of the new slaves and told him to memorize the name immediately.

MAX turned to face his men. Moments like this were central to MAX's spirit. His life was before him - these men and what they had achieved were MAX's life. He was proud.

"What is your name, slave?" MAX asked, pointing at one new slave.

"Sir, my name is V11, Sir," was the response from the man previously know as Alan. MAX knew that V11 would set the pattern for the younger two.

"And yours?"

"Sir, my name is M9, Sir," said the former Dick.

"And yours?"

"Sir, my name is D16, Sir," said the slave once called Little Mike.

"Excellent! New slaves, I am proud of you," MAX said. "Are you proud of yourselves?"

"Sir! Yes, Sir!" shouted M9, V11, and D16 as loud as they could.

"Your pride will only increase. Today is the most important day of your lives so far. The next few weeks will be challenging. You will grow. I salute you," MAX said, and he did. He saluted the three new slaves, as did every other man there. "Men, go about your duties, but find an opportunity to congratulate your new brothers. I order it. Dismissed."

"SIR! YES, SIR!" was the thunderous shout, heard now by the new slaves coming simultaneously from their own throats and their brother slaves' throats, their sergeants' throats, and the officers' throats, all together, as one.

M9 was overwhelmed by congratulation. Its platoon brothers were full of good wishes and sincere brotherhood. It was made to feel as if it were a part of something very large, as if it had made a good decision to join up, as if it were special. And all of this was true. Slaves from other platoons, other platoons' sergeants, officers, MAX himself, all congratulated M9 on its new status. Only Sergeant M held back, maintaining the distance which was necessary for the next phase of M9's training.

CHAPTER 15

Sergeant M told M9 to report to him at 1400 hrs. to begin formal training. It sought out its platoon sergeant at that time, saluted, and stated, "M9 reports, Sergeant." It had been coached by its brothers. It hoped it had gotten it right.

"OK, asshole," Sergeant M began. "This has been a big day for you. You think you're hot shit, that you've accomplished something. You're wrong. All you've done is get out of the fucking pit. Nothing more. And now you're mine. Mine."

M9 was confused. Where was MAX? Wasn't it going to be MAX's slave? Who was this new guy? Who was Sergeant M? M9 had the sense to say, "Yes, Sergeant." That was good.

"This is how it works, fuckhole. You are MAX's slave, that's true. But your day to day training is in my hands. You'll see MAX when he has time for you. And he will have time for you, particularly in the short term. But over the long term, you're mine. Get used to it. Accept it," Sergeant M stated.

Again, M9 had the sense to simply say, "Yes, Sergeant." Always a good answer.

Sergeant M was larger, older, and far more muscular than M9. Although it was disappointed that MAX was not going to be its one-on-one trainer, M9 was already feeling a clear need to serve its new sergeant. If MAX had delegated his authority to Sergeant M, well, that was all the information M9 needed. Sergeant M was the voice of authority if MAX said so. Sergeant M had a certain way about him, a cocky hardness, an edge that M9 found irrefusable. M was handsome in an unusual way, as if he would have been brutal if he weren't controlled by MAX. M9 had been deliberately placed under Sergeant M in order to learn control. Self-control and control over others. It was all part of MAX's plan.

Sergeant M attached a leash to M9's collar and led the slave, on all fours, into a private training room. M9 followed M, checking out the sergeant's cop boots the whole way. Sergeant M was close to promotion to Officer. It showed. M9 was quickly shifting over from its devotion to MAX to devotion to Sergeant M. Not losing devotion to MAX, just expanding the cadre of men above it which it would obey, to which it would be truthful, a broader slavery.

The training room was equipped with a fucking horse, to which Sergeant M strapped M9's arms, torso and legs. M9 could only squirm. Both its mouth and ass were held at cock level. It felt extremely vulnerable. Sergeant M unsnapped his breeches and hauled out his cock and balls. M9 began to sweat. There was no question that Sergeant M lacked the sophistication and large scale view which MAX brought to slave training. But sophistication and a large scale view are not always necessary. M had an erect penis, balls full of cum, a riding crop and an aggressive attitude which both frightened and enthralled M9. Sergeant M might not have the capacity to run an empire, but he damn sure had the capacity to get whatever he wanted out of M9 right now.

Sergeant M swaggered over in front of M9's face and slapped it with his prick. M9's history as a cocksucker flashed before its eyes. It wanted to suck this arrogant leather cop's cock in a major way. Forget its recent trend toward topping. That was over. M9 wanted dick, copdick right now, shoved down its throat, all the way down. It wanted training, copslave training. It wanted to serve its sergeant, its leather cop sergeant, to serve him in the same way it would serve MAX if he were here.

When Sergeant M barked, "Open up, fuckboy," M9 did. It opened up. Big and wide for its sergeant. Yes, Sergeant! M9's front fuckhole was filled with copdick as the sound of the door to the training room opening was heard. M9 checked the mirror. It was MAX! M9 could see very little. Out of the corner of its eye, in the mirror, it saw Sergeant M salute MAX, who returned the salute and said, "As you were, Sergeant. Continue with its training."

"Yes, Sir!" Sergeant M responded. An odd response, in a way, from a man whose erect penis still fully filled a slave's throat, but it made perfect sense in the context of the relationship between MAX and the sergeant. M had been MAX's slave for quite a while and had been trained by MAX and several ser-geants and officers in much same way that M9 was about to be trained. Now M was a sergeant, but MAX would always be "Sir." Even when M is promoted from sergeant to officer, MAX will still be "Sir." Officer Tracy Stockton refers to MAX as "Sir." That's how a copslave empire is run.

M9 began to struggle. Sergeants M's big prick had precluded breathing for many seconds as he greeted MAX. Once MAX returned M's salute, M pulled out of M9's throat and the slave gasped for air. Sergeant M's erect penis floated in the air in front of M9's face. After a few gulps of air, M9 stabilized and it began to hope that the organ would again plunge back down its throat.

M9 had quickly decided that it was very pleased that it had been assigned to Sergeant M. It felt that M was for sure the hottest of the sergeants and it hoped that M would allow it to suck his dick all the time from now on. It decided to serve its sergeant as well as it could, so it could get more dick down its throat, and just because it was coming to believe that Sergeant M was such a powerful man that he simply deserved the best service that his slave could provide. But no more dick for the moment. MAX took over.

"M - Take up your position at its rear fuckhole. I want to talk to it before we get started," MAX said.

"Yes, Sir," Sergeant M responded, obeying without any hesitation.

MAX came around in front of M9 and stood about six feet away, so that the slave could see its ultimate Master completely from head to toe. MAX knew slaves inside and out, backward and forward. He understood that it was essential to imprint their minds with an image at the very beginning, and then to reinforce that image over and over during training, so that they would remain enslaved forever. Even years later, even if they were promoted to sergeant or officer, they remain enslaved in the way that Sergeant M still was. The image to be imprinted today would be the image of MAX. MAX in his black leather police uniform, the uniform of the Capital City Motorcycle Detachment, the uniform M9 had seen in the video, the uniform MAX had worn this morning when M9 had been brought into MAX's system. The uniform symbolized the depth and breadth of MAX's total control over all the men under him, more power than any man had ever wielded before him.

MAX wore the white motorcycle helmet, the black leather shirt, and the black leather breeches with two white stripes down the sides which plunged into gleaming cop boots that nearly blinded M9. MAX's white leather tie was tucked into the slot between the second and third snaps on his shirt. His utility belt carried a holster, occupied by a large revolver, and a baton ring, occupied by a black side-handle baton. A shoulder strap crossed MAX's huge chest and back diagonally. A pair of cuffs rested in their pouch on MAX's belt as did a set of keys, hooked to a fob and an ammunition pouch. MAX's badge and chrome insignia glinted.

M9, of course, had been fully erect even before MAX had come in. It had found Sergeant M very exciting. But as M9 gazed at MAX, at this godlike black leather police icon, at the most powerful man on the planet, it thought its dick might explode. Additional training seemed superfluous. M9 felt that it was already totally enslaved, that it just wanted to obey and perform well, so maybe MAX might show it his cock, maybe might even let it suck that handsome cock!

MAX wore dark glasses so M9 could not see his eyes. These he now removed, and as M9 saw MAX's eyes, it let out a slight whimper. MAX's eyes were blue gray and deep and expressive. M9 could see deep into its Master's mind, deep into MAX's mind and soul, and it saw that it was valued. It knew that it was about to be handled far more roughly by MAX and M than it had ever before experienced, but it saw in MAX's eyes that the training, no matter how brutal, was a gift from its Master, an investment that the Master was making in his slave, and M9 was already very, very grateful. "Thank you, Sir," M9 said, quietly.

"You're welcome, slave," MAX responded, knowing exactly what M9 had meant. "You're entirely welcome." MAX moved closer to his slave's front fuckhole, so close that he could feel the slave's panting against the leather of his groin. MAX had done this hundreds of times, but it was always a thrill, because each new slave was different, although they all ended up much the same, all ended up as MAX's copslaves.

MAX's demeanor changed. "All right, Sergeant, let's get going. You know what to do."

"Sir, yes Sir!" M shouted, and M9 felt lubricant being shoved up its rear fuckhole. It figured out quickly what was about to happen. The first fuck from its new sergeant!

"Whose slave?" MAX asked.

"Your slave, Sir!" M9 responded.

"What about your sergeant, asshole. Aren't you his slave?" MAX demanded, moving still closer to M9's mouth, so close that M9 could have licked MAX's crotch, although it knew better than to try it.

M9 wasn't sure what to say. It didn't want to fuck up. So it just said, "Yes, Sir."

"'Yes, Sir'?" MAX mocked. "What the fuck does that mean, shithead? Whose slave are you?"

M9 began to get panicky. It wanted to get it right. It knew it was being fucked with, but still it wanted to do good, to please its Master, or its Masters. But how could it have two Masters? It got confused.

"Sir, I'm your slave, Sir," it said, pretty sure that it had gotten it wrong.

"Not good enough, asshole," MAX said, coldly. "Sergeant, three strokes."

M9 wasn't sure what Sergeant M used on its ass. It couldn't see very well in the mirror, but it did see the sergeant's arm rise and come down quickly delivering the first blow. The pain was like nothing M9 had ever experienced. Its whole body tensed, it broke out in a sweat and it let out a horrible sound, something between a roar and a scream. Then M struck it again, and again. M9 bleated and gargled something basic and unintelligible, both from the physical pain of having been cropped and from the far greater psychological pain of having displeased its Master.

MAX laid a gloved hand on M9's head and comforted it, rubbing its face gently into his groin. M9's immense pain continued, but then tapered off as the slave regained control of its emotions. It started to try to say something, but MAX cut it off. "Shut up, slave. Just listen. Your answer was correct as far as it went, but it was incomplete. You are my slave, that's true, but you are also Sergeant M's slave, because I have assigned you to his platoon and have ordered him to train you. Even though you are and always will be my slave, you simultaneously are and always will be the slave of any man I assign you to, on whatever basis. So let's try it again. Whose slave?" MAX asked.

M9 saw Sergeant M's arm rising. It trembled as it answered. "Sir, I am your slave and I am my sergeant's slave, Sir."

"Good, boy," MAX said, genuinely pleased that his slave could accept this dualism without more cropping. Any man can be taught anything given enough time and enough whipping, but the ones that pick it up fast are the ones who will go further. MAX had felt all along that M9 had high potential.

MAX spoke to Sergeant M. "Hand me your crop, Sergeant," he commanded. M obeyed. MAX held M's crop in front of M9's face for it to see. It was braided leather, with a loop on the end. "I want you to kiss your sergeant's crop," MAX said.

M9's lips kissed the crop deeply as MAX ran it back and forth so that its entire surface was cleaned and loved by the slave. It was just a crop, except it was Sergeant M's crop, and M9 had just learned that it belonged to M as well as to MAX, because MAX had said so. M9 got emotional, realizing that, by MAX's logic, MAX had wielded the crop himself, in a way, and that M was MAX's agent.

"Now, slave, thank the crop, then thank your sergeant, then thank me," MAX commanded.

"Thank you, crop. Thank you, Sergeant. Thank you, Sir," M9 responded.

"Good boy," MAX stated, and slipped Sergeant M's crop into his own boot. This act was intended, M9 thought, to reinforce again that the distinction between MAX and Sergeant M, as far as their slave was concerned, was to be ignored. Indeed, that the slave had one Master and also two Masters, simultaneously, was the lesson that was to be learned today.

"OK, Sergeant, fuck it," MAX said.

M9 felt pressure against its cherry. Then Sergeant M's penis entered M9's ass for the first time, the first of hundreds of times. That M9 was Sergeant M's slave was now undoubted. The sergeant's prick took control, enslaved, established ownership.

Sergeant M moved in and out slowly at first and M9 began making gurgling noises, feeling its ass being fucked by its Master while also staring directly at it Master's crotch. Two Masters who were really one. MAX unsnapped his fly and freed his magnificent cock and balls. M9 gasped. The fact that M9 had done the right thing by becoming MAX's copslave, even though it had hardly had any choice, was crystal clear to it as Sergeant M began to slam into its ass harder and harder, and MAX's cock came to attention with a little stimulation from his black leathered hand.

M9 wanted to taste MAX's prick more than anything it could think of. Wanted to tongue the glans, kiss the shaft, lick the base, get the whole thing slobbery and serve its Master better than any slave ever had. It wanted to be the best slave it could be, to pay MAX back for investing in it, to worship the leather cop who had taken control over it so totally. But there would be no penis worship, no licking, no kissing, no sucking, none of that. "Open up shithead," MAX demanded. M9 complied and its Master shoved the entire organ completely down its throat, burying the slave's nose in cop pubic hair and held it there, one, two, three, four, five, six, seven, eight, nine, ten.

When MAX pulled two-thirds of the way out, his slave snuffled and whinnied for breath, blowing spit onto MAX's balls, which then dripped down to the floor. MAX investigated this new fuckhole, finding the exact point where his cock would cut off the slave's breathing, then alternately shoving the whole thing in and removing it just far enough so M9 could suck air in around the massive organ. "Listen up, fuckhole. Your life is in my hands. I own you. I can kill you right here, right now using my dick. It's a deadly weapon. You need to fear it as well as love it. Think about that, about how you only continue to breathe, only continue to live because my dick permits it. You're a dickslave, fuckhole. A dickslave." Then MAX started fucking M9's throat in earnest, plunging all the way in and sliding all the way out, occasionally slapping the slave's cheeks either with his penis or with his black leather gloved hands. He called the slave "fuckhole" and "dickhead" and "slavemeat." All the while, Sergeant M had been using M9's rear fuckhole to entertain his own penis, pounding away at the slave's ass.

Suddenly, MAX snapped his fingers and both Masters pulled out simultaneously, switched places and continued to fuck both holes. They got their rhythm in sync, so both holes were either completely full or completely empty. They fucked and spoke between themselves, about what a worthless piece of shit the slave they were simultaneously fucking would be except for the fact that it was they who were fucking it. How all it was is what it derived from its slavery to them. How it had better get its shit together and perform well or they would whip the skin off it. How if it didn't obey immediately and correctly they would cut its fucking nuts off and send it off as a eunuch.

"Are you going to obey, slave?" Sergeant M yelled. M9 was almost to the point where it didn't know which Master was fucking which hole, but it could recognize its sergeant's voice, and thus realized that, at the moment, MAX was up its ass and M was down its throat.

"Yes Sergeant!" it squealed just as M's cock again thrust down its front fuckhole and cut off speech.

"Good, boy," Sergeant M stated. "Good boy."

They switched places again. M9 wondered if the two cops would ever get enough. The slave was near collapse, but its Masters were not quite finished. They had made eye contact and were intent of cumming simultaneously. MAX knew that the slave would be forever bound to the concept of two Masters and that M would forever be infected with the prestige of being, at least for the purposes of the training, a near-colleague. When both trainers nodded to one another that it was time, M9 felt the rhythm change, felt each man go where he needed to go in order to end the fuck. M9 felt them more as individuals for a moment, even as all three of them were about to be, just for then, as close as men can get.

"Nnnnghaahh! Ngyeeeeshah! Djyaaahah!!!" Sergeant M yelled. MAX also made a deep throated, resonant, rumbling noise of pure pleasure and pure dominance as M9 tightened up both holes and both trainers shot cum deep into their slave. Sergeant M was exultant. What a fuck! He was hugely proud. MAX had had confidence in him and he had not disappointed. He would always be MAX's slave, but now he was also a skilled slave trainer with the full confidence of his Master and had achieved something approaching the status of a colleague. It was complex, but deeply satisfying for the sergeant.

M9 was full of cum and already thoroughly enslaved. There was no difference between its two Masters that it could tell. They owned it. It was theirs. Their slave! What an honor!

MAX handed the crop back to Sergeant M after giving the slave a few light taps on its bruised butt. Three raised red lines were now very evident where it had been cropped earlier. "Whose slave?" MAX asked M9.

"My sergeant's slave and your slave, Sir," M9 cooed.

"Good boy," MAX said. "You are making some progress, boy." MAX addressed M. "You know, Sergeant, after you have fucked this piece of shit's two fuck-holes a couple thousand more times, it might make a half way decent slave."

Simultaneously, Sergeant M and M9 responded, "Yes, Sir!" as MAX put his equipment away preparing to move on. He patted M9 on the cheek and again told it that it was a good boy.

CHAPTER 16

MAX woke up late and lay in bed with his eyes closed for a few moments to collect his thoughts. The three new slaves were now inserted into his empire in slots he had chosen for them in order that they might thrive. He would, of course, monitor their progress closely. But by necessity, much of their training would be handled by the individual sergeants to whom they had been assigned. It had been many years since MAX had the time to do intensive one-on-one training. His job now was to coordinate, to keep everything on track, to oversee the activities of all the officers, sergeants, slaves, all of whom had come to depend upon his vision and his leadership.

He opened his eyes and looked down across his chest and abdomen to see his semi-hard penis. It stuck up and dominated his view. Beyond his penis was his world, a world MAX had created for himself and all the men he had trained. He was neither smug nor complacent, but he was proud of what he had achieved and what he had given his men. His gaze returned to his cock, his constant companion, his mentor, his buddy. It was a wise penis, MAX thought. Many men get into a lot of trouble by trusting their cock, but MAX was different. In his case, the brain and the penis worked in tandem - if both organs concurred, MAX went for it - an approach that had worked very well indeed.

MAX checked out the slave shackled face down next to him, still asleep. R3 was a good fuck, a slave with a tight hole and a lot of passion. R3 had been disappointed last night when, after MAX had summoned it, he merely strapped it down but did not fuck it. MAX was spent after the previous day's process of subordinating the three new trainees. That had required a lot of penis work on MAX's part, so he really needed a break and some rest. But morning was here and the sight of the sleeping, bound man had aroused MAX's dick to readiness once more, ready to dispel R3's disappointment.

MAX rolled over onto the slave and snapped it out of slumber. Its asshole had been lubed last night, so there was no need to deal with that. MAX applied a little spit to his prick, made several tentative light shoves against R3's cherry and then popped his glans just inside the slave's sphincter.

What a happy slave! Imagine how happy you'd be if you were awakened by a huge, rock solid man on your back, probing at your hole, and finally entering and taking control of your ass, your mind, and your future! You'd be as happy as R3. It let out a gurgling, sucking noise as MAX moved all the way in, then partly out, then back in, again out, and again in.

MAX whispered something tender in the slave's ear. R3 grinned and shouted, in response, "Your slave, Sir!"

Again tenderly, but now audibly, MAX rejoined, "That's right, fuckhole. My slave. Mine."

R3 wanted nothing more than to be MAX's fuckhole, MAX's slave. To serve MAX. To be fucked by MAX. So R3 was happy, very happy, and it shouted, "Yes, Sir! Thank you, Sir!"

MAX took his time. He ground his body into the slave's, knowing how excited the slave would be to have MAX's musculature pressing roughly against it. He didn't take sex from his slaves as much as he gave sex to them. Same with everything else. MAX knew what slaves wanted, what they needed and he gave it to them. It was pretty simple. In return, slaves gave MAX their souls.

MAX did not have a nickname for all his slaves. Hell, that would have been dozens of nicknames. But he did for a few, usually signifying, some special quality or useful attribute. "OK, peewee," MAX said. "Get ready. A few more strokes and I'll load you up." MAX pumped hard, got focused, stopped being tender, thought about his power, his strength, his ability to enslave virtually any man at will and his big dick making R3's hole into a receptacle for sweet cum. Wordlessly MAX shuddered and jerked. Peewee felt it, tightened up as much as it could and imagined it could feel MAX's spunk shooting out of his prick and splashing against the slave's insides.

"Yes, Sir!" R3 shouted. "Sir, yes Sir!"

MAX slumped onto the slave, spent for the moment. He fell briefly asleep. He always did when he could, even if just for 15 or 20 seconds. Not really asleep, but certainly not awake either. Time enough to change gears. MAX's and R3's breathing returned to normal. MAX slowly exited his penis from the slave's hole - a difficult moment for any slave, for how long would it be until the next fuck? MAX raised his mass off the slave and unfastened it from its bonds. They showered together, something MAX liked to do for his slaves, because he realized that slaves need a cooling off period after getting fucked. After a fuck, a slave craves its Master a great deal and it is cruel to rip it away too quickly. It needs to know that it is special, at least for the moment.

In the shower, cleaning its Master, R3 became erect and it was clear how it had gotten its nickname. MAX was smart about such things. He celebrated peewee's diminutive equipment by singling it out for special duty. MAX called on peewee every time a new slave was brought in who wasn't used to being fucked. Although 100% slave, peewee was a hot little fucker and got huge prestige out of beginning a new cock-shy slave's asshole training, training it to work up to larger organs, such as MAX's. It was this kind of intelligent slave management, leadership if you will, that explained the scale and durability of MAX's empire. He did what the Army claimed it did. He made his slaves all they could be. He was a leader and a true slavemaster.

"Permission to inform, please, Sir," R3 requested.

"Granted," MAX responded.

"Sir, I saw in the newspaper the story of Benjamin, the Rottweiler who sniffed out explosives in a Sa'udi princess's luggage at SFO and saved the Golden Gate Bridge," R3 began.

"Yes, I read that. What about it?" MAX asked.

"Well, Sir, Benjamin and the handsome paramilitary cop he works with have become celebrities and have made appearances at events. I wonder if they would come to Trough for a 'dog show.' Benjamin's handler, it looked to me, might be our kind of guy. I sort-of sensed it from his appearance, the attention to detail in his uniform, and his demeanor," R3 said.

"It's interesting that you caught that," MAX said. "I saw it as well. And I like the dog show idea. There are several 'dogs' here which could be shown. You, for example."

R3 blushed. It was one of several of the slaves which had been fitted for dog hoods, and it found K-9 to be very exciting. "Truthfully, Sir, I had thought of that. I'd like to compete and also to meet Benjamin!"

"Take it easy, peewee," MAX cautioned. "I know what you're thinking. Forget about it."

Now R3 REALLY blushed. It hadn't realized where its fantasy had been taking it. But MAX had. He always thought ahead of his slaves, a big part of dominating them.

"Sergeant J has been put in charge of Trough. I'll make arrangements for you to inform him of your idea. Meanwhile, keep it to yourself," MAX said.

"Yes, Sir. Thank you, Sir," R3 responded. The shower was over, slaves were summoned to towel MAX off and to dress him for the day's action. R3, happy for the attention, returned to its normal duties awaiting an interview with Sergeant J.

Chapter 17

Leather Officer was pleased with the new slave line-up at his facility. The run-away was long gone, having been replaced by 1 as head slave. At first, having the former head slave escape had bothered Leather Officer quite a bit, but he eventually got over it, especially since 1's performance was so outstanding. 1 had truly been brought to a higher level of slavery when Leather Officer nearly drowned it during its interrogation. Something snapped with the slave, and it came to realize that its dependence on Leather Officer for guidance and support was total. It no longer had any will of its own. Its sole function was to implement Leather Officer's will. 3 and 4 found the new head slave to be less savvy and sophisticated than its predecessor, while more strict. Unlike under the old system, where the head slave had functioned as a sort of second-in-command and had taken an interest in the welfare of the other slaves, 1's approach was fairly cold. It listened carefully to Leather Officer's orders and implemented them fully and immediately, with no modification or interpretation. The regime had become more authoritarian.

The most recently recruited trainee took slot 2 - became the new 2. It turned out to be easily enslaved - a surprise, perhaps, since it had successfully topped other men until so recently. At first it thought a lot about Dick, about fucking Dick. But slavery in Leather Officer's system had a way of cleansing slaves' minds of the past, so 2's world shrank down to one centered on its cage, its chores, its punishment and Leather Officer's dick.

In many ways 3 came to be Leather Officer's favorite. It was selected to spend nights with the cop more than the others put together. Leather Officer enjoyed fucking right after waking up, and 3 was good at this, quickly wakening and squeezing tight as the cop ploughed it and shot. The others generally got fucked sometime during the day, usually more dramatically. But 3 was a convenient receptacle to deal with Leather Officer's inevitable morning erection.

4, to everyone's surprise, finally began to make progress. Its boot blacking wasn't bad, it could prepare simple food, and do OK on many chores. Finally it learned to pay attention, therefore it could obey. It had always been wired for complete obedience - indeed it had the best slave wiring of all of them - but it had just been so emotional and adoring that it couldn't think straight. 4 calmed down and turned into a pretty good slave. As a reward, Leather Officer purchased 4 a custom dog hood, complete with pointy ears and a removable snout. 4 was very excited about its job as the cop's K-9. It yearned for the day when it would be taken out in public to do tricks and wag its tail.

Yet, although things were running smoothly, there were only four slaves. Leather Officer continued to feel that the pressure on the four of having a trainee preparing to replace one was good for them. He decided once again to seek a new recruit.

About 2200hrs. on a Friday evening, 3 got Leather Officer dressed in the cop's current favorite leather uniform, all black with a white stripe down the breeches' side, the newest custom uniform that he always wore out to the bar. He'd had it modeled on the ones worn by those motorcycle cops written up in the Chronicle who got busted up in Capital City. This uniform, once animated by the cop's body and mind, was a virtually irresistible tool for converting any leatherman into a slave. Leather Officer's slave.

It was relatively warm for San Francisco, but Leather Officer wore a motorcycle jacket for the trip to check out the new bar. Impersonating an officer was not a huge concern, but it was best not to show a badge. Nothing other than some socializing and hunting were on his mind as he neared Trough. This would be his first visit since the big change. As he turned off Folsom onto 13th he saw a red light in his rear-view mirror. Shit! What the fuck was this?

Leather Officer pulled his bike over to the curb, shut it down, and dismounted. A California Highway Patrol motorcycle officer pulled up behind him. Leather Officer held the CHP in contempt. He had outgrown them. At one time, like most leathermen, Leather Officer had admired the CHP bike cops a lot, but the organization had changed in a bad way, he felt. When the blue nylon jackets replaced black leather, Leather Officer began to lose interest in the CHP. Then, he'd read somewhere, they actually were fielding a female motor officer in Santa Cruz. He decided that the heavy emphasis on traffic enforcement was not real police work. It was more like AAA with a gun. He also began to lose interest in their uniforms. He was moving toward black leather, but CHP were mostly tan, sometimes with khaki Eisenhower jackets, even bow ties sometimes. Some local bike cops had maintained standards, but, well, Leather Officer was just over the CHP. He had trumped them long ago. The Highway Patrolman approached Leather Officer. "May I see your license and registration, sir?" he asked.

Leather Officer's attitude about the CHP in general notwithstanding, this particular officer, it had to be admitted, was doing it right. He was several inches taller than Leather Officer, a few years older, probably 45 lbs. heavier, obviously muscular, and drop dead handsome. This guy was doing it like Leather

Officer remembered from years ago. His jacket was shiny black leather, not blue nylon, and his boots were incredibly shined, slave-shined it almost appeared, although this could hardly be. A passing truck's headlights were reflected momentarily by the cop's boots, nearly blinding Leather Officer. The gold badge shone brilliantly as well, as did all the shiny brass hardware on the cop's belt. His breeches were tight, crammed full of muscular legs and ass, bulging in front, suggesting that the cop must either be well endowed or excited about something. Or both. "I said, may I see your license and registration?" the cop repeated. Leather Officer felt his face redden, realizing that he had not yet responded to this standard request, having been so involved in checking out the details of the cop's body and uniform.

"Oh, yes. Yes. Sorry. Yes, here they are," Leather Officer said presenting the documents. He began to perspire a bit. He was quite nervous. He had an odd, queasy feeling in the pit of his stomach, a feeling vaguely remembered from long ago.

As the Highway Patrolman accepted the license and registration, he stepped forward toward Leather Officer and stood just inches away while reviewing the documents. Leather Officer imagined that the cop's body was giving off a kind of heat or radiant energy, making his own body heat up and causing him to perspire profusely. He pulled off his helmet to cool down, but it didn't do any good. He felt feverish, as if he were suddenly coming down with something, as if he had caught something from the cop. But how could that be? Leather Officer noted that the cop's name tag said "T. Stockton." After what seemed like an unusually long review, Officer Stockton returned the license and registration to Leather Officer, reached into his inside jacket pocket, and pulled out what looked to be a missing person flyer. "Have you ever seen this man?" Stockton asked, showing the flyer to Leather Officer.

It was a picture of a handsome, muscular man, seated in the corner of a metal room, or large metal box, or maybe the interior of a van. The man wore virtually nothing, only short lace-up boots, leather shorts, and a collar around his neck. The man looked up at the camera in apparent disbelief. In the foreground of the picture, only partially visible, was the top of a leather boot, a portion of a pair of leather breeches covering a muscular right thigh, and a large revolver in a holster. It almost seemed more like an erotic photograph than a missing person flyer, as if the seated man were the captive of, at least, the man wearing the gun, and perhaps the photographer as well. But further analysis was impossible for Leather Officer, who went from being overheated to a major chill as he recognized the collared man. It was 2! The former 2! The runaway!

"I asked you whether you had ever seen this man. Have you?" T. Stockton demanded.

Leather Officer's brain was using a great deal of glucose at this moment. He had to process quickly what he was seeing, regain control of his emotions, formulate an answer and not allow this cop to take control of the situation. He hesitated, tried to regulate his body temperature, inhaled, and attempted to extricate himself. Leather Officer produced a grin. "No, I haven't, although I'd like to. It's a hot photo!" Not a bad response. Perhaps with intelligence and finesse it would be possible to get this situation back under control, Leather Officer thought.

T. Stockton shifted his weight from one foot to the other and moved even nearer to Leather Officer, standing toe to toe. The cop grabbed Leather Officer by the lapels of his leather jacket, jerked the jacket upward, nearly lifting Leather Officer off the ground and said, coldly, "You're lying, asshole."

There was no clever rejoinder. None was possible. Leather Officer knew it. He was losing control of the situation. There was nothing he could do. T. Stockton was in charge. "Open your jacket up, asshole," the cop demanded. "I want to see your shirt."

Leather Officer obeyed, not even thinking about the fact that what was going down here had increasingly little to do with legitimate law enforcement. T. Stockton touched Leather Officer's badge, inspecting it, tugging at it, as if his next move might be to rip it off the shirt altogether.

The cop sneered. "Fuck," he muttered. "Zip it up," he ordered. Leather Officer obeyed. Officer Stockton removed his side handle baton from the ring attached to the left side of his gun belt. The handle was held in his hand, the shaft below, in the extended position. He poked at Leather Officer's thighs, then circled around and slapped the baton against his ass, then returned and thumped the groin repeatedly, not hard enough to really hurt, but hard enough to get Leather Officer's full attention.

"You're vulnerable, asshole. Very vulnerable," Stockton stated. "Why don't you resist arrest, so I can show you how talented I am with the baton? So I can teach you not to lie to a police officer?"

Leather Officer said nothing. He felt completely humiliated, completely subordinated. With no way out. And fuck! - he had gotten an erection! And the cop saw it, and was outlining Leather Officer's cock and balls with the end of the baton. Could it get worse?

"If I were to arrest you for impersonating a police officer, which I easily could, they'd eat you alive at the county jail, and I don't want that. I want something else," the cop said, replacing his baton in its ring.

"What, Sir?" Leather Officer asked, only realizing when Stockton flashed a triumphant grin, that using the word "Sir" had put the situation in a whole new category altogether.

Officer Stockton responded. "From now on, I own you. You are vulnerable to arrest at any time. Any time I want you. You are no longer independent. You are working for me, and the extent to which you continue with your activities is governed by limits which I set. Keep it in mind at all times if you value your freedom. Got it, asshole?"

"Yes, Sir," Leather Officer answered. He knew he was stuck, that there was no way that he could stop what he was doing, give up his leather and his slaves, but that unless he were to, Stockton could bust him at any time. He felt conquered.

"Get your ass over here, fuckhead," Stockton demanded, moving toward Leather Officer's motorcycle. "I'm going to issue you a fix-it ticket."

"What for, Sir?" Leather Officer asked, knowing that the bike was in perfect condition.

"Non-operating right rear turn signal," the cop answered, quickly filling out the citation.

"I think it works fine. Let me check," Leather Officer said. He started the bike up and activated the turn signal which, indeed, functioned properly.

Officer Stockton handed Leather Officer the citation. The cop then pulled the baton once again from its ring, flashed the same triumphant grin, and spun the baton quickly and forcefully around, pivoting on the side handle, cleanly snapping the signal light off, and leaving it dangling by colored wires. "You were wrong, shithead. It's not working. Get it fixed fast and report back to me for inspection. There's only one way for you to play from now on - my way. Otherwise, you're out of business." The cop spun the baton again, and used the short end as a prod to poke Leather Officer hard in the chest for emphasis, so there would be bruises to remember the incident. Stockton then circled back behind Leather Officer and jabbed with the baton between the leather covered ass cheeks. This gesture left nothing more to be said. The cop remounted his bike, sped off toward South Van Ness and zipped up onto 101.

Leather Officer remounted his motorcycle as well. He felt sick, really ill. He threw up in the gutter, vomit splashing on his boots. Then tears came. Multiple emotions, braided together with confusion. Nowhere to go. He couldn't go to the bar now, he couldn't return to his slaves and he couldn't just ride around. He'd get pulled over again for the signal light.

So he shut the bike down and sat on it, just sat there, trying to figure out what had happened and what to do next. Trying to figure out why his prick was rock hard and was staying that way, and why images of Officer Stockton and his baton could not be removed from Leather Officer's mind's eye no matter how hard he tried. Leather Officer continued to straddle his quiet machine for some while. He needed time to think. He needed time to pull himself together before returning to his slaves.

Who was Officer Stockton? Why had he had such an overpowering effect on Leather Officer? Why had Leather Officer become Stockton's subordinate so readily? Why was Leather Officer's dick still hard, uncomfortably, unrelentingly hard? Why did his asshole tingle in a manner he had not felt for decades? Why had he become nauseous? Why had his body temperature been out of control? Why was everything crumbling? Why did he yearn for Stockton to return, cuff him and take him away?

Leather Officer hated these emotions. He had worked hard, very hard to create himself. He was proud of what he was and wanted to stay that way. As a very young boy he had become aware of the attraction he had to hyper-masculine men - heroes, leaders, conquerors. He had been confused. Did he want to be a hero, or be with a hero? Both, really. Or at least both at different times. He discovered leathermen and found that he would gravitate toward big, muscular, take-charge kinds of men, particularly cops. He'd sweat and swallow hard and go up to these overwhelming men and introduce himself and offer himself. He also emulated them, and soon guys were offering themselves to him. He could go either way at first, but in the end, he got laid a whole lot more when he was the top. When he tried subordinating himself to men who seemed initially to be his superiors, it never seemed to work out. He ended up turning the tables on them. He finally figured out that the ideal for whom he would bottom out just didn't exist and that he was the closest approximation. He became his own fantasy, in a way, and refined himself into his heroic ideal.

Leather Officer understood exactly what had just happened. He had just had an encounter with a man that was closer to his ideal than he was, and he'd melted. He wanted to erase the whole thing, go back to where he had been when he pulled the bike out of the garage. But he also wanted Officer Stockton to return, so that...that what? Did he want to get fucked? Did he want the cop to fuck him? *Oh, Christ!,* he thought. He hadn't been fucked for twenty years! No, he didn't want to get fucked! Didn't! Except, he did want Officer Stockton to come back, to come back to get him, so he could be with the cop forever and ever. And they would...what? Well, they would...

He felt sick again, spinning out of control, controlled from without, controlled by another man, controlled by the cop. Yes, he did want to get fucked, because it was a sure thing that the cop would demand it - of course he would - and if Leather Officer was going to be with Officer Stockton forever, then he would have to obey him, to submit to him, to submit to his dick, to submit to his baton. Leather Officer thought he might lose consciousness at this point, as he remembered Stockton's parting gesture, remembered that the cop had taken his fucking baton and jabbed it at Leather Officer's asshole. *The baton.* Shit. *The baton.*

This was the most difficult moment for Leather Officer. The moment he realized that, one way or another, at some point, the baton was going up his ass and he was powerless to stop it. *Powerless.* Officer Stockton had simply pulled the power out of Leather Officer, increasing Stockton's power, feeding off Leather Officer, just like Leather Officer had fed off so many men himself. Having passed the most difficult moment, the moment when he figured out where the baton would eventually go, he began to rebuild, reconfigure his world and find a place for himself in it. He remembered what Officer Stockton had said, that he was no longer independent, that he was working for Stockton now and that the extent to which he could continue with his activities would be governed by limits which Stockton would set. To keep this in mind if he valued his freedom. So it seemed that, if he played by Stockton's rules, he could pretty much continue as he had been. Maybe Stockton's limits wouldn't be that constraining. Maybe he could keep his slaves and his facility and his whole program. Maybe Stockton's limits would actually be good advice. After all, the cop certainly had his shit together.

This was bullshit of course, but it was bullshit that Leather Officer needed to believe right now in order to get going. The reality was that Officer Stockton had taken full control of Leather Officer, the four slaves, the facility, everything, and that the cop would do what he pleased with all of it. The baton would get shoved up Leather Officer's ass at a time and place of Stockton's choosing. That's the way it is when you are another man's slave. Whether you are ready to accept it or not. Whether you want it or not. Leather Officer started his motorcycle and rode to a gas station. He cleaned up in the restroom. Not too much the worse, apparently, for his experience. He'd be OK. He was tough, a survivor. He had weathered the head slave running away. He'd survive this as well.

He rode back to his slaves. It was after bar closing time now. He was surprised how long he had sat astride the quiet bike thinking through this. As he pulled into the garage, 3 appeared, penis erect. He gave the slave his helmet and slapped it on the ass to get it moving up the stairs. It grinned. The other slaves were in their cages, asleep long ago.

He took 3 upstairs to his quarters. He decided to sleep in uniform as he often did, because he enjoyed the power. 3 removed the Sam Browne Leather Officer was wearing - one appropriate for the bar - and replaced it with one that had a holster and baton ring. 3 brought the .44 Mag, slipped it into the cop's holster, and slipped the baton into its ring as well. Leather Officer hauled out his big copdick, already semi-hard. The big furry balls hung underneath, overfull with cum.

"Lick my boots, slave," Leather Officer barked. "Clean 'em up."

"Yes, Sir!" 3 squealed. Bootlicking was a real treat. Unless the copboots were pretty fucked up, bootlicking was not permitted, because it was bad for the shine. 3 slurped greedily wherever spots appeared. Not piss, it noted. Wonder what it is?"

"Suck my dick," the cop ordered, coldly, when the boots were done. 3 leapt to the task and immediately swallowed the entire organ. The cop's groin hair tickled 3's nose. It pulled off slowly, giving a special service that you would like if you could get it, tongue darting all over, slurping lips, very light teeth action. Heaven! "Good sucking, slave. Really good," Leather Officer said. The slave's eyes looked up at its Master with adoration. Important. Slave eyes are how you know that the slave is truly yours.

After a little more sucking, 3 was shackled to the bed. Leather Officer had fleetingly considered shoving the baton up 3's ass, but dropped the plan. That was more daytime stuff, something meant for an audience, so he knelt behind his slave, spread its legs wide, teased its asshole briefly with the tip of his copdick, and then inserted the head an inch or two inside. He held it there for a moment, then pulled out abruptly, again teasing the outside of the hole. "You want it, boy?" Leather Officer asked.

"Yes, Sir! Please fuck me, Sir!" was the response.

"Louder! Beg for it! I've got three other assholes downstairs fidgeting in their cages right now because they need fucking."

"Sir! Yes Sir! Please fuck me, Sir! Please! Please fuck me hard with your big copdick now, Sir! Please fuck me, Sir!"

The cop loved begging, loved to hear how his slave needed copdick and needed it up its ass right now. Begging was great power flow, sucking power out of the slave and into the Master, filling the Master's balls with the power to fuck. He shoved the big dick back in, about half way. 3 hissed, as if the copdick had directly caused air to whistle through its teeth. It let out a sort of sigh, a sort of whimper, but one of pleasure, of belonging.

"Sure you want it, fuckhole?"

"Yes, Sir. Please, Sir, give me your whole copdick, Sir. Show me how to be the best slave I can be, Sir," 3 said, dropping the fuck-rhetoric and speaking from its heart. It wanted to be with its Master, to be a part of its Master, and the only way to do that would be for the Master to go inside it and unite with it, to fuck it.

Leather Officer shoved all the way in and 3 could feel cop balls, hairy cop balls, slap up against its shaved slave balls. It could feel the wiry ball hair. It knew the cop was all the way in. It felt owned, safe, important and prestigious. It knew it was being fucked by the best, by the ultimate leather cop, therefore it must be the best copslave, the ultimate as well. There is no greater pride than that felt by a slave being fucked.

Leather Officer pulled nearly all the way out of 3's ass, then shoved back in, then all the way out, then back in half way, then out almost all the way, then back in 2/3 of the way, then all the way out, then all the way in, slapping cop balls against slave balls once more. The slave was being played with, tormented, not knowing what was coming next and unable to rhythmically respond. It informed 3 that the man on top was in charge and that the slave's hole was merely a receptacle for the big copdick to fool around in. Almost all the way out, hesitate, all the way out, barely back in, all the way out, repeated sphincter jabs, then all the way in, cop balls and slave balls slamming together, 1/4 way out and then back in balls to balls.

3 began to feel warm breath on its neck as Leather Officer's pace picked up and his rhythm smoothed out. More of the cop's weight now rested directly on the slave's body. 3 felt the leather uniform rub back and forth on its hairless skin, felt the cold metal of the badge, the boots pinning its legs and the big revolver, too, as Leather Officer turned slightly to abrade the left side of 3's rectum more vigorously. 3 heard the baton clinking in the chromed steel ring and at times it could feel the cold metal rub against its hairless leg. 3 checked out the mirror and could see the cop on its back, pumping and beginning to

sweat. Leather Officer was pulling power out of the slave with every stroke, storing up the power inside the cop's body, storing it in the uniform, animating the leather, getting feedback from the leather, from the uniform, from the weapons. Anything other than this would have been of no interest to 3. It was totally ruined for anything other than copsex - it was a true copslave. It had to be fucked by a leather cop frequently or it would surely die. It needed its Master like grass needs water. Its whole existence depended on having copdick up its ass. Right now was the moment it lived for, the moment that sustained it.

3 felt the pace quicken. Leather Officer began to groan in a manner 3 knew well. It felt the cop pump and felt its hole on fire. It felt that feeling where it would want the fuck to end because the stimulation was getting unbearable, but also want it never to end. It felt sweat splattering on its neck and the back of its shaved head, felt spit spraying out of its Master's mouth as his breathing came up to maximum rate and his heart pounded. Leather Officer was losing control, control was being taken over by the automatic pilot which forces a male to continue pumping, possibly beyond what he can endure, but pump on none-the-less until the release comes. 3 knew that its skin would be all abraded by the cop's hardware and weapons, but it didn't care. Even if he killed it, it didn't care. It wanted as much of its Master as it could get and to feel the man slamming into its back, the copdick slamming into its hole. Full, long strokes now, simple rhythm, no games.

Leather Officer now started to hiss. He needed to cum, to get release and to squirt into his slave. He was close, very close, pumping, pumping, pumping. He was aware of the power he exercised over his slave, sustained by the power he drew from the slave, drew out of the interior of its guts, drew up through his copdick, the power that fueled his mastery. His cop balls smashed into his slave's hairless nut sac, pulling the power out of there as well. The cop was feeding off his slave, getting what he needed and could only get from an obsequious, totally owned fuckhole. No man did this better than Leather Officer. He was the top. The top of tops. Top cop. He felt a burst of power flash out of his slave's body and jolt him, like electricity conducted through the leather and then held within him by the leather. 3 felt it, too, as if the cop's whole body, his whole being got kicked into high gear just as there was a tremendous exhalation from 3's body. 3 felt it had given everything to its Master, perhaps too much, so much that it would die, that life had been sucked out of it.

For a second they teetered on the edge, the cop still pumping, but now pumping jerkily, rhythm left behind. Leather Officer let out an animal-like cry, an octave higher in pitch than his usual baritone. His body jerked, controlled entirely by his copdick, his copballs and all the apparatus that makes and delivers cum. He shot inside his slave's ass. Much cum. Much cop cum. He quivered and shook, his entire body, as he shot again and again up the slave's ass, giving it what would sustain it, giving it what it needed to replace the power that the cop had drawn out of it. The power that had kept the cop going through the fuck and allowed the payback.

3 was exhausted. Leather Officer had fucked it many times, but never before quite like this. It truly had feared for its life just before the cop shot, but now it was blissful, filled up with sweet cum. The copdick was still gently pumping, slow, cool-off strokes, shoving all the cum up high into the slave where it could nourish it, rebuild it and fill it with exquisite pride.

Leather Officer felt great, felt that he was at the top of his game, that he had just fucked better than any man ever had before. Maybe he had. He rested his full weight on his slave, felt strong feelings of ownership, knew that he controlled the slave utterly, that it would gladly die for him. It was great to be alive, to be a man, to be a top, to own slaves, to fuck them, and watch their dicks come to attention whenever they saw him. His breathing and heart rate returned to normal. He began to get drowsy. He could feel 3's breathing develop a quality which informed him that the slave had fallen asleep. He thought about pulling his prick out and rolling off 3, but decided to just fall asleep like this, in uniform, penis inserted, armed. He briefly touched the revolver. Good. Then the baton.

The baton.

Leather Officer's eyes snapped wide open. The baton! The fucking baton! Shit!

The baton.

He continued to lie on his slave. He was wide awake. His dick became erect again inside the slave, causing it to stir. The same confusing stew of thoughts he had wrestled with earlier returned, as they would again and again. He knew he had never fucked any slave better than what he had just done to 3, but he also knew that his independence was gone, that power was now flowing in new directions, and he wasn't at all sure where or how.

But the baton was pretty straightforward. This piece of aluminum attached to his belt, which had been attached all during the fuck, now had an entirely new meaning and function, although he wasn't at all clear what. Officer Stockton's baton had figured importantly earlier, especially when it wrecked his signal light and probed at his asshole. Now his own baton had taken part in this best of all fucks. He lay awake for some time, trying to figure out what was happening, decide whether it was good or bad, and figure some sort of plan. But his thoughts just went around in circles. Exhaustion finally drove him to sleep. As he dropped off, he was still fully erect, wondering when he would see Officer Stockton again.

CHAPTER 18

Morning came too soon. The image of the wrecked signal light came to the front of Leather Officer's mind as he awakened. A task for today would be to get the light replaced and then...well, what? Then seek out Officer Stockton to sign off on the ticket? No. Wait. How could Stockton be found? Where would he be? Leather Officer jumped up, awakening 3. He pulled the ticket out of his jacket pocket and reviewed it. It appeared that any Highway Patrolman could sign off on the thing. It didn't have to be Stockton himself, although it had seemed that the cop had more-or-less ordered Leather Officer to report back to him personally once the light was fixed. Ambiguity upon ambiguity.

It was clear that 3 was hoping for a morning fuck, but not today. Last night would not be repeated. Too much was on Leather Officer's mind right now to service the slave further. It was unshackled and ordered to remove the cop's uniform. They showered together, the slave cleaning its Master's body, becoming erect as its hands spread soap all over, cleaning its Master's cock and balls especially well and also cleaning the cop's asshole, using its tongue to make sure no residue remained.

The slave dressed its Master for the morning workout, dressed itself, and the two descended the stairs to join the other three slaves for coffee. The others had arisen earlier and had been busy with their chores. Each sprang an erection at the sight of Leather Officer. None had even an inkling of what happened the previous evening. If anything, Leather Officer gave the appearance of increased strength and control, no hint that a profound change had occurred. The cop did feel strangely empowered by his encounter with Officer Stockton. Perhaps it was the sense that everything would continue more-or-less the same, that regardless the body blow Stockton had delivered, still Leather Officer had withstood it and would continue. As the hours passed, Leather Officer was able to increasingly successfully convince himself that what had happened would have no long lasting effect. Just a bump in the road.

After the workout and feeding, 2 and 4 were dispatched in the pickup down to the bike shop to fetch a new signal light. Lucky to live in San Francisco, where the arrival of two men wearing combat boots, bondage shorts, and dog collars at a motorcycle dealership parts department would cause little stir. Slaves shopping. Big deal. Upon returning with the new light, it was only a few minutes wrench time to do the repair, and nothing was left of the event other than fixing the ticket. 1 considered it a special honor to get leathered up and take Leather Officer's bike down to the CHP office on 8th Street, obtain the signature of an officer it spotted there, and finalize the issue.

Leather Officer had lied to his slaves. He told them the damage had occurred while he had been in the bar, that the motherfucker who had broken the signal light didn't even had the balls to come in and report it and had just run off. It was not his practice to lie, and certainly he tolerated no slave that lied. Lying had been the cause of innumerable whippings, innumerable punishments. But the cop could hardly inform the slaves about the incident with Officer Stockton. So he lied. He deceived them. And he deceived himself, convincing himself of what he chose to believe, that Officer Stockton was just an aberration and that the Highway Patrolman could be forgotten quickly. Life would continue.

Several days later 1 approached its Master and said, "Sir, I have information which you might find of value."

"What's up, fuckhole," the cop responded.

"Sir, perhaps you saw an announcement of this when you were at Trough last Friday, but I thought I should make sure you are aware," the slave began.

"OK, drop the intro, slave. What have you got?" Leather Officer demanded.

"An e-mail came. Trough is having a Dog Show next Saturday, with that hero dog Benjamin as a special guest. I know that 4 has been excited about its new dog hood and its new role as your K-9, Sir," 1 suggested.

"Print the announcement, fuckhole, and I'll take a look," Leather Officer said.

"I have, Sir," 1 responded, and handed the cop the new bar's announcement of the event.

The text read: "AARF! AARF! WOOF! WOOF! Trough announces an opportunity for dog handlers to show off their pooches! Who's got the best mutt? The truest K-9 attitude? Find out by entering your tail-wagger in a contest to be judged by Benjamin and his handler, the team that saved the Golden Gate Bridge. Your dog will enjoy meeting Benjamin! Be there, at Trough, 2200hrs., 30 May 03."

"I had not been aware of this," Leather Officer stated truthfully, glossing over the fact that he had not actually made it to Trough yet, so therefore could not have been aware. "This sounds like an excellent opportunity. Don't inform the other slaves, but make sure that 4's gear is ready. This looks like a good event."

"Yes, Sir!" the head slave responded. It was pleased that it had provided good and timely information. It was extremely proud of its status as Leather Officer's second-in-command. Top of the heap, it knew, worldwide, among slaves.

"Good work. You'll sleep with me tonight - you deserve a reward," Leather Officer said.

1 beamed and grinned. To be of service to its Master, to get fucked by its Master! These were the best days of 1's life. Leather Officer's head slave! 1 was very happy, as you would be if you were in its boots. But things can change quickly for a slave, very quickly. That's why it's always a good idea for a slave to serve fully right now - things can change fast.

4 remained clueless until an hour before the dog show. Leather Officer summoned both 1 and 4 to his quarters. The two slaves dressed their Master in his current favorite uniform; the black leather breeches, single white stripe, black leather shirt with white tie, tucked in like an MP. Slave shined cop boots, cop gun belt with shoulder strap, badge, cap. This was the uniform that had enthralled 2 and started its slavery; that had torn 2 away from Dick; that had lured Little Mike into real brutality; that had caused such turmoil in so many men's lives. This leather uniform, based on that of the busted cops from Capital City, was the current culmination of what Leather Officer conceived to be the uniform of the ultimate leather cop. It worked in tandem with Leather Officer's body and mind and became an irresistible weapon of enslavement: slavery for those chosen, unfulfilled masochistic yearning for those not.

"Get the new K9 brassard," Leather Officer commanded. This was 4's first clue that something was up. K9! 4's eyes and ears pricked up. The new armband was mostly red leather, but trimmed at the top and bottom with a band of black, then white, then black, referring to the stripe on Leather Officer's breeches. The same pattern, black, white, black was employed to show block letters: K9. It was sort of like an MP armband, but more striking. 1 affixed the brassard to Leather Officer's left arm.

"Get Fido ready," Leather Officer said to 1, referring to 4. The head slave quickly produced the needed equipment and started to get 4 geared up. 4 was excited and sprang an erection. It knew something was going on when it caught sight of the dog hood. Slave boots protected the hind paws. 1 strapped knee protectors onto 4's legs and then slipped mitts over the front paws and locked these on. Then the hood.

4 understood intuitively that a slave derives pride from its humiliation. Much blood has been shed to teach this fact; there are many slaves or slave wannabes have a tremendously difficult time with humiliation. Some have a difficult time understanding that humiliation exalts the Master. The Master that has chosen the slave as his property. Anything that raises the prestige of the Master also raises the prestige of his slave. Humiliating the slave raises the Master's prestige, so likewise, the slave's prestige. Simple, no? Well, yes it is simple. But in spite of the simplicity, it is often necessary to beat the hell out a slave before it can accept it. Slaves that cannot accept humiliation and derive pride forthwith better find another line of work.

The hood: it had been custom made for 4 as a reward for its progress. It had eye holes so 4 could see, and tiny invisible holes where the leather covered 4's slave ears, so it could hear. It included a built-in collar, thick, with a lock and d-ring for leash attachment. Nothing really unusual, but here was the dog part: pointy leather ears stuck up from the hood just where a German shepherd's ears would stick up, or a Boxer's. And 4's nose and mouth were covered by a heavy leather snout, openable in case access to the slave mouth might be needed, but otherwise giving the hood, and therefore the slave, an utterly canine appearance. 1 slipped the hood onto 4's head, zipped it up, buckled the collar and locked it.

4's humiliation was exquisite! It yearned to sit dog-style at its Master's boot, at its trainer's left boot, leashed! 4's dog prick was near to explosion. "Center!" Leather Officer yelled. 4 immediately zoomed in and knelt in front of its Master, facing the cop's groin, snout only a fraction of an inch away from Leather Officer's bulging codpiece. 4 was incredibly excited, but it knew that it must perform. It must listen carefully and obey fully, not allowing itself to fall back into its old bad habit of becoming overwhelmed by its own emotions and failing to focus totally on its Master. It needed to show that it deserved the dog hood and that it could perform well.

Leather Officer removed his codpiece and handed it to 1. He slapped his copdick repeatedly against the snout of his dog. 4 wanted nothing more than to swallow the swelling organ whole, but it could not, for it was in dog mode and its snout was a barrier. Leather Officer could easily have opened the snout and slipped his rod down the slave's throat, but that would have been too easy. Teasing was much better. Inflaming the pooch, re-emphasizing the limits of being a dog. Not a slave, not a cocksucking slave…but a dog, denied its Master's cock!

The cop petted his pup. "Good boy," he stated matter-of-factly. "1 - Take it down and put it in the cage in the bed of the pickup." 1 replaced Leather

Officer's codpiece, affixed a leash to the dog's collar and led it to the garage for transport. Leather Officer checked himself out in the mirror. Slave-shined cop boots shone. The leather uniform fit perfectly. Tie straight. Belt and gear fine. Cap. Badge. And the new K9 brassard! His own design. First time out on the street. Leather Officer knew that he was at the top of the heap, that no other man was even close. It had been a struggle at times, particularly lately, but he had survived and succeeded. He had every intention and expectation that he and his dog would easily win the contest and therefore, first place on all the radar screens of all the leathermen present. And should he choose to collar a new trainee, every man in the place would be available. No man could say "no." No man.

Chapter 19

Peewee was excited! The dog show was finally happening! Sergeant J had interviewed R3 some time ago to extract from the slave its idea for the show. R3 had then heard no more about it. MAX had taken R3 aside to fuck it once during the interim, but peewee had known better than to bring up the topic. R3 was a well trained slave and knew better than to question. Finally it saw the printed announcement for the show. It hoped that it would be allowed to participate. But who would handle it?

MAX certainly did not have enough time to appear at Trough on a nightly basis. He dropped in now and then, leaving the day-to-day operation to Sergeant J and J's platoon. The bar was only a small part of MAX's empire. MAX had informed Sergeant R, R3's Sergeant, well in advance that R3 would be a contestant, but had deliberately not bothered to have R3 learn a routine of any kind. So on the night of the event, Sergeant R had R3 put in its dog hood and had its hands converted to paws with mitts. The three, MAX, Sergeant R, and R3 emerged from the tunnel at precisely 2200hrs. MAX's plan, to the extent that there was a plan, was to allow the event to develop its own dynamic, either allow R to run R3 through some easy, impromptu routine, or handle the mutt himself. In other words, no agenda at all other than to be ready to fill in if it appeared that the event need spark. A host's role.

As MAX emerged from the tunnel accompanied by Sergeant R and peewee, he immediately focused on a man with a dog - a leather cop - and MAX's game plan changed totally. MAX, by this time, was familiar with Leather Officer. Leather Officer's runaway head slave had been incorporated into MAX's empire within minutes of its capture. It would soon make sergeant. It had provided MAX with much information. The three new slaves, M9, VII, and D16, had each had markedly different experiences with Leather Officer which had come out under interrogation and which had coalesced into a profile which MAX had found unacceptable yet exciting. Officer Tracy Stockton was not only a recruiter for MAX, but also eyes and ears. MAX's dossier on Leather Officer had been greatly thickened by the handsome Highway Patrolman, a veteran of MAX's Motorcycle Detachment in Capital City. MAX knew what to do, what had to be done.

The show had not yet gotten underway. Sergeant J would be the MC and would be assisted by the slaves of his platoon in running the event. MAX signaled for J to approach. "Don't begin the contest until I give you permission. I have a treat for the crowd," MAX said. Sergeant J did not question. He merely obeyed. Suddenly, there was some hubbub at the door. Benjamin and his handler, the handsome paramilitary cop who R3 had felt was "our kind of guy." Well, apparently so. There was no doubt that Benjamin's handler was as excited to be at Trough as anyone else who was there. Probably his first leather bar. Certainly not his last. The two made a striking team, very military, very STRAC (Strategic, Tactical and Ready for Action in Combat). Benjamin must have picked up on his handler's excitement. He sprang a rod, which only increased the crowd's excitement. It was already a great event!

MAX unclipped R3's leash from its collar. "Go have some fun, peewee! Check out your idol Benjamin, and check out the mutt with the handsome leather cop as well, the one with the red K9 brassard."

R3 shot over to the center of the action, to check out Benjamin. But Benjamin was a bit cold - more than likely he was straight. And Benjamin was not fooled by the dog hoods - he could see through the get-up. He was just here to support his handler - nothing more. R3 moved on and checked out the leather cop and his mutt. Leather Officer had struck up a conversation with Benjamin's handler, momentarily distracting him from the dogs. R3 and 4 took an immediate liking to one another. Both were hard and began sniffing each other's cocks, balls and assholes. R3 was getting from 4 what he had hoped for. R3 wondered if he could get 4 to fuck him - forgetting where he was, who he was with, all of it.

At this point, Leather Officer interceded. He cropped his pup's ass with several sharp strokes and commanded, "Home!" 4 squatted obediently at its Master's left leg and wrapped a paw around the glistening boot. R3 squatted in front of Leather Officer as well, trying to be a part of the action. It put a paw up on Leather Officer's right thigh. "Be down! Get away!" the cop snorted. This other pup was being a pest.

R3 was still keen on interacting with 4. Additionally, it found the leather cop exciting. So it again put its paw up on Leather Officer's thigh. "Bad dog!" Leather Officer struck viciously with his crop. The pup let out a yelp and ran back to MAX and Sergeant R. It assumed home position, at its Sergeant's left heel, and whimpered. The crop had hurt, a lot. And it had been unexpected. R3 had merely been being playful.

"Take care of the dog," MAX growled to Sergeant R. "Calm it down." R held R3 tight to his breeched thigh and petted it. MAX moved over adjacent to Leather Officer. "You whipped my puppy. Why?" MAX asked.

Leather Officer had not noticed MAX or Sergeant R before. Suddenly he was being confronted by a huge leather cop, uniformed in most ways identically to himself and demanding an answer. Leather Officer felt a familiar set of emotions. Well, not familiar, exactly. Foreign, but recently experienced. He felt the same set of emotions he had during his encounter with Officer Tracy Stockton. A sort of giddy/queasy feeling. A tingling asshole. A combination of comfortableness, apprehension, excitement, and fear. As if another man were about to take control of him.

His questioner was four inches taller, somewhat more mature, carried 60 pounds more muscle and gave every appearance of being capable of raping Leather Officer right now, right here. Or killing him. All the emotions of the encounter with Officer Stockton flooded back, because the circuits had so recently been reactivated. Leather Officer began to feel weak and exhilarated simultaneously. He paled, sweated, felt his pulse race. He needed to summon all his strength just to keep standing.

Even though Officer Stockton had been able to overpower Leather Officer in the street, Leather Officer had remained contemptuous of the CHP uniform - AAA with a gun. But now he was confronting something different. His questioner was wearing the uniform of the outfit in Capital City which Leather Officer had used a model for his own uniform, but this man's uniform was authentic and complete. And he was armed! Leather Officer knew it was an S&W .44 mag. And – Oh, Christ! – He had a baton!"

"You haven't answered my question, asshole," MAX said.

"I'm sorry. I didn't get the question," Leather Officer responded, now experiencing the kind of confusion that had been so troublesome for 4 for so long. Maybe it was time to go, to say "You can't call me 'asshole'" and go. Leather Officer tried to think how to extricate himself. He thought too long.

Most men probably won't see this very often in a bar, but what happened next was the stuff of every man's remembrance from then on. MAX pulled his big .44 mag from its holster, stuck the end of the barrel against Leather Officer's neck, just below the ear. He said very quietly, "Slowly lie down prone on the floor or I'll blow your fucking head off."

Leather Officer lowered himself to the floor, feeling the pressure of the huge revolver's barrel against his neck. "Hands behind your back, asshole!" MAX barked. Leather Officer obeyed, and handcuffs were quickly snapped around his wrists. MAX then placed his boot on the back of Leather Officer's neck and pinned him to the floor. Leather Officer heard the revolver being reholstered.

"Slaves, bring a carton of beer and the pruners," MAX commanded. The patrons were utterly silent. What the fuck was about to happen here?

The pair of pruners was kept behind the bar, useful to cut through rope when bondage demonstrations got tedious, the same pruners Alan had used to remove Dick's collar the night Leather Officer had stolen Dan. The blades were curved but powerful, designed to sever small tree limbs, and yet another example of why the hardware store is such a resource.

Leather Officer was pinned at the neck under MAX's gleaming cop boot. MAX reached down under his captive, grabbed hold of Leather Officer's badge, ripped it off and threw it across the room, where it smacked against the wall and clattered to the floor. As MAX continued to pin Leather Officer to the floor, a slave inserted one of the hooked cutting blades of the pruners under Leather Officer's shirt collar at the back of his neck and began to cut through the collar and the leather tie. And then down the back of the shirt, along the backbone, to cut through the utility belt and then down to the level of Leather Officer's asshole. The cutting continued out both arms and legs, through the backs of the slave-shined boots, through the gloves and through the new K-9 brassard. Several slaves tugged at the cut pieces of leather uniform and they fell away from Leather Officer's body.

"Put the beer carton under its ass," MAX commanded, continuing to hold Leather Officer by the neck. Then the words Leather Officer would never forget: "Peewee - front and center!" The beer carton raised Leather Officer's asshole to just the right height for a dog fuck, and peewee was the pup for the job.

4 was beside itself. What was happening? Its world was crashing down. Its Master! It tried to intervene, but was quickly leashed by Sergeant R and dragged into the tunnel.

Leather Officer's cap had fallen off. It had gotten trampled by the patrons of the bar as they pressed forward to get a better look at the rape. Peewee spat into Leather Officer's asshole, spat again in its hand, rubbed the spit on its erect penis, and made several tentative teasing probes toward the cop's hole.

"No. No! Please. Please! Don't do this to me," Leather Officer begged.

MAX was cold. His only response was to grind his boot more roughly into Leather Officer's neck. There would be ample time later to explain in full detail what the cop's sins had been, how he had failed to care properly for his slaves, how he had been unethical. But now it was time for peewee to administer the humiliation. "Fuck it, peewee! Make it scream!" MAX yelled.

Peewee did. It shoved its little slave dick into the cop's asshole, an asshole not fucked for twenty years, an asshole not ready to be fucked, the ass of a man for whom this treatment arguably may have been necessary, but certainly was not wanted. It was rape, pure and simple.

Leather Officer did not relax. He fought it, and therefore it hurt. So he screamed. Screamed horribly. Cried out. And begged not to be fucked any more. But he was. Peewee didn't get to fuck enough, it thought, so it made the most of it. The slave was exultant, fucking the shit out of the former leather cop, humiliating it, making it MAX's slave, serving MAX.

Leather Officer whined and yelled. How could this possibly be happening? And why? Had he been a fraud all along? Had he been so uncaring about his slaves, so uncaring about everyone else in the leather world because he had been a fraud? Overcompensating to mask his self-doubt, his fear that he really was slavemeat all along? Why had he let this happen to him? Why hadn't he escaped when he could have?

MAX removed his boot from the neck and stood back. Leather Officer could see the gleaming slave-shined copboots clearly. Less distinctly he could see the huge leather cop standing in triumph over him, the man who was so easily conquering him, the man he now wished to serve. The slave dick pumping his ass became a pleasure, a pleasure because it was his new Master's will that he be fucked. Leather Officer's big dick became swollen and much harder than ever before, filled with pent up need to serve the leather cop who had taken control of him so easily, this God he had waited 40 years to find. Leather Officer could barely see high enough to glimpse MAX's cock as it was hauled out. Warm, sweet piss shot down and bathed Leather Officer's body and the remnants of his uniform. The slave fucking him began to lose its rhythm, to get spasmodic and to shoot hot cum into Leather Officer's ass. Leather Officer heard both peewee and himself scream simultaneously as the slave became totally the instrument of MAX and infected Leather Officer with slavery.

"OK," MAX said. "Get this piece of shit out of here." With that, Leather Officer, or the slave trainee which used to be Leather Officer, was dragged feet first, cum oozing from its raw ass, drenched in piss, the tatters of its leather uniform falling off its body, through the tunnel to the edge of the pit, where it was uncuffed, ordered in and then covered by the grate. Leather Officer, the hottest top in town. Now inserted at the very bottom of MAX's empire. A top no more. Total slavemeat. Penis erect. Awaiting its Master.

A Boner Book

CHAPTER 20

"A9 reports, Sir," the slave stated, saluting MAX smartly and trying to control its erection. Always a difficult thing to do for slaves in MAX's presence.

"Be at ease, slave," MAX stated, matter-of-factly, in the military way, but again, for the slave, it was extremely difficult to be "at ease" in MAX's presence. A9 may very well have been MAX's best trained slave at the moment. It was close to making Sergeant and undoubtedly would rise quickly through MAX's hierarchy to assume a place of great importance within the Officer Corps. But right now A9 was as subordinate as they come and absolutely thrilled to have been called in to see MAX. What was up, A9 wondered?

"You have a rather unusual biography," MAX said.

Oh shit, A9 thought. It knew what MAX meant, knew that its Master was referring to the fact that it had come into MAX's system as a runaway slave. That it had run away from Leather Officer, had been free for less than hour and had then allowed itself to be captured by Officer Tracy Stockton and quickly re-enslaved. It knew that many of the other slaves were jealous of it, that several Sergeants were apprehensive about its rapid rise and that even some Officers had issues concerning its almost superstar quality. But what did MAX think?

"Yes, Sir, I guess I do have an unusual biography, SIR, but I've just tried to be the best slave I can be and to serve you as well as I can, Sir," A9 said.

"Relax, boy. This isn't about what you think. This isn't about anything that you are likely to have imagined," MAX assured the slave, glancing at A9's engorged penis, and then grinning at his slave to express a type of conspiratorial amusement. A9 blushed deeply. MAX knew how to handle men. He utterly dominated his slave, yet at the same time instilled in it a sort of man-to-man bond like buddies, which only served to deepen the slave's allegiance and slavery.

MAX came around from behind his desk and cemented A9 to him forever. MAX played lightly with the slave's dick, watching A9's mind through its eyes as the slave was overwhelmed by the feel of MAX's skin-tight black leather cop gloves. MAX grinned. A9 grinned, too. MAX put his muscular arm around A9's shoulders and said, "Pardner, I've got a special job for you."

A9 didn't know what to say. So, as a well trained slave will, it said, "Yes, Sir."

"The fact that you ran away from a weak master indicates to me a reflective quality about the nature of slavery which you, unlike many slaves, possess. Indeed, for most slaves, excessive reflection on slavery in the abstract is detrimental to effective functioning. In your case, during your tenure as my slave, whatever energy you may have expended analyzing and critiquing my methods has not impeded your service or your advancement. In fact, the opposite has apparently been the case," MAX explained.

A9 was astounded. It had never heard MAX speak in this manner. It wondered whether MAX had ever spoken to ANY slave this way before. What was up?

"Are you aware that I have been considering promoting you to Sergeant?" MAX continued.

"Yes, Sir, I am," A9 responded, hoping that it would not be thought presumptuous. But also knowing that it had no choice but to be completely truthful with its Master, and that to be other than completely truthful was unthinkable.

"As you know, my Sergeants are task oriented, and are assigned slaves based on the skills and slave power needed to accomplish the task. A rather unusual task has arisen and I have decided that now is the time for your promotion. I will assign you slaves to accomplish the task as you develop your plan for task-accomplishment," MAX said.

A9 tried to say calm and, outwardly, was largely successful. Its mind quickly wandered to the hot Sergeant's uniform that it would now wear, very much like an Officer's uniform. Instead of being all black leather, the breeches, shirt and cap were of tan leather. The boots, tie, and Sam Browne belt and gear were black. It was a stunning uniform, and A9 had longed to wear it and wield the power that went with it from its first day as MAX's slave. A9 had even figured out ahead what kind of whip it would choose, since each Sergeant was allowed to choose the type of whip he felt would accomplish the task most effectively. A9 had long ago decided on a short, flexible single-tail bullwhip. The thought of wielding that whip in order to elicit obedience from the slaves assigned to him made the new Sergeant's cock swell even more. MAX noticed.

"You're thinking about your new uniform, aren't you, boy," MAX said. Again A9 blushed deep crimson. It adored MAX, would be MAX's slave for the rest of its life, was being promoted to serve MAX better, and felt a sense of huge transition and belonging.

"Yes, Sir," A9 admitted.

"You're going to enjoy the looks in the slaves' eyes when they see your muscular body clothed in perfectly tailored tan leather, with gleaming slave-shined black boots, hot cop gear, and your new whip, aren't you, slave," MAX taunted.

A9 realized that the promotion increased its level of slavery. It would obey MAX even more quickly and unquestioningly than ever before. It would do its damnedest to be allowed to continue to wear its new uniform, to wield its whip and its power over its slaves. It would obey MAX fully and immediately. "Yes, Sir," A9 responded.

MAX touched A9's collar as if he were inspecting it. In many ways, moments like this were more important for MAX than for the men he controlled. Except for periodic replacement of slave collars which had become so worn that they were no longer soldierly, removal of a collar either attended promotion or termination from MAX's system. Neither was voluntary. Always it was MAX who decided. MAX produced a steel clippers and cut cleanly through A9's collar. A9 was very emotional, but maintained control. MAX hung on to the collar for a moment, as if to pull the power out it so it could rest and then laid it on his desk.

"You are now Sergeant T. You will serve me at a higher level than you have before. You are now more my slave than ever, regardless of the fact that your collar has been removed from your neck. Your slavery is now total, and you no longer need a collar. I congratulate you," MAX said. "Kneel before me, slave!"

Sergeant T understood. He knelt. He had half understood all along, but now he understood fully. The slaves surely didn't think of their Sergeants as fellow slaves. Hell, the Sergeants were constantly on the slaves' asses, forcing them to perform, whipping when the performance fell short. But the Sergeants were MAX's slaves just the same. Performing a different kind of service, in a different role. They would always be MAX's slaves.

"Check this out, T," MAX ordered. "This is your task. A task for which you are peculiarly suited. A task which will test you in terms of your capacity to enslave the men beneath you and to serve me." MAX clicked on a TV monitor which quickly came in focus to reveal a scene which Sergeant T realized was live, not far away, and which defined a task for which he was "peculiarly suited."

Sergeant T's brain snapped into "rewind." It rewound back through the period when he had been A9 and then further back into the time when he had been 2, the head slave who had run away. Sergeant T saw the man he had known as Leather Officer, his former Master from whom he had fled, the Master whom he had served for so long, so well. There he was, completely naked and on his knees in the drain pit with a big hard-on.

"He's now my slave, he thinks," MAX said. "That's why his dick is hard. Whether he will ever become my slave is up to him and up to you, Sergeant. It will be your task to teach slavery to this piece of shit which got it so wrong for so long."

Sergeant T was astounded. Truly astounded. But there was no time for questioning or unproductive emotion. He quickly shifted gears, understood that his promotion was dependant upon successfully enslaving his former Master and began immediately to formulate his plan of action. "Yes, Sir! Thank you, Sir!" Sergeant T half shouted. He saluted MAX and held the salute until his Master returned it.

"Dismissed, Sergeant," MAX said, dropping his salute. T responded, pivoted abruptly, and left MAX. T was entirely focused on his task. He knew that his entire future was resting on a successful enslavement. He would succeed.

CHAPTER 21

The man previously known as Leather Officer was enduring a psychic crisis of such profundity that perhaps he should have been congratulated for simply continuing to keep his heart beating. His fall had begun years ago when he had, to a large extent, misapprehended the nature of slavery and what it meant to own slaves. Perhaps he had erected his slave empire too quickly, without sufficient foundation, too much in isolation. Perhaps he had been induced to do this because he was too handsome, too hung, too spectacularly uniformed, and too hot. Perhaps if he had had to struggle a bit more to build his empire it would have been more substantial. Perhaps.

The encounter with Officer Tracy Stockton had left him shaken. Shaken, but not destroyed. It should have been a wake up call, but he had pressed the "snooze" button and not obeyed Stockton, not plugged into Stockton's program. If he had, he might have been able to have profited from what Stockton knows about running slaves. Might have been able to have applied it to his own set up. Might have grown, matured, accepted the responsibility that goes with slave ownership, solidified his mastery and avoided his subsequent fall. But he hadn't. Instead of obeying Stockton and working with the Officer on the fix-it ticket like he was fucking told, he slid sideways and sent 1 out to get the job done. As if the "job" had had anything to do with signal lights or tickets.

If he had simply subordinated himself to Stockton, which was only right since Stockton was ten times the man Leather Officer had ever been, he would have been protected from MAX. By having already subordinated himself to a man who was MAX's subordinate. Like it or not, that's the way it works. You can either do it the easy way or the hard way, and he would do it the hard way. Whether he had chosen the hard way or whether it was just inevitable like the ends that befall Wagnerian characters is an interesting question which will remain unanswered for now. For now, we investigate the consequences of the hard way.

He was no longer a Master. That was clear. His set up was in some kind of receivership. Swallowed whole by MAX and administered by a satrap. One of MAX's Officers had been dispatched to the Mission District Victorian to keep the four slaves from suffering unduly and to keep the little principality going until MAX could find a new use for it.

Nor was he a slave. He had yet to be enslaved. His training had not begun. He had not even met his trainer. But although he had lost his whole world, and although he had yet become part of another in any meaningful way, one step forward had been taken. He had stopped thinking about how to extricate himself and return to what he had been and keep it afloat, somehow. He knew it was gone. He wasn't even thinking about it. All he thought about was MAX. He had no history before he had heard the words "Peewee, front and center." Raped by the randy little slave on MAX's command, the now non-slave, non-Master had already learned what was normally taught by many days in the pit. So he squatted there in the pit, penis close to explosion, hoping for his God to return and take possession of him.

Sergeant T's plan, which was MAX's plan, did not presume that the not-even-yet-a-slave in the pit would be ready to serve MAX in any valuable way for quite some time. The questions would be whether he would ever be ready and, if so, when. Questions to which he and T would develop answers as his training progressed.

He was kept waiting for some time. With the standard deliveries of waste-water, random feedings, occasional hosings. But no visits from MAX to give structure. Structure would be provided by Sergeant T and the cadre of trainers he was assembling, once T was ready.

Sergeant T had struck Leather Officer's new trainees, Dan, Little Mike, and all the rest, as a particularly handsome, powerful, hung and competent head slave. All that was still true. T's new Sergeant's uniform was impeccable and his body was better developed than ever (since MAX had taken better care of him than Leather Officer had). His big dick was hard most of the time, easily seen through the tight uniform breeches. Because he was at last moving where he was destined to go, Sergeant T would end up a legendary slave trainer and a legendary Master, only at this point about to enslave the first man of his career.

At Sergeant T's convenience and under his command, four slaves entered the pit, removed the inhabitant, scrubbed it thoroughly, shaved it completely, leaving only the eyebrows, scrubbed it again to make it pink, and then applied a light coat of oil to make it glisten. Now that it was a slave trainee, it was entitled to be referred to as "it," and when it heard that reference, it became erect. It was taken to a metal room, all stainless steel, and shackled to a chair by its ankles, wrists, and neck. It was no longer hard. It hadn't seen MAX for days and wasn't sure it ever would again. It was completely disoriented and wasn't even sure who it was. But then it was given cause to remember.

The proceedings were structured like a trial or tribunal. A group of men, also completely shaved, but wearing collars, leather shorts, and slave boots, entered the room and took their places standing at parade rest against a far wall. The trainee was astounded by whom it saw. Alan the bartender, Dick the barback, Little Mike, Dan (the new 2), 1, 3, and 4! What were they doing here? What was going on?

It only got worse - or better - or both. Officer Tracy Stockton came in. Full and totally strac CHP bike cop uniform and gear as always, including, the trainee saw immediately, the PR-24 side handle baton in its ring on the Officer's belt. Stockton came up to the bound trainee with a big smile on his face and began to caress his baton with one black leathered hand in a suggestive way, as if to imply that the inevitable penetration of the trainee's asshole had only been delayed. Stockton slapped the trainee across the mouth. "When are you going to report back to me to sign off on the ticket, asshole?" the cop asked. "Isn't that what you were ordered to do?"

"Yes, Sir, but the ticket said that any CHP Officer could sign off on it, so I thought..."

Another slap across the mouth. "But what did I tell you to do, shithead?" Stockton asked.

"Sir, you told me to report back to you, Sir."

"And did you?"

"No, Sir, I didn't."

"And why didn't you," Stockton asked.

"I...I...I don't know, Sir" the trainee said.

"Yes you do, fuckhead, and so do I. You didn't obey me because you thought you didn't have to. That you could disobey without consequences. But guess what? Here are the consequences," Stockton said, and pulled the PR-24 side handle baton out of its ring, flashing the same triumphant grin the trainee remembered from their previous encounter at 13th and Folsom. "Open up, fuckhole."

Stockton pressed the short end of the baton against the trainee's teeth, threatening to crush them if they were not opened out of the way. The trainee opened up and allowed the baton to be inserted down its throat past the

169

sphincter to the point where breathing was impossible. "If you had obeyed me fully and immediately before, we might not be here now. You can't run, boy. You can't."

Just then MAX entered the court. The trainee caught itself being relieved that MAX had showed up and might prevent Stockton from escalating the situation and raping it with the baton. But the trainee had no friends here. MAX came up to Stockton and they did a kind of bad cop / bad cop, derisive, chuckling routine emphasizing the helplessness of the trainee and the inevitability of severe repercussions for its numerous transgressions.

Stockton and MAX began interrogating the slaves who, predictably, recited a litany of brutalities, overreactions, inhumanities, and shortfalls which, taken singly, could possibly have been forgiven. But collectively, they described a program which needed to be terminated.

After the testimony, Stockton summarized. "Here's where you fucked up, shit-head. You missed part of slave training because you were isolated. You ran it like a porn novel rather than like real men living real lives. You couldn't under-stand what your slaves and trainees were feeling because you had never been there. Your shallow experience lead to shallow responses to situations that demanded sophisticated responses because of the complexities of slave emotion," Stockton said.

MAX stepped in: "You had the power to enslave. You were handsome, hung, and perfectly uniformed. No man could resist you. But you took no care for the men you enslaved or for those whom you left with unfulfilled need. You abrogated the responsibility that you assumed by accepting your position as a Master. You failed to understand that your job was to build your slaves. You treated a two way street like a one way street and you crashed. I had to take you out before you hurt again. And now, since I have done to you what you did to so many men, I'll show you what you should have done. I'll rebuild you. I'll make you into much more than what you were. I'll make you all you can be, and in gratitude, you will be my slave forever."

The trainee did not need to be asked whether this analysis was correct. It knew it was. By failing to nurture its former slaves, to build them into the best they could be or invest in them, it had not received the dividends of Mastery which would have strengthened it and made it impregnable to Stockton's initial weakening attack and MAX's coup de grace. If only it had adequate training itself early on, it might have been far more successful and not hurt so many men. Stockton's baton should have gone up its ass years ago, so it would know a slave's emotions and therefore how to build its slaves. But the baton had not, so there had been a lot of wasted time and hurt slaves. Now it was time to make a break with the past.

If bad cop / bad cop weren't enough, a third cop entered the room. At first the trainee did not recognize the third cop. He was muscular, handsome, and wore a tan full leather motorcycle cop uniform, with black boots and gear and cap. He seemed familiar, somehow, but it would be a moment before the trainee would be able to ID him.

MAX spoke. "Sergeant T, these slaves have given their testimony and Officer Stockton and I have summarized the gravity of the offense. Two questions now remain: what to do in terms of justice for the injured slaves, and how to rehabilitate the offender."

"Sir, what punishment and rehab do you and Officer Stockton propose?" Sergeant T asked.

The trainee had begun to shake. The baton had been in the back of its mind for weeks, ever since being stopped by Stockton at 13th and Folsom. It began to yell. "No! No! Please! Please! Don't shove the baton up my ass! Don't. I'll obey you completely. Immediately. I want to be trained to serve you. But please, not the baton. Please, not the baton."

Stockton pulled out his baton. MAX unshackled the trainee from its chair, put it in a headlock, and forced it to the floor. The slaves were summoned to hold it down. It began to scream. It finally recognized Sergeant T. "2! 2! Please help me! Don't let this happen! You were right! I understand why you ran away and you were right! I understand now. I want training. I want to submit. I need to. But please! Not the baton! Not the baton!"

Stockton began to probe at its asshole. It screamed, horribly.

"Officer Stockton, I think that my training of this piece of shit and its ultimate rehabilitation and capacity to obey will be better served if its punishment is left to me, Sir," Sergeant T said.

"Bullshit," Tracy Stockton said. "Fuckhead deserves the baton! It needs to be hurt, like it hurt."

One of the slaves then exclaimed, risking punishment itself for speaking when not spoken to, "Please, Sir, don't hurt him! He was my Master! Maybe he was as bad as you say, but he was my Master! He always will be! Don't take more of that from me than you have already taken!" It was the former 4 who had lost control and tried to intervene in behalf of its former Master and itself, even as it had tried to intervene at the dog show.

Then the former 3 also lost control and, addressing MAX, pleaded, "Please, Sir, he fucked me a thousand times and he is a part of me, of my life. Let me keep that. Don't destroy him before my eyes." There was a general murmur of agreement from the trainee's other two former slaves as well, although not from Dick, Alan, or Little Mike. They agreed with Stockton. They wanted to see the baton up the shithead's ass.

If it seems that this situation is coming unglued, remember that structuring men's emotions and subsequent actions is the essence of Mastery. This wasn't a staged drama. It's a real-time challenge designed to teach and have long lasting effect. Consider the number of men involved here, all of whom are MAX's slaves, all of whom he is training, and his motive of trying to squeeze as much training out of every interaction with every man.

It was more or less a hung jury. All the jurors had been brutalized both physically and emotionally by the defendant, but, interestingly, those that had been its slaves were begging for leniency. Tracy Stockton was ready to punish. He was pissed that his hard-ass tactic at 13th and Folsom had been brushed aside. Simple as that. Punish it now. Sergeant T wanted the trainee unpunished, or at least not so brutally humiliated in front of its former slaves that its spirit might be broken, rendering it untrainable. Besides, T had been its slave himself. T had felt that he, as the head slave, was a better judge of how to handle the other slaves than the Master, and this had caused him to run. But clearly, he had been the trainee's slave for years. This could not be swept aside as if it were nothing.

MAX took charge. It was his job to make the final decision when his subordinates were at loggerheads, and to teach them by his example of cool deliberation, clear concern for their well-being, and intelligent choice considering the long term and the larger good. "Slaves, thank you for your testimony. Rejoin your platoons," MAX commanded. This was not received with immediate acceptance by any of the slaves, for each had an immense stake in the outcome of the proceedings. But none was so involved in the trainee's case that it would damage its slavery to MAX in any way. Blind, immediate, willing obedience was something MAX had earned not through brutality, but through prestige. So they left, leaving MAX, Stockton, and Sergeant T to handle the now relatively free-to-resist trainee.

Tracy Stockton could see that, without the slaves to hold the trainee down, baton rape, which he would have enjoyed administering immensely, was looking less and less likely. But Tracy knew that he himself was a hot head, MAX was far cooler and that it would be better in the long run for cooler heads to prevail. He slid the baton back into the ring on his belt. He knew from experience where MAX was going, and remembered that he, Officer Tracy Stockton, State Traffic Officer, California Highway Patrol, was, in the end, still MAX's slave.

MAX began: "I'm ready to see a police side handle baton shoved up this motherfucker's ass and kept up there until the tears cease to flow only because they have dried up. I'm ready for justice for all the men who have been treated unethically, who have been damaged or used without having learned anything or become better men. I'm ready to terminate the life of a man who has dishonored all Slavemasters and perpetuated the false myth of brutality and unethical exploitation."

Stockton fingered his baton, wondering whether he hadn't missed a signal. Maybe it was stick time after all.

Sergeant T got concerned. He had been the trainee's slave for many years. The bond had been very deep. The shortcomings were substantial, but T felt that to destroy the man would be to destroy the time T had spent as its slave. And the time of the other slaves. And T's opportunity to prove its skill as a trainer. "Sir, I...," T began.

"At ease, Sergeant. I've made my decision. No more testimony is required," MAX said. "Take the trainee away and train it to serve me. Make it useful. Create something from it that will outweigh the transgressions of its past. Make it into something that will make its former slaves proud of their tenure under its heel. You are the best man for the job. Do it well."

Sergeant T locked a collar around the neck of his former Master, attached a leash, and led the trainee out on all fours.

MAX turned to Officer Tracy Stockton. He put a beefy arm around the Highway Patrolman's equally beefy shoulders and said, "You know, pardner, I'm a little surprised at the narrowness of your view."

"What do you mean, Sir?" Stockton asked, genuinely puzzled.

"I mean, Tracy, that you had decided several weeks ago that this guy needed your baton up his ass, and you clung to this idea in spite of a lot of clear evidence that a more rehabilitative approach would produce better results in the long run. You completely ignored the effect that such humiliation would've had on its former slaves, all of whom are now my slaves."

Tracy Stockton began to get nervous. Not having his point of view sustained was bad enough. But MAX was beginning to sound rough. Tracy had been MAX's slave for long enough to recognize the tone.

"You need to understand, boy, the larger picture," MAX continued. "No man is immortal. Nor is any organization. But all men strive and fight to have what they have created succeed them. I will fight to have this organization I have created continue for as long as I can, because the finest men I have known are my Officers, my Sergeants, and my slaves. You are the finest among the fine. You are my heir. You will take over this organization when I am no longer able to lead."

"Sir! Yes, Sir!" Tracy stammered.

"But boy, I wonder if you are ready, if you are adequately trained."

"What do you mean, Sir?"

MAX's demeanor changed. "I mean, fuckhole, I wonder whether the man who will lead an organization composed of hundreds of slaves is adequate to the job if he sets aside the larger and long term good in favor of shoving his fucking baton up some slave's ass just because his attempt to hard ass the guy failed."

"Yes Sir," Stockton murmured.

"How long has it been since I've fucked you, boy?" MAX asked.

"Several years, Sir," Tracy responded.

"Then, probably, you're pretty tight just like the trainee you were so willing to hurt in front of its former slaves," MAX said.

"Yes Sir, I am pretty tight, Sir, but..."

"But what, boy?"

"But...nothing, Sir. Nothing."

"That's right, boy. That's right. You have nothing to say. Nothing at all. Now give me your baton. Drop your breeches. Kneel."

Officer Tracy Stockton obeyed. "Please, Sir, I'm not sure I can take this," he said.

"Whoa, pardner! Isn't that what the trainee was saying?" MAX asked.

"Yes, Sir, but the trainee had abused its slaves! I haven't abused any slaves," Tracy said.

"Only because I didn't permit it, boy. You were ready and willing," MAX responded.

Officer Stockton hesitated and thought this through. He then responded.

"Yes Sir, you're right. I wanted to rape him with the baton and it was because I was angry that my initial attempt to control him had failed. He ignored me and I was pissed. I wanted to hurt him, Sir," Tracy Stockton admitted. "I did."

MAX slipped the baton back into the ring on Tracy's belt. "Good boy," he said. "Get up." Stockton exhaled.

"But Sir, it *has* been a long time since you fucked me. Maybe my perspective would broaden if you took some time and opened me up again," Tracy said, beginning to crack a grin.

MAX looked deep into his slave's eyes and remembered the hot young boy he had recruited decades ago and realized that the hot young boy stood next to him now. The same boy. MAX put his arm around Tracy's shoulders. "You're right, pardner. I've neglected the finishing touches on your training. We'll go take care of it right now."

Tracy grinned broadly. He'd come to think he'd outgrown this. He hadn't. He needed it.

MAX grinned, too. He'd just learned something new about slave management, after all these years. He had just become even more powerful. He felt his dick begin to swell.

A Boner Book

ABOUT THE AUTHOR

Alan G. Goes was born in Chicago in 1946 and was educated there and at Berkeley. He has resided in coastal Northern California since 1965. His several careers have included Military Policeman (US Army – Viet-Nam and New York City), Forester, Bus Driver, Leathercop Escort, and now, Author.

The author's boyhood obsessions with soldiers, bodybuilders, gunslingers, brutal paramilitary police, weapons, tall boots, black leather, and big motorcycles have only become more intense with time. He discovered Folsom Street in San Francisco in 1974 in much the same way as does the character Little Mike in *Copslaves*. Several decades of hanging out in leather-bars and investigating dimly lit back alleys have proved that the reality of leathermen and their interactions definitely exceeds fantasy.

The author now resides just off Folsom Street in San Francisco's Mission District. He is happily partnered to one of the top men on the planet and enjoys the friendship of a fine circle of men and women whose enrichment is his main focus.

www.ingramcontent.com/pod-product-compliance
Lightning Source LLC
Chambersburg PA
CBHW071217260626
47162CB00004B/1327